JEST AND DIE

JEST AND DIE

Stella Whitelaw

severn
House

This first world edition published in Great Britain 2004 by
SEVERN HOUSE PUBLISHERS LTD of
9–15 High Street, Sutton, Surrey SM1 1DF.
This first world edition published in the USA 2004 by
SEVERN HOUSE PUBLISHERS INC of
595 Madison Avenue, New York, N.Y. 10022.

British Library Cataloguing in Publication Data

Whitelaw, Stella, 1941-
    Jest and die. - (Jordan Lacey series ; 5)
    1.   Lacey, Jordan (Fictitious character) - Fiction
    2.   Women private investigators - Fiction
    3.   Detective and mystery stories
    I.   Title
    823.9'14 [F]

    ISBN 0-7278-5980-3

Typeset by Hewer Text Ltd.,
Edinburgh, Scotland.
Printed and bound in Great Britain by
MPG Books Ltd., Bodmin, Cornwall.

To Alvina,
long lost friend, now found

Acknowledgements

L ong overdue thanks to a certain station officer in the Fire Service; a certain, now retired, detective chief inspector; and to a wonderful windmill preservation guide for answering all my questions.

Also warm thanks to the staff of both Oxted and Worthing libraries for finding endless books and newspaper microfilm.

And my thanks again to Anna Telfer, for her enthusiasm and helpful editorial work; and to Edwin Buckhalter for his confidence and support for the Jordan Lacey series.

One

S ummer was still on a roll along the West Sussex coast and the seaside town of Latching was caught in a soporific haze which did not improve my current lack of work. Even the villains were snoozing on the beach, clad in factor 30 and little else.

Since various bits of me still needed time for healing, it was not all groom and tomb. The warmth of the sun on my bare arms was the gentlest of massages, the waft of sea breeze a kind of aromatherapy. Not exactly oil of seaweed, but near. My mind was coasting along on some internal thought wave that was half daydream, half sleep. A fringe area of consciousness that I could not name.

This delightful state was broken by the low-key ringing tone of my new mobile. Having lost count of the number of mobiles I have owned and mislaid recently, it took me a few moments to remember the new procedure to log on.

'Hello,' I said. 'Jordan Lacey.'

'Are you the lady private investigator?'

'Yes, that's me. How can I help you?'

The caller hesitated. The voice of the man was county, polished, professional. I put him in his fifties, fairly well off, solicitor, doctor, architect. No clues, just an instinct.

'My name is Samuel Steel. My wife and I live on Updown Hill.'

The picture grew. Updown Hill is an area of large houses with large gardens on the outskirts of Latching. Its quaint name comes from the medieval past when traders and merchants struggled up and down the hill with their sacks and bundles.

Now the owners of the spacious properties have BMWs and Jaguars and four-wheel drives to save them the uphill climb.

'Yes, Mr Steel.'

'I am at my wit's end and I just don't know what to do.'

I was beginning to doze again in the sun.

'You see, my lawn is being killed off.'

I wondered if I had misheard. His firstborn? His fawn? A pet prawn? 'Your what, Mr Steel?'

'My lawn. I have a very beautiful garden and my lawn is being decimated. Someone is doing it on purpose. I know we have had a lot of sunshine and very little rain, but this is most peculiar, not normal at all. And now there's a footprint.'

'Footprint? What sort of footprint? Where?'

'On the verge outside the garden. A sort of burnt out footprint. Quite definitely in the shape of a boot.'

'Who wears boots in this weather?' I remarked.

'Exactly. That's why I'd like you to come and talk to me. I know it may not be the kind of criminal investigation that you usually take on, but I would appreciate your opinion.'

He obviously did not know that I live on serving court papers, finding lost animals, lost husbands, lost anything, and surveillance cases. A dying lawn might be refreshingly different.

'Have you spoken to the police?'

'Yes, but it's not really up their street, they said. Vandalism is rife in town. But the detective I spoke to gave me your number. He seemed to think you were the right person.'

Detective Inspector James or Detective Sergeant Evans. It could be either. My two musketeers. One who barely tolerated the sight of me and the other longing to take me on an exclusive twin-bedded holiday. I was in the middle between them, caught in a trap of my own making.

'Give me your address, Mr Steel, and I'll come round and see you right away.'

'We live at Denbury Court, Updown Hill. It's at the top of the hill, on the right-hand side. I hope you have a car.'

'I have a ladybird,' I said mysteriously. 'I'll be with you in half an hour.'

Half an hour was an optimistic guess so it was skates-on time. I half ran, half jogged back to my two bedsits. No time to explain why I live in two bedsits. I changed into summer working gear, clean jeans, clean T-shirt, leather sandals and scraped my hair back with a tortoiseshell claw.

I grabbed a notebook, a banana and keys to the ladybird, then sprinted to my shop, First Class Junk. My shop is on a corner site with two small optician-style windows and it sells what it says, first class junk. Hours of combing the charity shops, going to house clearances and spotting a bargain, provide my stock. As the shop windows are small, I can change the display in minutes. Only a few choice items go in the windows, always with a theme. Nostalgia, war, music, herbs, the sea . . . The ladybird is parked in the backyard of my shop. She is a classic red Morris Minor, 1100cc, with huge black spots and goes like a dream with minimal attention, as long as I remember to put in petrol and talk to her occasionally. I looked at the fuel gauge. Almost full. Thank the Lord. I had barely fifteen minutes left.

I know Latching like the underside of my foot. Updown Hill is past the golf course and up a steep hill towards the South Downs, my second favourite walking area. The four miles of promenade and sea shore is always my first. Updown Hill is very select. You can hardly see the houses, lost behind trees, shrubbery and long drives. I bet the trick-or-treat kids never come here.

Denbury Court was on the right-hand side, as Mr Steel said, a discreet hand-carved name at the drive entrance. I drove slowly, first taking in the absolute tranquillity and beauty of the garden, and then the signs of a garden dying. The once gracious lawn that swept up to the house was turning brown in lines. The herbaceous borders were shrunken and withered. Roses were drop-headed and liquid black. I could almost smell the decay.

The house was a dream. Could I live there, please? An attic would do. It was a long L-shaped house, low roof, old stone, slate tiles, creeper, square-paned windows like rows of watchful eyes. The front door was oak, heavily barred with wooden dowels, and a long bell pull on a rope. The door opened before I even got out of my car.

Samuel Steel was in his fifties, tall, a mass of grey hair brushed back from a high forehead, light-blue eyes, cleft in a firm chin, casually dressed in an open-necked shirt and chinos. He looked successful. Money oozed from his gold watch and hand-made leather tooled shoes.

'Miss Lacey,' he smiled, holding out his hand. 'I'm very glad to see you. This garden means a lot to me and my wife. And someone or something is destroying it.'

'Mr Steel,' I said. His handshake was firm and not sweaty. 'There certainly seems to be something wrong with your garden. Will you take me on a tour and tell me everything that you've noticed.'

'It's dying before my eyes,' he said, turning away and shaking his head. 'We've spent hours working on this garden. It's our main interest outside the family.'

I could see what he meant. The green lawn was disfigured with patches of scorched brown as if someone had painted out the grass. Mr Steel, talking all the time, pointed out the plants that were dying. Roses, peonies, begonias, dahlias and delphiniums, all drooping and curling into decay. Even the herb garden was affected. Every clump of herbs was shrivelling, tiny leaves burnt and blackened.

'I know there's the usual summer drought but this doesn't look natural,' I said.

'No way. We have been conserving water and throwing it on the garden. The other gardens nearby are not affected. We are at the top of the hill and water drains down, but not to this extent. This destruction is heartbreaking. We've lost 42 plants already. Anne and I spent hours transporting and replanting shrubs which we grew in our former home and they were taking well. They had great sentimental value which can never be replaced.'

I did not question the sentiment. I couldn't see myself getting fond of a busy Lizzie.

'Do you know if you have any enemies or perhaps jealous gardeners in your circle of friends or neighbours?'

4

'No, never. I don't know of anyone.' He managed a grin. 'We are all keen gardeners up here. My first wife never liked gardening but Anne loves it.'

'Could you show me the footprint, please,' I said.

It was one bootmark burnt into the verge outside the house. I crouched down to look at it. The grass had been scorched as if someone had stepped into chemicals and left a footprint behind. I'm no good at guessing sizes so I asked Mr Steel to put his foot carefully beside the faint mark.

'I take a size nine,' he said.

'And this is a good two sizes larger?'

'Probably.'

'OK. Someone is targeting your garden. They are using a chemical sprayer, the kind council workers use to kill weeds,' I said confidently, knowing nothing whatever about chemical sprayers.

'Glyphosate is the only weedkiller that kills grass,' said Mr Steel, who clearly knew more than I did.

'He's dangerous,' I said. 'We ought to be able to find out the exact chemical from a sample. I have friends in Forensic who would help.' This was sheer boasting. I have friends of a sort in Forensic who might, with a bit of arm twisting, help. 'But I need to take a plaster cast of the bootmark first. It could be valuable evidence. Like a fingerprint.'

'Excellent. What a good idea.' Mr Steel looked much cheered by my efficiency. 'I suppose we ought to cover it up so that it doesn't get damaged?'

'Right. Any sort of plastic sheeting would do, weighed down at the corners. Have you got one of those frame things? We don't want any accidental damage. By the way, Mr Steel, do you have any pets?'

He looked surprised. 'We have two dogs, Jack Russells. We call them Jack and Russell.'

'Jack and Russell.' I wrote it down.

'Yes, I know it's daft,' he went on, 'but at the time we both thought it rather clever and funny. We have lived to regret it.'

'They are lovely names,' I said to reassure him. 'And what does it matter if people laugh? But while this damage is being done to your garden, you should make sure that your dogs are kept in at night. If you have to let them out after dark, then take them for a walk on a lead.'

'You don't think that they could get hurt?' Mr Steel looked shocked.

'It might happen. Intruders don't like dogs, especially the small yapping kind. He might turn the spray on to them.'

'How awful. We'll make sure they are kept in although they won't like it. They like rushing about in the dark, chasing shadows.'

'And I would like to have a word with your wife before I leave,' I said. I cut an area of scorched grass with nail scissors and put the samples into a plastic specimen bag. Then dead-headed some roses and let them drop into bags. 'That is, if you want me to take on this case.'

Mr Steel stopped in his tracks. 'Miss Lacey, of course we want you to take this case. There's absolutely no doubt you are the right person.'

'You haven't asked how much I charge.' At that moment, I was not quite sure what to charge. I normally charge £10 an hour or £50 a day, but I did not want Mr Steel to think I came cheap. My brain went into a mathematical spin.

'I don't care what you charge,' said Mr Steel. 'Just send me a bill at the end.'

'I'll have to ask you to sign a contract and pay a retainer. It's customary,' I said, not believing my luck. I always carry a spare contract. I might fall over a lost tortoise.

'Naturally. I'll make out a cheque for £200 right now. Will that do as a retainer?'

I took a deep breath, pure odourless Updown oxygen. 'Thank you.'

We walked back to the house and I took in the extent of the damage. Mr Steel had not shown me the garden at the back of the house. It was the same there. Long lines of scorched and burnt grass and plants.

'Someone has been creeping into your garden in the dead of night with a lethal herbicide spray,' I said.

'Perhaps I ought to stay up all night and keep watch. I've got an air rifle. And a licence,' he added.

'No,' I said. 'Don't let him know that you are on to him. We'll let him think he is safe from being identified for the time being. I wonder if I could meet your wife.'

Mr Steel left me waiting in a sort of hall, part study, while he went to find his wife. It was a room with character, long slim windows and beamed ceilings, classy furniture and heavy curtains draped and folded. His desk was a partner's desk made of oak, leather-topped. On it was the newest flat screen computer and keyboard. A man with a business to run.

'I'm sorry,' he said, returning. 'I can't find Anne. She must have gone out somewhere. She probably didn't think you would want to talk to her. Can I offer you a drink?' he said, going over to a cabinet.

'Coke or juice would be nice,' I said.

'Orange or pineapple?'

'Pineapple, please.' I'd had enough orange juice to tint myself a delicate shade of carrot.

He poured out a juice into a crystal goblet and added ice.

'Thank you.'

He made himself something stronger with ice. I reckoned from the waft that it was whisky or maybe rum. I'm not an expert on spirits. Memo: become an expert.

'I'll make out this retainer for you now. Who do I make it out to?'

'First Class Investigations,' I said.

He switched on the computer, fed a cheque into a printer, keyed in the name and amount and pressed enter. It came out immaculately printed. I still write my cheques long hand, joined-up writing, biro.

'Thank you, Miss Lacey,' he said, signing the cheque in a normal, human fashion. 'I take it that you will return soon to make a plaster cast?'

'Almost immediately,' I said, folding the cheque and putting it into my back pocket. 'I have to collect some plaster.'

'I'll cover the print with some plastic sheeting in the meantime,' he said. 'And get a frame from the potting shed.'

Mr Steel walked me down to where I had parked the ladybird. He was interested in my car, walked round it, but was too polite to say very much. I got into the driving seat and wound down the window. It was boiling hot inside the metalwork. The seat was burning my seat.

'May I ask what you do for a living?' I said, my hand on the brake, expecting architect, solicitor, stockbroker.

'I'm a butcher,' he said.

People can surprise you. I was surprised. Samuel Steel was nothing like a butcher. I could not imagine him in an apron, chopping up chops, feeding pork scraps into a sausage machine, hacking great carcasses into weekend joints. Still, that is what he had said. I'm a butcher. Whatever kind of butchery he did, he'd made enough money from it to live on Updown Hill in Denbury Court. And someone was bent on destroying his garden.

I knew how to make a plaster cast from my WPC career. I was once a WPC in the days when a certain detective inspector let a rape suspect go free when I knew there was enough evidence for an arrest. He did not like it when I filed a complaint. Guess who got suspended? No prizes.

Let me explain, this was not the present hard-working Detective Inspector James whom I rate pretty highly even on an off day. DI James replaced the scumbag who has moved up north now. I hope I will never see scumbag again. He lost me my job and my living. If I had not pulled up my socks, I might be sleeping in the beach shelters like Gracie. Maybe even alongside Gracie and her six supermarket trolleys piled with loot. Heaven help me.

I drove back to Latching, blinded by the sun, hot and sweaty, hungry, already asphyxiated by chemicals. What a strange case. Still, the retainer was burning a patch in my jeans and I could not wait to get it to the bank. My last cases had not exactly made my bank manager glad to see me.

My two bedsits were cool and welcoming. The side-by-side rooms have high ceilings and sloping roof corners. I have two doorbells, two keys and two kitchen sinks; unusual but ideal for my needs. I threw myself into the bathroom, shed clothes and stood under a lukewarm shower. Twenty-five Celsius with a sea breeze. It had been a long cool spring, a slow summer and now a tropical heat had burst on us with volcanic violence. A crazy climate but I was not complaining.

I knew how to do acceptable impressions of footwear on a floor. Zinc powder and specialized lighting equipment. But plaster work had always been in the hands of a technician. Sergeant Rawlings would know. My clean casuals were still clean and I walked round to the station. It was my lucky day and the sarge was on the duty desk, looking hot and uncomfortable.

'Jordan,' he said. 'This is a surprise. I thought you were sunning yourself on the beach, not like us cretins, working our butts off.'

'Try getting yourself suspended and then you'll have all the time in the world.'

'Spare me the sob story, Jordan. We've heard it all before. How can I be of help?'

'I need to make a plaster cast of a bootprint. How do you do it these days? Where do I get the plaster? Are you still using plaster of Paris?'

'Your memory is correct. But we also use a new quick-setting plaster.'

'Trust in progress when my back's turned.'

'I daresay I could find a bag of the quick-setting, if you are in a hurry. Footwear prints get walked over so you've gotta be quick. You can replace it when you've got a spare tenner.'

'What a tiger,' I said, grinning. 'You're a star. My client will pay.'

'Careful, Jordan. A star *and* a tiger. It could go to my head.'

He got up and walked heavily towards the back of the station.

He did not look too well. Perhaps the heat was getting to him. DI James was not around. I did a quick check but no tall, granite-jawed detective on the premises.

I drove back to Denbury Court with a cut-out cardboard box for the framework and a ruler for scale. I also had the equipment for mixing the quick-setting plaster. According to the instructions, I would have to be pretty quick to not set myself too. I did not fancy a weekend in plaster.

The lean figure of Mr Steel was waiting for me at the end of the drive of Denbury Court. I could see he was distraught. He was pacing up and down, his arms folded across his chest. I hoped it wasn't Jack or Russell, two sick doggies after inhaling fumes or eating grass. That would be really unpleasant.

He came towards me as soon as he saw the distinctive ladybird climbing the steep road. He was waving his arms so I slowed down and stopped.

'What's the matter, Mr Steel?' I asked, winding down the window.

'Look what they've done! Look what someone has done! Driven right over it and I was so careful to protect it with a piece of plastic sheeting and a cloche from the greenhouse. Smashed, all smashed to pieces.'

Now I could see what Mr Steel was talking about. Someone had driven over the cloche and the bootprint, flattening the whole lot. No doubt the print underneath would be a mash of tyre, plastic and crushed grass. Not a lot of help.

'Did you see who did it?'

'No, I thought I heard this lorry or big car chuntering up the hill. We don't get many lorries. It's plain hooliganism.'

'Maybe or maybe not. I'll see what I can rescue of the print and the tyre. It might come in useful.'

'I am so sorry,' said Mr Steel.

'Don't worry. It's not your fault. We'll find the mystery sprayer, even if I have to stay up all night, perched in a tree in your garden.' I sounded braver than I felt. No tree was going to feel safe.

'You don't mean that?'

'I do. I'm Latching's number one surveillance expert. Give me something to watch and I'll watch it. A nice tuna sandwich and a thermos of coffee and I'm there till dawn.'

'You deserve wild smoked salmon,' said Samuel Steel. 'I'll get Anne to make some. Are you going to start tonight? I mean, right away? That would be brilliant.'

What could I do? My big mouth had led me into it again. I had not planned to do any night surveillance, and certainly not that night, but some fool talked me into agreeing.

'Yes, tonight,' I said. Pin a medal on me. Call me a heroine. I'd probably lose my mobile up a tree.

Two

H ere am I, up a tree with the sharp branches prickling through my jeans. This was ridiculous. Why couldn't I have done my surveillance from a deckchair in the greenhouse? The view, of course. I had a bird's-eye view of Latching – if I didn't fall off.

I'd come a roundabout way so that no one saw me arrive. A bus to the back of Latching, up a few lanes and then across a field to the lower edge of Updown Hill. Quite a walk.

Anne Steel had left a cling-film wrapped packet of smoked salmon sandwiches for me and a thermos of coffee. It was a kind gesture. She was out again and I had not met her yet.

'This is Anne's bridge evening,' said Samuel Steel apologetically.

'Players get addicted to bridge,' I said.

'Anne's group is addicted. The house could be falling down around them but they'd have to finish a rubber.'

We selected the best tree for viewing. It was a sturdy pedunculate oak with a large crooked crown some distance back from the drive entrance but with views in both directions. The only drawback was that I needed to be a bodybuilder, or a squirrel, to climb the rough, furrowed and rugged trunk. There were no holds.

'Once I'm up, I'll be alright. There's masses of foliage. And I'll be able to get down using a fireman's drop.'

'A fireman's drop?'

'Holding on with your hands, using your height and arm's length to minimize the distance of drop.'

'Useful to know.'

'Bend your knees on landing and roll over,' I added.

A ladder was the answer. Mr Steel held it steady while I climbed up into the heart of the tree. I hoped this was not going to be a regular occurrence. My camera was tucked into my back pocket and I'd checked the number of shots left after taking a few snaps of the damage to the garden.

'Are you sure you'll be all right?' said Mr Steel. He was obviously dubious about leaving a young woman up one of his trees. Maybe he was not insured. 'I'll be indoors if you need me. And Anne will be returning home about eleven. She drives a white Mazda coupé.'

I nodded through the branches. There was a strong branch that I could sit astride with the main trunk as a backrest. 'Don't forget to take away the ladder.'

This was new to me, being up a tree (*quercus robur*). Most surveillance cases were on foot or in the car. You could do something, keep yourself occupied. Read or listen to the radio, write up notes, draw pretty pictures. There was nothing to do in the encroaching night gloom except count leaves. I wondered if acorns were edible. Squirrels and pigs eat them.

Biology: the name *oak* comes from the Anglo-Saxon *ac* and Teutonic *aiks*. *Acorn* means oak-corn. How come I could remember this from my schooldays but was quite unable to remember any mobile phone number? Only James had a mobile identity that I could remember. But then James was special, even when he was not talking to me.

He was talking to me these days, in a restrained, aloof manner. He had not completely forgiven me for arranging to go on holiday to Cyprus with DS Ben Evans. That we did not actually go, he had brushed aside. He thought it was because all leave was cancelled due to a red alert in London. I knew that I had also missed the plane check-in time at Gatwick airport entirely. One day I would tell him the whole story. I could visualize his reaction now, those dark eyebrows raised in disbelief, the curved mouth sardonic, the blue eyes boring into me for the truth.

It was easy to think about DI James, stuck up a tree, only the prickles making me fidget. This surveillance was so boring. I was reduced to filing my nails.

Anne Steel arrived home at 11.08. Punctual lady. The low white car swept up the drive. Butchery must be doing well despite the various beef scares. The garage door opened automatically and she drove inside. I never caught more than the briefest glimpse of her. She looked slim and elegant.

Pouring coffee from a thermos whilst up a tree and holding a torch is not easy. I dropped the lid and spilt scalding coffee on my knee. Burnt lower lip with same scalding coffee. Decided that a bottle of water was a safer idea. Shopping list: blow-up cushion, game of peg solitaire, fruit gums.

The smoked salmon sandwiches were gourmet. Making them last was the main problem. I rationed myself to one dainty triangle, hostage-style, every half hour. It was starvation by numbers.

A few cars went by, their headlamps sweeping past the curve of the drive. There was a beauty spot on the top of the hill and a favourite parking place for courting couples who wanted to admire the views of Latching. Or any other twinkling views.

The lights in the house went out. I was in for a long wait if this spray merchant was a dawn riser. I peered down through the mosaic of foliage. The moon was casting silvery streaks across the lawn and distant sea. I had not checked on the moon. He would not come if there was moonlight to illuminate his antics.

I'd give it another two hours. The retainer had been generous and I had to earn it. Car lights swept down the hill, heading for home, a travel lodge, or a more secluded parking spot. DI James never took me to a secluded parking spot. Come to that, neither had Ben Evans.

The night was full of noises. Scamperings in the undergrowth, bats swooping, night owls hooting. I saw a fox in full glory loping across the lawn, his tail the colour of fire, his high-pitched barking unnerving. I thought I saw the majestic striped head of a badger, but he moved quickly through the shrubbery despite his bulk.

I nearly forgot why I was there.

I think I had almost fallen asleep.

There was a sudden flurry of cars accelerating up the hill, turning into the drive. I jerked awake. I recognized the flashing lights and garish green and yellow stripes on the cars. It was the police. Uniformed men got out of the cars and started racing towards the tree. My tree. The sturdy oak. They flashed lamps up into the branches. I was completely blinded. I forgot all about the fireman's drop and fell out of the tree.

In a split moment of impact, I remembered to bend my knees and roll over. I lay on the grass, face squashed, my heart pounding, wondering what I had broken.

'I should have known it was you,' said DI James.

He went down on his knees and peered into my face. 'How are you?'

'I don't know,' I gasped. 'Winded.'

He told his men to back off. I could not see what was happening. He came back to me and started to feel me all over. It was a purely medical examination. 'Does this hurt?'

'No.'

'Why were you lurking up a tree?'

'I do not lurk.'

'What were you doing up a tree?'

'I'm on surveillance.'

'Up a tree?'

'Yes, I was. For Samuel Steel who lives here. This is his house. Remember, the lawn spraying case.'

'Ah. We got a call from a couple who said they thought they saw a prowler at Denbury Court.'

'But was it me or someone else? I don't think they could have seen me. Perhaps there is a prowler. You'd better check, hadn't you?'

DI James sent his men round the house and garden. Lights came on. I ached all over but I did not think I had broken anything.

I pushed myself up into a sitting position and caught my breath. Aaah . . . it felt as if I had cracked a rib. There was a numbing pain in my side somewhere, about where the ninth, or floating rib exists. I said nothing. There was no way I was going to any more hospitals. They'd think I was a malingerer or had a crush on one of the doctors.

Mr Steel came hurrying out of the house, flashing a torch. A navy striped silk dressing gown flapped round his legs.

'What's going on?' he was saying. 'Have you caught him?'

'Detective Inspector James,' said James, showing his badge. 'We were called to investigate a reported intruder and your garden is being searched now. Unfortunately Miss Lacey fell out of a tree and somewhat delayed matters.'

Now I did not like that remark. He was putting the blame on me and that was not fair.

'My falling out of a tree took up all of ten seconds,' I said. 'You can hardly register that as a delay.'

'I had to check that you were not injured.'

'Two patrol cars full of uniformed police to check on the health of one winded female detective? Isn't that slightly over-doing your concern?'

DI James decided to ignore me, as he often does. He turned to Mr Steel. 'Miss Lacey is obviously uninjured. Her tongue is as sharp as usual.'

Mr Steel remembered his manners which was nice. 'You'd better come indoors, Miss Lacey,' he said. 'You need a cup of tea laced with brandy.'

'Thank you,' I said faintly, hoping I'd make it to the house. I held my side. It seemed a very long walk. I hardly noticed where I was going. Mr Steel took me through to a kitchen at the back. It was one of those gorgeous French farmhouse type kitchens with hanging brass pans and garlands of garlic and herbs strung from the oak beams.

'This is the oldest part of the house,' he said, seeing the interest in my eyes. 'Did you know that Denbury Court is classed as a Grade II manor house? Look at the floor, it's the original stone flagging.'

'Beautiful,' I said.

'Although the kitchen has every modern appliance, we have tried not to spoil the authentic atmosphere.'

'It's perfect.' I thought of the tiny corner kitchen unit in my living-room bedsit. Just enough room to shred a lettuce or make some soup. You could have prepared a banquet in this kitchen. They probably did in years past.

Samuel Steel made me a large cup of tea and added a generous dispensation of brandy. I sat down at a long, polished pine table, still holding my side. The tea was navy brew, strong enough to stand a spoon in, too strong for my taste but I acted the polite visitor and sipped. The brandy was pretty fiery, burning my throat.

'And you saw nothing at all?' he asked.

'No, I think there was too much moon. I need to check dates of damage with moons. Maybe he prefers the darker nights.'

'Of course. I've kept a random log of the damage during the latter part, not at first, because it did not dawn on me that someone was doing it. I just thought it was the dry summer. I'll fetch my diary for you. We can soon check.'

Still no Mrs Steel around. She had not appeared. How odd. I began to wonder why. I would have thought she might have got up to find out what was going on. Police cars flashing lights in a drive and burly officers tramping round the garden are enough to wake anyone from the deepest sleep.

Mr Steel returned with his diary. He'd scribbled in things like: '4 more plants dead' and 'another area of lawn lined brown'. His diary had little symbols for the size of the moon each week, and sure enough, the sprayer worked mostly during the last quarter of the moon and the first when the light was poor.

'Now we know the best time for me to keep watch,' I said.

'That's helpful. I'll be back in a week's time. Meanwhile I'd like to talk to a few people. Could you give me the name and address of the people who owned Denbury Court before you?' He nodded and began writing it down on a kitchen pad. 'And perhaps the people who bought your old house?'

I was not quite sure why I added them on to the list. It seemed to broaden the investigation, an investigation which at the moment went nowhere. I had to look as if I was doing something for his retainer.

'No problem,' he said, handing me a sheet of paper. 'All very nice people. Nothing to do with this, I'm sure.'

'Of course not. I'd like to check that it hasn't happened before,' I said, improvising fast. 'There could be a chain of events.'

'Ah,' said Mr Steel, not really understanding.

'Thank you for the tea. I'd like to go home now but I'll keep in touch.'

'Thank you, Miss Lacey. I hope you remembered your fireman's drop.'

I winced. My side was hurting with every breath. 'I remembered the roll.'

The police officers had gathered outside. They had found nothing and no one. DI James did not look as if he was going to offer me a lift. I would have to grovel. I rehearsed some grovelling words.

'Thank you, Mr Steel,' I said at the door. 'May I ask you one thing? I would have expected your wife to have got up and come downstairs. I would like to meet her. Did she not hear all this commotion?'

'I doubt it. Anne has trouble sleeping so she takes sleeping tablets, prescribed from the doctor. She's always dead to the world.'

'I see. Goodnight then, Mr Steel, or rather good morning. And thank you for the brandy.'

I strolled towards the first patrol car. DI James was waiting with the passenger door open.

'Do you want a lift?' he said, sparing me the humiliation of asking. His heart had that much generosity in it.

'Thank you,' I said, getting in carefully.

He slid into the driver's seat and started the engine. 'They don't do anything for cracked ribs these days,' he said, checking the rear-view mirror. 'Once they used to wrap an adhesive bandage round the chest which helped support the ribcage but was sheer agony to rip off. Now they don't bother.'

'What makes you think I have a cracked rib?' I said, holding on to my side as the car reversed down the drive.

'I could feel the tenderness. Don't worry. Six weeks and it will have healed. The first two weeks are the worst.'

I groaned. 'Thank you for the encouraging news. I still have to work and it hurts.'

'Painkillers and a deep support bra, that's the answer.' He said it with an edge of suppressed amusement as if he thought I deserved every sharp twinge and agonizing breath. Or perhaps it was the deep support bra. 'Remember not to cough or laugh.'

I extracted a shape from my back pocket.

'Would you like a squashed sandwich?' I said. 'Smoked salmon. I didn't get a chance to thank Mrs Steel when she came home.'

DI James was right, as always. A packet of 16 painkilling tablets diminished rapidly. They would not sell me a larger quantity in case I topped myself. Anyone wanting to quit this world could have gone into three adjacent chemist shops along the pedestrian walkway and bought enough tablets in ten minutes to send them off to everlasting dreams.

The waist-length bra was harder to buy. Only the older winceyette-type draper's shops stocked them. I pretended it was for my mother and that we were the same size. It was expensive. I chose a plain one, no lace, no rosebuds, work-manlike cotton and latex. It felt like putting on plated armour but the support did help. I could breathe with minimal pain. Don't make me laugh or cough or ask me to bend in any direction.

I wrapped myself in mythical cottonwool for a couple of days and dusted my shop. There were a few customers, mostly browsers. I had invested in one of those magnetic fibre dusters and cleaning was a doddle. My shop had never been so dust free. I was round the entire shop, without lifting a thing, removing dust, flicking at cobwebs, spiders and mould, in minutes. It was magic. I felt like a saviour.

'So,' said Doris, passing by with an armful of shopping. 'You are in the wars again?'

'I fell out of a tree.'

'One of them bird watching twitchers, are you?'

'Something like that, only I was observing a human variety of rare bird.'

'So I heard.'

'Tell me, Doris, how is it that you know everything that I do and I know nothing?'

'Mavis and I are old friends, from schooldays. Mavis has a neighbour who cleans up at Denbury Court. Very short grapevine. This cleaner found a thermos on the grass under a tree. Heard about the police taking someone into custody. She passed it on. Mavis and I can spot one of your cases a mile off.'

'I was not taken into custody. I was given a lift home,' I said, with restraint. Tawny hair has a temper too, even when it is tied back with a scrunchie. 'What can this grapevine tell me about Mrs Steel? I haven't met her yet.'

'Nothing at all,' said Doris, moving on. 'It doesn't work backwards.'

I was not convinced. I shut shop early and took my lunch break right then at Maeve's Cafe, the best seafood and chips cafe in Latching. It was busy, height of the season. My regular window table was taken by a couple of wheelchair tourists. I did not begrudge them the view. The tide was out and they could enjoy the vast sand, endless sea and therapeutic sunshine.

Mavis did not mention my ribs. She nodded towards a corner table at the back. 'They'll be going soon. They're on their second coffees. You won't have to wait long.'

'I'll wait here,' I said, leaning on the counter for support. 'It won't hurt too much.'

'I could start cooking your order.'

'Brilliant,' I said. 'Grilled haddock fillet and chips, please. I won't have cod as stocks are running out. Weak tea, if you've time.'

'With honey.'

'Please.'

It was impossible to pin an age on Mavis. She could have been a worn-out thirty or a well-preserved fifty. The colour of her dark blonde hair changed with the seasons. She had a fondness for the bronzed fishermen who enhanced Latching's shores with their muscular bodies. I envied her such a rampant love life.

'I hear you have a friend who works up at Denbury Court for the Steels,' I said casually.

'Not exactly a friend. She's my next-door neighbour, Joan Broseley. I met her this morning when I was out walking Jasper. She told me all about the shemozzle up at the house. It sounded like you. Thank you very much, sir. That comes to six pounds fifty. I hope you enjoyed your meal.' She dealt quickly with a departing customer.

The couple in the corner were collecting their belongings and leaving. I was only too happy to sit down and rest. Mavis would bring my lunch over when it was cooked. I wiped the table clean with a paper napkin. It was the least I could do.

Mavis came over with a steaming plate of fish and golden chips. It looked succulent and the smell was enough to make me faint. I'd lived on cheese rolls for several days. Stodgily boring even with excellent apple chutney bought at a summer fete.

'Thank you, Mavis,' I said. 'Do you think Joan Broseley would talk to me?'

'I'm sure she would. She likes visitors. Take her a box of chocolate mints. Only don't tell her I told you.'

I nodded my thanks and tucked into the delicious food. I ate like someone on the verge of malnutrition. Chips with fingers, fish on fork. Don't ask me to pass no etiquette test.

DI James came in the cafe and straight over to where I was sitting. My heart missed half a beat. Where did he get those dark, brooding looks?

'How come you get a seat?' he asked, eyeing my chair.

'Because I am nice to Mavis,' I said. 'And I'm an invalid.'

'So bribing Mavis is my only chance today.'

'She's busy. But you could sit at this table if you bring over a stool. There's room. Someone's taken the other chair.'

He sat down and rubbed his cropped hair. His tie was loosened and hanging at half-mast, shirtsleeves rolled up. 'It's hot. How is your rib? The cracked one?'

'Painful. The only way I can sleep is to hug a pillow. It's the one thing that helps.'

'You could merchandise the idea. Cracked rib pillows.'

'I'm not sure that there is exactly a vibrant market out there,' I said, offering him a chip. My pounding heart had settled down. He looked so handsome, but dark and distant. His skin had tanned with the summer days. His hands and bare arms were a darker shade than his face. Very touchable but out of bounds. I found I could cope if I concentrated on the food.

'Do you want to hear some odd news?' he asked, reluctantly, as if I was the last person he ought to tell.

'Sure. Shoot.'

'Samuel Steel has reported a missing person. It's his wife, Mrs Anne Steel. She has not been seen since the night of your tree incident. Yet you saw her arrive home, didn't you?'

'Yes.' A chip stopped halfway. 'I definitely saw her.'

Three

Mrs Joan Broseley lived in the same terrace of small Victorian cottages at East Latching as Mavis. Nesta Simons and her charming son, Dwain, also had one of the small houses. I was beginning to know the whole row. The Simons house looked closed up, windows dusty. They had either gone away, been sent away or removed entirely. Mrs Broseley's house, in contrast, was bright and sparkling with whiter than white net curtains and a brass door knocker that outshone the sun.

The duck pond and its inhabitants were surviving the arrival of Jasper, the untamable puppy who now lived with Mavis. Perhaps they had come to some doggy–duck agreement that he could chase them as long as he did not catch them.

It seemed reasonable to me. I knocked gingerly, concerned about leaving fingermarks on the polished brass. I heard brisk footsteps coming to the door and it opened.

'Yes?'

'Mrs Broseley?'

'Yes.'

'I'm Jordan Lacey, a private investigator. I'm at present working for Mr Samuel Steel and as you work for Mrs Steel, it seemed a good idea if we could have a chat.'

'Of course, that dreadful business of the garden. Come in, miss. I've never talked to a real detective before.'

I was not sure if I could be classed as a real detective but I was not going to argue and it was a pleasant thought. Mrs Broseley was a roly-poly, small mountain of a woman. Her flesh was a miniature landslide. Somewhere hidden in her face were twinkling eyes, button nose and a smiley mouth covered in glossy lipstick. She wore a brightly flowered tent and flip-flops.

'It's cooler in the kitchen with the back door open,' she said. 'I was making a cold drink. Would you like one?'

'Thank you,' I said, following her along a narrow corridor. It was painted white with lots of colourful pictures on the walls and souvenirs from holidays in Majorca. The kitchen was yellow with white tiles, curtains and work tops. Everything was spotless. You could have eaten off her kitchen table.

'Your house is a great advertisement for your work,' I had to say. 'I've never seen anywhere so clean and tidy.'

'That's very kind of you, miss,' she said, getting out a jug and starting to pour juice into it. 'I really like housework. I'm never happier than when making a place look polished.'

'I'm sure Mrs Steel appreciates your work.'

'It's a lovely house. They've got some really nice things. But the kitchen is a bit of a bugbear. I don't go for that old-fashioned look. All them garlics hanging from the beams, gathering dust. I wouldn't cook with that garlic. Is this enquiry about their lovely garden being wrecked?'

'Yes. Someone is intent on destroying it.'

I was fascinated by the cold drink in the making. Orange juice, pineapple juice, lemonade, cascades of ice and now a generous tumblerful of rum. Mrs Broseley was stirring vigorously, talking all the time.

'This is my rum punch,' she said. 'I learned how to make it in Barbados. We were on holiday there last year. I got a proper recipe but I usually put in anything that's handy.' She poured the punch into two long glasses, added some sliced fruit and then two paper umbrellas. She handed one to me. 'Down the hatch,' she said cheerfully.

'Down the hatch,' I agreed.

Phew. It was some drink. Tangy, tingy and icy cold. It went down like a glacier stream. I coughed on the alcohol as it hit the back of my throat. For a nanosecond I forgot why I was there. A breeze wafted in from the garden. I bet the garden was as tidy as her house. Petals ordered to stay attached till midnight.

'Mrs Anne Steel,' I reminded myself, twiddling the umbrella. 'Is she a nice lady to work for? Do you get on well with her?' 'Oh, yes. We get on very well, but I rarely see her. She leaves me alone and I don't see her around much. She's always out somewhere, bridge, workouts at the gym, golf, shopping. Mr Steel lets her do exactly what she likes. She's very independent.' And now Mrs Steel had disappeared. I said nothing. Mrs Broseley did not know yet apparently.

'Do you work at Denbury Court every day?' 'No, five days a week. I have every Sunday off and one day midweek. I'm taking today this week. It's a very good arrangement. Flexible, you know. Would you like another drink?' 'Thank you.' The rum was cooling on a hot day. 'Does Mrs Steel ever go off for days on her own?'

'Oh, those weekends at the health farm? Yes, she loves doing that. Every few months, she's off. Comes back looking really fit. She's got such a lovely figure but she works at it.'

Mrs Broseley needed no encouragement to talk. I was getting a good picture of Mrs Steel with every word. She would be blonde, slender and smart, wearing lovely clothes and lots of gold jewellery, driving her white coupé round the leafy lanes of West Sussex every day. Yet Mr Steel had given me a more homely picture, all this compatible hoeing and weeding. He said his wife had helped in the garden, that they enjoyed working there together. The gardening Mrs Steel sounded a different woman.

When I eventually decided to leave, the kitchen had a fuzzy edge and my asthma was becoming addicted to the punch. I thanked Mrs Broseley, quite forgot to give her the mints, and went looking for my car. No way was I in a state to drive my ladybird. I'd have to walk first. I'd take the coastal path and enjoy the sea air. Clear away the fumes of the rum punch. It had been enjoyable but not conducive to solving local crime.

Shopping list: water.

The heat coming off the beach was blissful. I took off my sandals and walked in the shallows, the water cooling my overheated feet. (Does alcohol go to the feet?) The tide was coming in and I had to walk fast to get round the end of each groyne before a deeper wave made it impossible. It was a contest between me and the sea. I had to judge each receeding wave and the amount of time it gave me to reach and scramble round the end post of the next groyne. My jeans got splashed as the tide entered into the spirit of the game, determined to beat me. Who was this mere human? Taking on the mighty pull of the moon. What impudence.

Several dogs entered into the fun, racing me, leaping up with playful paws. I was still apprehensive about dogs since a violent encounter with a bull mastiff, but these were sweet-faced, long-boned collies and without a single vicious streak in them.

'Good boys,' I said, encouragingly. 'Let's beat the next one!'

The dogs were not so worried about getting wet. But I was quite wet already. Sandy paw marks on my white T-shirt adding to my general disarray.

'Hi, Jordan. Don't you wish we were in Cyprus?' a man shouted from the shelf of shingle. His jacket was flung over his shoulder. It was Detective Sergeant Ben Evans, my fervent admirer. I hoped he would not start kissing me on the beach. One could never tell. Even police behaviour is unpredictable on a hot day.

'This is just as sunny,' I said, not giving him the answer he wanted. He was not the paddling type. He kept walking along-side on the lowest rim of the pebbles.

'We'll make it another time,' he said confidently. 'I've still got some leave to come. It'll be great.'

'Sure. Are you busy?'

'Usual mindless crimes. Robberies, muggings, car thefts. Latching's normal happy holiday scene. What are you doing?'

'Vandalism of a lovely garden on Updown Hill. Isn't that exciting? No clues as yet apart from a crushed bootprint.'

'I'm sure you will give it your best.'

'Of course, don't I always?'

Ben flashed his attractive grin at me. It was such a pity that I was not in love with him. It would have been so easy. But you can't turn on love to order. I liked him, liked him very much. That was as far as it went. I sent him a return smile.

'You are going to get soaked,' he shouted as the tide raced in. 'Bet you can't make the next one.'

The dogs made it, their legs deep in water but I did not. The waves swept over my knees, dragging me back as they receded, heels dug in swirling sand. I'd had enough. I staggered ashore, very wet indeed, laughing.

'That last wave served me right,' I said. 'You put me off my calculations.'

'Sorry. I did not realize the great mind was at work.'

That's what I liked about Ben. This casual ragging. As if he was my brother. The thought consolidated. Yes, I liked him as a brother, not a lover. But he was not in brother mode. Was I falling into incest? I did not have a brother. This was becoming too complicated for me to cope with.

He took my arm as I staggered up to the shingle, pulled me towards his chest, kissed me quite thoroughly. My sore ribs winced in the embrace. I hoped he could not feel the long-line bra. But his mouth was both gentle and seeking.

'Jordan,' he said, the word coming from the pit of his stomach. 'Darling . . .'

It was the rum punch, of course, but I kissed him back in broad daylight. All of Latching could watch. A semi-porn video was showing on the beach. No, not quite. Not a stitch came off. It was all in the mind.

'Ben,' I said, disentangling myself.

'Still love me?' he asked.

What could I say? I have never loved him in the same insanely passionate way that I feel about DI James. But I could not hurt him. Ben was nice, attractive, a dish. The sort of upright man that any normal woman would be thankful for. He was second-best for me and it was wrong to give him any encouragement.

'I care very much,' I said. 'But I'm not going to say that I love you until I'm sure.' It was the best I could do.

He seemed satisfied. I felt as guilty as hell. We walked along the shingle, slipping and sliding. He took my hand.

'How's the rib?' he asked.

'Healing. As long as I am not grabbed by hunky men.'

'Sorry. I forgot.'

'I won't breathe for a few minutes.'

'Like to go out for a drink tonight?' Ben asked.

'Dancing, jazz, razzmatazz?'

'Can't promise more than a sober glass of red.'

'Give me a call.' I did not want to say yes. I could pretend to be out, not answer the phone. I'm such a coward.

We said goodbye and I walked back to collect my car. On the way I bought a bottle of mineral water from a kiosk and drank the lot. Ben had not tasted the rum in my mouth. Life was taking me in strange directions. The tide was high now, pounding the shore in a dominant don't-argue-with-me way. It was hissing and growling.

'OK. You win,' I said.

The sea sucked itself back and returned with a smooth reflex action, washing over the pebbles, shining them with sea-gloss, strands of seaweed and dewdrops from a distant ocean. The sky was a reflective ceiling of blue with rags of clouds scattered like wings of angels. Sometimes I thought I had a guardian angel, but I was not sure. I might have seen him once.

I walked back, wondering who could be so vindictive that they would want to destroy a quite beautiful hilltop garden. What ever kind of chemical spray they were using, it had already killed the former glory of Denbury Court gardens. There was little left. Only dead and dying plants and scorched grass.

Who would do such a thing? I made a list:

1. Former employee of successful millionaire butcher.
2. Former owner of Denbury Court.
3. Present owner of Steel's previous home, but why?
4. Ex-lovers of either Mr or Mrs Steel. ???

The possibilities made me feel quite ill. How could I possibly track down all these people, find out what made them tick, discover if they had a hidden agenda? I preferred being up a tree. I'd bring my own sandwiches.

And the disappearance of Mrs Steel was not my case load though I had an uncanny feeling it was going to become so. I drove back to Updown Hill, carefully. The potent punch had worn off but blood tests these days are pretty scary. You can still be over the limit hours later.

I turned into the drive of Denbury Court and caught my breath. The monster had made another overnight visit. Whole new areas of lawn were burnt brown. Where had I been while it was happening? I should have been here.

Mr Steel came out to meet me. He was distressed, pale-faced, hands flapping and wringing. The whole atmosphere of the place had changed. Shafts of light were making crazy patterns and the acrid smell was overpowering.

'My wife has gone, disappeared, without leaving a word. She didn't say where she was going. I don't know where she is and now this . . . What is happening, Miss Lacey? Please help me. I don't know what to do. This is driving me mad.'

I knew how he felt.

'Please try to stay calm, Mr Steel. I'll do all I can. You have informed the police, haven't you? Perhaps Mrs Steel has taken a sudden visit to a health farm, something to surprise you?'

'Yes, she might have but she always tells me. I informed the police as soon as I realized she'd gone.'

'I'll take some more samples,' I said. 'Try to date this stuff and identify the chemicals.'

I put on gloves and found a patch, out of sight, that was still slightly burning, and dug around it, lifting the sod into one of my larger plastic specimen bags. I needed my own forensic expert. Some hope. Perhaps I ought to chat up a scientist.

The garden smelt bad. It had that last breath feeling about it. Any moment it would turn over and expire. It was horrendous and pointless. What did it achieve? Nothing. Fortunately, no human bones around. I had a sudden nightmare vision of Mrs Steel immersed in a vat of chemicals.

'I take it that the police are making all the right enquiries following Mrs Steel's disappearance? Hospitals, ferries, airport? Did she take her passport?'

'She took nothing, no money, no clothes, not her passport or credit cards. Only the car. The car has gone. Her white Mazda coupé. And I've phoned everywhere that I can think of, the hospitals, her friends. No one seems to know anything.'

'And the police are searching for her car?'

'Yes. It must be somewhere.'

'Would Mrs Steel have sold it? It must be worth a lot of money.'

'She might have sold it but only under duress. It was her pride and joy and she was very fond of it.'

Samuel Steel was clearly distraught. This was no play-acting. He was pacing about like an animal, a film of sweat on his face, his hands clenched. His hilltop garden was a scene of desecration, shredded like an old secret. The sweeping lawns were scarred with ancient lava paths, burnt earth and long lost rituals. This was about the past. Some Iron Age fort. Bones long buried. I could feel an old animosity searing the air itself.

'I can't believe this is happening.' He was talking to himself now, quite unaware that I was present. 'Anne, Anne . . . where are you? Please come home. Please get in touch with me, wherever you are. Dearest, don't leave me like this.'

'Have you had any strange communications? A letter or phone calls? No threats? Had Mrs Steel received anything odd in the post in the last few days? A parcel or delivery?'

'No, no, I don't think so. Nothing.'

'Does Mrs Steel have a mobile? Have you phoned her mobile?'

'I've tried. There's no answer. I don't think it's switched on or the battery has run out.' Mr Steel was running his hands through his hair. I was starting to worry about the man. And I did not like the feeling in the garden. Lawns one night, house the next?

'Have you got someone who could come and stay with you, Mr Steel? I don't think you should be on your own.'

'There's my daughter, Michelle.'

'Would she come over? Where does she live?'

'Chichester. Half an hour's drive and she'd be here. That is, if she's in. She's an actress.'

'How lovely. Why don't you give her a ring?' I had a second thought. 'You have told her, Michelle, haven't you, I mean, about her mother?'

'Anne is not her real mother. Anne is my second wife and no, I haven't told her, but I will now. Michelle will come if she can, I'm sure of that.'

So Anne was a second wife, probably younger and prettier, Botox and Barbie. I'd heard it all before. I did not ask about Michelle's mother. It could wait.

He hurried into his study and I heard him on the phone but the words were not audible. It was a long conversation. Michelle had a lot to say. I wandered about the garden looking for signs of entry, any indication of how the intruder arrived and left. He must have left something genetic behind. No one goes anywhere without leaving something of themselves behind. But what? I could hardly send the whole garden for DNA testing.

A scrap of silver paper caught my eye. It was the screwed up wrapper of a Penguin chocolate bar. Not Mr Steel's style. Nor would he have thrown the wrapper away in his own garden. I scooped it into a specimen bag without touching. People bite bars. There might be saliva on the inside folds of the wrapper.

Mr Steel came out into the garden. He had a belled brandy glass in his hand and seemed steadier. 'Michelle's coming over,' he said. 'She's not working at the moment. The acting profession is very volatile. She's resting more often than she is acting.'

'A bit like detecting,' I said. 'It comes in seasons. I either have a lot of cases or none.'

'What do you do in between?'

'I run a shop.'

'How very sensible,' he said, his voice full of shop-keeping approval. 'I wish Michelle would do something like that. She just lounges about, drinking a vast amount of coffee.'

'Could you tell me a little about your work?' I said. 'I don't imagine that you are an actual butcher in a white and navy striped apron, serving in a shop or butchering out the back.'

'No,' said Samuel Steel. 'Although I did wear one when I was younger, that is, when I was working in my father's shop. I did learn the trade. But then I discovered that I was better at running shops rather than chopping chops, and began to expand. There's now a whole chain of our shops and I have gone into retail supply. I supply big supermarkets with fresh meat.'

'I don't eat meat,' I told him.

'Very wise,' he agreed.

'Have you any competitors who might have a vendetta against you? Have you trodden on any toes?'

'Heavens, no! What an idea. We all get on very well, play golf together. Anne is more likely to have a bridge friend who does not like being beaten.' His face clouded over as he thought of his wife. He gulped at his brandy; not the way to drink it. He saw my eyes on the drink. 'Would you like one?'

I shook my head. 'No, thank you, I'm working,' I said, like a police officer on duty. I was also driving on Mrs Broseley's punch.

'Coffee?'

'Yes, please. Black.'

We went back into the house and through to the kitchen. I could see Mrs Broseley's handiwork. The gleaming pans and sparkling surfaces. Mr Steel knew how to make real coffee. Ground some Brazilan beans. I was addicted to the smell. As I drank the mug of coffee, we went through the possibilities of why Anne might have disappeared.

'I hate to ask this, Mr Steel, but do you think she might have met another man? It does happen.'

'Never. Out of the question. We are so happy together, always have been. No, that has never crossed my mind. We've been married eight years and they have been the happiest ever. Truly, Miss Lacey, there is no one else for either of us.'

For a moment his face was uplifted, perhaps momentarily

flushed by the brandy. He was, truly Miss Lacey, devoted to his wife. I only hoped that she was as devoted to him. She might be halfway to Sorrento with a darkly Italian lover.

'And how about Mrs Joan Broseley, your cleaning lady? Could she know where Mrs Steel has gone?'

'Joan? Heavens no. She'd have no idea. Wonderful cleaning lady, an absolute treasure, but they were not close, never were.'

I hoped Michelle would arrive soon. I was running out of consoling-type conversation. DI James was supposed to be looking into this. He should be here, saying all the right things, looking severe and intense. I knew he was doing all the right things, but back at the station. Mrs Anne Steel was one case among many. Latching might be a sleepy seaside town, only a ghost of its former Georgian glory after Princess Amelia visited it in 1798. Before then it had been a small fishing village with night-time smugglers. But now, in its new growing catalyst, crime was expanding alongside commerce.

My shop, First Class Junk, was an expansion. First Class Investigations was an expansion. Latching had not had a private investigator before. I was the first. One day they would put up a blue plaque on my shop:

JORDAN LACEY
LATCHING'S FIRST
PRIVATE INVESTIGATOR

I hoped they spelt my name right.

We heard a loud roaring noise heading up the drive. It could only be one of those little open roadsters with souped up engines. Samuel Steel nodded.

'That's Michelle, my daughter,' he said, putting down his glass and hurrying out.

I followed him outside. The roadster was bright yellow, open topped, and Michelle was climbing out without opening the door. She was a dark-haired beauty, finely built, face like a bird. She was wearing skinny jodhpurs and a skimpy top that showed off her tanned shoulders. She came striding over to her father, all pent-up energy.

'So she's gone, has she? The robotic Barbie wife? Not before time. Well, all I can say is, good riddance!'

Four

M ichelle launched into a passionate tirade as soon as her father went indoors to answer the phone. Most of it was vitriolic, anti-Anne stuff. It was like a scene from a play and I wanted to leave after the first act. Although I knew I should stay on in case any useful or useless information came up accidentally. I'd rather surf the Internet.

'I'm not surprised she's cleared off. Not exactly Lady of the Manor material. More Barbie of the Bar. With or without the extensions, Botox, the laser. Did she take a meat cleaver with her? She might find it handy in her next career.'

'I've no idea.'

'I expect the family silver has gone. Have you counted the spoons? She's partial to the odd heirloom.'

'I guess I ought to go soon,' I said, interrupting the flow. 'I've other work to do.' Liar.

'You'd better find out who's done all this vile damage to my father's beautiful garden,' said Michelle. 'Don't bother about the ubiquitous Anne. She's all right. She'll make her own bed. Probably shacked up with one of those gorgeous fishermen on the beach.'

No, I didn't think so. Mavis had a monopoly.

'I wonder if I could have a contact number for you, Michelle? There may be several points to check.' She handed me a flamboyant deckle-edged gold card which had a flash face photo on it and detailed CV. Michelle had apparently appeared in several soaps. Bubble acting.

'Wow,' I said, feigning impressed. 'Well done. TV. What are you doing at the moment? Chichester Theatre is right on your doorstep. Do you ever get any work there?'

'I've been in a few pantos,' she said, not going into which pantos or when. Back row of the chorus? 'I'm reading scripts at the moment. The rubbish they send me. It's heartbreaking.'

Actor-speak for resting.

'Your father must be very proud of you,' I said, walking towards my ladybird. 'I shall watch out for you on television.'

'Don't hold your breath,' she said with a tinge of bitterness. She was a very pretty girl but I guessed they were a dime a dozen at auditions. It was that extra special something that made one hopeful stand out, and perhaps Michelle did not have that quality. I would never stand out despite my hair. They'd think I was merely a shadow or something washed up by the tide.

A magpie strutted across the lawn like a male model. There was some folk poem about one magpie or several magpies but I could not remember what it was. They were either good luck or bad luck. You took your choice.

'I'll be in touch,' I said, getting into my car.

'Please yourself,' said Michelle. She swung away, tiny hips swinging in tight jodhpurs, bikini line in view. 'She damned well did this, you know. She didn't care a jot about Dad's garden. Or perhaps she paid someone else to do it. She'd know how to hire a thug or two. It's probably charged to him on one of his cards. Bet she signed her name somewhere.'

'Give me a motive,' I said sharply, leaning out of the window. 'She would have to have a motive.'

Michelle's face was twisted. It was not a pretty sight. The mauve shadowed eyes were hooded. 'It was revenge, Miss Lacey. Revenge, pure and simple.'

'Revenge for what? Mrs Steel has everything. A doting husband, a lovely home, car, money. Why should she want to ruin everything? I don't understand. Revenge for what?'

'Find that out and you've solved the mystery,' she snapped.

This was too enigmatic for me, yet I knew that things were often not what they appeared. 'Thank you, Miss Steel. You've been a great help. Keep reading those scripts.'

I was not sure if Mr Steel's retainer covered investigating the activities of his wife. It did not seem ethical. I had never met the woman. Perhaps I had to find her and that would not be easy if she had disappeared. My resources were one spotted car, one mountain bike, a mobile and a clapped out portable typewriter. DI James: I need your help. One word might point me in the right direction. Phone me, please. He didn't.

I added two more names to my list of suspects. Mrs Anne Steel and Miss Michelle Steel or Michelle Tapley as she was professionally known. I had read the card before stowing it on the passenger seat.

Michelle had a stronger motive than Anne Steel. She disliked the new Mrs Steel intensely and might do anything to drive a giant stake between her father and the woman. Even at the cost of his precious garden.

Perhaps I should start by investigating Michelle Steel's background and current pursuits. Ladybird was revving to go but I had not yet let off the handbrake.

'By the way,' I added, still leaning on the open window. It was hot. 'Where did you train? Did you go to RADA?'

'No, I trained at the Italia International School of Drama. I went there to combine normal schooling with drama training. It's very well known.'

'I have heard of it. So you took A Levels?'

'I got three A Levels: French, Biology and Science. I was no good at English or Maths.'

'Me neither,' I agreed. 'Still hopeless at Maths. I have to use all my fingers and toes, ears as well sometimes. Bye.'

The ladybird was tired of waiting and leaped away as soon as I eased off the handbrake. Her interior was intense with heat and I could feel the backs of my legs prickling with sweat. The breeze through the open window was like a hairdryer on top volume. It lifted the hair round my neck, dried off my skin. The sky was a well of blue, limpid and lucid. Not a cloud in sight.

Biology and science. Diverse subjects for an artistic drama student. Still, she'd know a few chemicals, paraquat and nicotine in particular, both highly toxic pesticides.

*   *   *

The light was changing and the air charged with a coming storm. I could feel it. So could every cat in Latching. Their fur stood on end, whiskers twitching, eyes watchful. Dogs, on the other hand, romped around on the beach, chasing seagulls, with their usual indifference to the weather.

A man was pacing the pavement outside my shop. He was athletic looking, broad-shouldered and narrow-hipped, over 6 ft, wearing immaculate white jeans and short-sleeved white shirt. His dark hair was tied back in a ponytail, his forearms tattooed with serpents. His appearance was a mass of contradictions.

'Hello,' he said. 'Don't you ever open your shop?'

'Sorry,' I said, fishing for my keys. 'Won't be a moment. Is there something you want to buy?'

I had not sold anything for several days. No wonder shops are always changing hands or closing down. You had to sell a lot of stuff to cover overheads. Thank goodness my staff are unpaid and not prone to complaining. Staff = me.

'I want to buy your time,' he said.

He had a really nice voice. Warm, deep, a pleasantly light baritone and casual. He held the door open for me. And manners . . . this was almost over the top. I was tempted to go back and see if he did it twice.

'Please come in,' I said politely, hoping the dust would not show. Me and my magnetic duster had not seen each other today. And I couldn't feel sexy in a long-line bra. 'Have a look round.'

'I don't have much time for shopping. Just lead me to the detective agency and the lady detective. Is that you?'

'That's me,' I said modestly. 'Please come through to my office.' I needed another case. Desecrated gardens are static and somewhat unsatisfactory to work on. I put on the coffee percolator and asked my hunky visitor how he liked it.

'Black, no sugar, thank you.' Same as me.

I got out a notebook, crossed my legs and tried to look calm and professional. He was disturbingly good-looking. He had the brightest of eyes, colour indecipherable, somewhere between grey and brown, flecked with gold.

'How can I help you?'

'I have had a stalker for months and she's driving me nearly mental.'

It was the last thing I expected to hear. He looked so capable of taking care of himself. He could flick off a stalker with a toss of that ponytail. But apparently not.

I poured out the coffee and handed him a mug. 'I'd like to take some notes,' I said. 'Please begin with your name.'

'My name is George Hill, George the Jester in the trade. I'm in show business. I'm a comedian. I tell jokes. Hire me for any event and I'll make it swing.'

This was disappointing, and it hurt swallowing the disappointment. I had expected a higher profile, stockbroker, lawyer. airline pilot. And here was an end-of-the-pier act, telling jokes at any event, making it swing.

'Go on, Mr Hill.'

'I'm well known on the South Coast circuit. People like me. I've bookings right into next year. But this woman is stalking me. She's always there, at every function, every event. There she is, out front, looking at me. I can't get away from her. Now she has found out where I live.'

'Do you live in Latching?'

'Yes, I live at Chapel Court. It's a block of flats behind the Co-op supermarket. Newish built. Brick boxes. Nothing special.'

'I know the block. And the number, please.'

'Seventeen. That's on the top floor. It's small, just a home base. I work away a lot of the time and live in hotels.'

'Tell me about this woman,' I said.

'I've just told you. She sits in the front row, staring at me. Everywhere I go, she's there. Now she stands outside the flats, waiting for me to leave. The other day she was behind me in the queue at the Co-op. I nearly dropped the basket and ran.'

'Hey,' I said. 'You're a grown man. Surely you could cope with a woman in a queue? That's not so difficult.'

He gave a snort of pure annoyance. 'You don't seem to understand. She's stalking me and I don't like it at all. It's an infringement on my privacy. I'm a very private man. I want to know who she is and what is going on.'

'She probably has a crush on you, Mr Hill. You are a very attractive man and she may be lonely.'

He was mollified for five and a half seconds. 'That is not the point, Miss Lacey, and it's far more than that. I want you to find out who she is and I want her to stop. No more. You tell her. I've had enough and am ready to go to the police.'

George Hill gulped down the coffee. He was obviously annoyed. Artistic temperament. Two show business people in one day, an actress and a comedian. Perhaps I should specialize. PI to the Stars. I sat back in a momentary glow of career escalation.

'So you would like me to find out who she is?' I said, floating back to earth, my office, my shop.

'Of course, that's the whole point of coming to you. Find out who this woman is and get rid of her.' His voice was unexpectedly edged with steel. The flecks of gold in his eyes had hardened.

'My fee is £10 an hour or £50 for a day.'

'I'll take the day rate. I want it done quickly.'

I had no scruples. Mr Steel had paid me a retainer. No rate or time specified. So the work might overlap. Well, so what, I told myself. I wrote out a contract and George Hill signed it with a flamboyant signature.

'Tell me exactly any dates and times that you can remember,' I said.

He got out a slimline diary, the kind I gave DI James for Christmas. Coward. I had wanted to give him the moon.

'I've been making a note. Here are some of the dates and times that I wrote down. There's lots more that I can't remember. This is serious, I tell you. The woman is no teenage crush. She's dangerous. I could be knifed on the street.'

I was impressed. I wrote down a series of dates and times. George Hill was right. This was no ordinary crush. I hoped it was nothing sinister. Women go through hormonal changes which send them off balance. There was even an illness called

De Clerambault's syndrome. Perhaps it was one of those things.

'And can you describe her?'

'Easily. About forty, well-built, brown hair twisted up in a French pleat, good clothes, loads of jewellery. Maybe a face lift.'

She sounded a lot like Anne Steel.

'I'll work on this straight away,' I said. 'But it may take longer than you think. Stalkers are often very devious people.'

'Would you come with me to some gig?' he asked suddenly. 'Do yourself up, wear something snazzy. She might think you are my girlfriend and clear off.'

I was not sure if this was a compliment or not. Do myself up? I'd rather go out with Jack from the Pier Amusements. He never tells me what to wear, bless him. And my jazz trumpeter, the man with the top F, is pleased that I am there, listening to his music.

'Hello sweetheart,' he always says.

'We'll see,' I said. 'If absolutely necessary, it could be arranged. If you think it would work.' Shopping list: take black dress to the cleaners.

It was the best I could do. Gorgeous hunk rose and shook my hand. He was in the wrong profession. He should be standing for Parliament. I would vote for him anytime. So would the entire female population of Latching.

'It's worth a try.'

'Tell me a joke,' I said.

He looked at me in surprise. There was a theatrical pause, then he raised an eyebrow. 'How many politicians does it take to change a light bulb?'

'I don't know.'

'Eleven. One to change the bulb and the rest to form a committee.'

I raised a smile.

'Not one of my best but you did catch me on the hop,' he grinned.

My office felt empty after George Hill had left. There was no doubt that he was a super stud. And he would improve with age. It was not fair. Men got better looking as they matured. DI James is à la carte now. In ten years' time he would be an outrageous, hormone-racing, irresistible six foot plus of pulsing manhood with streaks of silver in his hair. And that was on a bad day.

A distant rumble of thunder gave notice of the coming storm. I put a couple of umbrellas in the window. They always sold well. They did not merit a £6 price ticket as you could get brollies for a couple of pounds at Woolworths now.

A woman came into the shop almost immediately. She was thin, hawk-like, wearing a long dress, floaty scarves and gloves. 'That umbrella in the window, the one you've just put in, the one with the silver handle,' she began without stopping for breath. 'Where did you get it?'

'The old black one? I didn't notice that it had a silver handle.' I was still in Hill haze.

'Yes, but where did you get it from?'

'I've no idea, from some house clearance perhaps. I've had it ages. I think it's got a split.'

She leaned against the counter, clutching the edge. 'It's my mother's. How much is it? I'll pay anything.'

The £6 price tag swam back into view. A silver handle was worth £6. But it was her mother's . . . My conscience wrestled with my acute business acumen.

I went to the window and took out the umbrella. The black silk was faded, almost fawn in places. The silver handle was tarnished but a scrolled pattern was still visible. I could imagine some lady in the Thirties or even Edwardian days carrying this very elegant brolly along the front to shield her delicate skin from the sun's rays.

'Are you sure it is your mother's?'

'I'm sure. She's dead now. But I remember this umbrella so well from when I was a little girl. She was very fond of it.'

It was no contest. I took off the price tag and handed it to the woman. She looked at me in amazement. 'Here you are,' I said.

'It's yours. I couldn't charge you for your mother's umbrella. It's full of memories, your memories.'

'I don't believe this,' she said, touching the silk. 'I feel I ought to pay you.'

'Buy something another time,' I said, much cheered by my own generosity. 'You'll need the brolly. It's going to pour any minute now. Look at that cloud.'

The sky had darkened. The Cornish coast was sending Sussex the clouds that it didn't want. A strong wind hurried them along, streaking the sky with long arms of menace. I did not like the look of it. Thunder rumbled again, near this time.

'You'd better get home.'

But she seemed rooted to the spot and I almost had to push her out of the door.

'I can't thank you enough,' she managed to say.

'That's OK.' This was one of my halo days.

'You're really very kind. Maybe one day I will be able to repay you.'

It was starting to spit as she went down the two steps to the pavement. She hurried away, all fluttering scarves and thin legs. She did not look back, already lost in her childhood memories. I wondered what her name was. I should have asked. Contacts of any kind are always useful.

The heavens opened, large drops splattering the pavement, and I drew back, standing in the shelter of my doorway, feeling the chill of the cloud burst. This rain might just revive Mr Steel's lawn. It depended on whether the weedkiller had reached the roots.

I pulled on a waterproof, blinked at the lightning, locked up my shop and set out for the Co-op. The thunderclaps were overhead, loud as an explosion, making me jump every time. It was not far to walk even when it was chucking it down and the rain bounced back off the pavements, so you got wet twice.

Chapel Court was a lacklustre block of concrete flats designed by architects with no imagination and built by builders with even less. Plain, characterless identical windows. No balconies. No interesting stonework. Number 17 was on the top floor. It had a high-tech answerphone entrance. I pressed the button for number 17 but no one was in as I expected.

I hovered, searching the area for similarly hovering woman with intense look. There was no one about. Only a woman walking a dog and she did not look once in my direction.

I did a quick tour of the Co-op. George Hill had said she shopped there, but maybe only occasionally. I bought a tin of mixed salad beans and a jar of curry sauce. Curried bean soup? Every shopper had the normal frazzled look of busy, tired, irritated mums with whining children, legs hurting, depressed, complaining, or like me, passing through in a haze of boredom.

It was still raining and the storm was right overhead, thunder stalking the Downs, lightning zagging the dark with electrical slashes. I was not frightened of lightning but I didn't like the crack of thunder. It was awesome. As if a bit of heaven broke off and hurtled towards earth. Straight towards me.

As I drifted away, wet hair wrapped round my neck, head down, a shadow crossed my vision. A woman had come out of Chapel Court and merged into the swirling rain. She crossed the road and then hurried into the supermarket entrance. There was something vaguely familiar about her although I knew no one who lived in the flats except George Hill.

I went back into the Co-op and scanned the aisles but she had disappeared into the crowd of shoppers. People hung around in the entrance, not wanting to make a dash for their cars.

A line was nagging me. Was it something George Hill had said? Or something that Michelle had said? It's annoying when a thought nags. I couldn't shrug it off.

Five

T he ladybird had been through a complimentary rainwash. Her spots gleamed, and the red of her paintwork glistened as new. Unfortunately I had not closed the passenger window properly and the upholstered seat was damp. I picked up Michelle's sodden business card and took it indoors to dry off.

I propped it on a windowsill so some air would get to it. The heavy clouds were rolling off in a different direction and the storm was clearing. The coolness had a tinge of autumn in it. Ah, were we being told that summer was over? Surely not already? We had not had our fair share of summery days this year. The heat had been a passing wonder, a haze of sea merging with sky.

I stripped off my wet outer clothes and hung them up to drip. The card fluttered off the windowsill and landed at my feet. I picked it up and was about to stand it again, when I caught sight of some writing on the back.

I turned it over. '*Who's next?*'

It was written in biro, the question mark smudged as if the writer's hand had been sweating. *Who's next?* I stared at the words. Who's next for what? A wayward thought came unbidden and I caught my breath. Disappearing, desecration, stalking? Which of the three? My three cases. The hairs on the back of my neck cringed. The words had not been there when Michelle gave me the card. I'd looked on the back to see if the stagey CV continued. It had been blank.

The words had been added while the card was lying on the seat in my car. It made me feel sick that someone had invaded my car, touched any part of it while I was not there. Someone who knew what was going on, perhaps a person who knew of my cases, someone who was involved in some way.

Was it me next? And how? Acid on my car? Paint sloshed over my shop or worse, burning rags stuffed through the letterbox? Me being stalked and watched? Me mysteriously disappearing?

On the other hand, it could be a nutter with nothing better to do. There were people like that.

I hurried into some dry clothes, squeezed my feet back into clammy sandals. The discomfort went unnoticed. Now perhaps DI James would listen, take me seriously. I was desperate. I prayed for help. It was auto-pilot to the police station.

The station was packed wall to wall with people. They were the feuding families of some domestic punch-up; both sets of relatives still arguing among themselves while a pregnant young woman was weeping in a corner and a young man was holding a bleeding nose.

'I'm not having it,' he was shouting. 'You're all f****** morons.'

'Don't you dare touch her,' threatened a heavyweight mother, arms akimbo. 'Leave her alone.'

'She's my wife.'

'I'll knock your bleeding head off,' growled an equally heavyweight father, glowering. 'You f****** her up.'

'You leave my son alone! You ignorant bastard!'

It sounded potentially dangerous. I bleeped the swear words out of my head, left the desk sergeant and the WPCs to deal with the party and wandered off to look for DI James. He would not be involved in a domestic. The same old notices hung on the corridor walls. Upstairs was out of bounds for the public but I was not public. Surely an ex-WPC had special privileges?

He was sitting at his desk, body swung away from the door, talking on the phone. He did not hear me come in. I could stand and drink in the broad shoulders and dark, cropped head without anyone wondering. Just being there and watching him at work calmed my nerves. I even felt a twinge of lust. The back of his neck was strong and muscled though he was rubbing it with one hand as if it was stiff. My fingers knew exactly where to find those tense muscles.

'I want that information by tomorrow morning,' he was saying. 'On my desk. No more excuses. You've had enough time.' His voice was firm, authoritative with a hint of menace. But no swearing, no blustering, my man in charge. I like a man in charge.

He put the phone down, swung his chair round to face his desk and opened a file.

'No,' he said, without looking up.

'I didn't say I wanted anything,' I said.

'You always want something.'

'Sheer exaggeration and unfair to age and gender.'

'I don't see what your age has got to do with it.'

Neither did I but it was the kind of repartee that I used as a defence. 'It's got everything to do with it,' I went on determinedly. 'Take a look at this. I found it in my car.'

The sodden card was drying deckled everywhere. But Michelle's photograph was still recognizable though the CV was nearly unreadable.

'Who's this?' DI James asked, looking at the photograph.

'That's Michelle Steel, daughter of Samuel Steel whose garden on Updown Hill has been rubbished. She's the step-daughter of Anne Steel, the wife who has since disappeared. Michelle gave me her card. Then, hours later, after the storm, I found that someone had written this on the back.'

DI James turned it over. ' "*Who's next?*" Are you sure it was not already there, when she gave the card to you?'

'Positive. It was blank. I know, I looked. Someone has nipped into my car and written on the card. They left the passenger window half open in their haste. Is it a threat?'

'Unfortunately I am not clairvoyant.'

'Nor are you polite, caring or interested.' The violence of the brawl downstairs had rubbed off on me. I glared at him. James did not seem to notice.

'Did you leave your car unattended at all?'

'Of course, several times. I have not been sitting in it all day.

If I had, I would have noticed someone getting in and writing on the card. My eyesight is not that bad.'

'It could be a joke.'

A joke. I simmered down. George the Jester. Could it have been George Hill? His light bulb joke had not been very good. But I had the feeling that his stage act would be smooth and sophisticated, the result of hours of scriptwriting, rewriting, rehearsal, timing and delivery.

'I'm not laughing,' I said.

'Would you feel happier if I took a photocopy of the card and put it in the Steel file?'

It was a gesture, even a slim one. I nodded. James got up and went over to the photocopying machine. Just those lean movements were enough to send my pulse racing. I could watch him for ever. In that instant, I understood stalking now. I had the genes of a stalker too. Perhaps I might be driven to following James everywhere, standing outside the station, his home, waiting for a glimpse of him, except that I did not know where he lived.

'Where do you live?' I asked.

'Why do you want to know?'

'In case I decide to stalk you.'

'In that case, I won't tell you,' he replied. 'I couldn't stand the thought of you out there in the street, day and night, in the cold, in the rain, getting pins and needles, chilblains, a red nose.' He was laughing at me now. A silent kind of laughter. It was one degree better than being ignored.

'Have you any news about Mrs Anne Steel?'

'None. We've checked the ports, airports, stations, hospitals, car parks. Not a sign of her or her white car. She's done an Agatha.'

'An Agatha?'

'Agatha Christie, the author. She stage-managed her own disappearance for ten days or thereabouts in the Thirties. I'm not sure of the details. Harrowgate, I believe, was where she was found, the spa town. Perhaps Mrs Steel has signed into a health farm in a different name. Or she's having a face lift at a discreet cosmetic surgery clinic and will return a new woman. That's a strong possibility.'

'Michelle and her stepmother do not seem the best of friends. Quite the reverse. Michelle does not have one kind word to say about Anne.'

'That's interesting,' said James, handing the card back to me. I did not want to touch it but dropped it straight into a plastic envelope. I am paranoid about prints. 'Perhaps I ought to talk to her. She might tell me if Mrs Steel has a secret life.'

'She'd invent a secret life for sure,' I said. 'Michelle is an actress. She might have been putting on an act for me. It has just struck me that this might be an elaborate piece of play-acting to pull the wool over the eyes of innocent private investigator.'

'Did you say innocent?'

'OK, ignorant. I'm still learning, James. How deep do we have to dig?'

'As far as it takes. You ought to know, you've worked here. It's a long slog, turning over every minute detail and it all takes time. Relish your freedom, Jordan. You don't have a tightrope to walk or a treadmill under your feet.'

'I don't have a pension either,' I said.

James slammed the file shut and stood up. He pulled on a lightweight jacket, loosened his tie. There was a momentary look of amusement. 'Then I'd better buy you an iced coffee,' he said. 'At Maeve's Cafe. We could both do with a break.'

'You're bribing me.'

'It's a sweetener. I might want a favour.'

Doris was outside my shop. As usual, she was laden with bags of produce from a cheaper supermarket which she sold on. I was not sure if this was legitimate but then I was not an inspector.

'Jordan. Your shop has been shut for days. What is happening? Are you having an affair with Miguel?'

'No, I'm not. I haven't seen Miguel for weeks.'

'Then it's about time that you did. He's the only man who is any good for you. You never take my advice. His restaurant is doing great business and he's so generous. You're wasting your opportunities. He'd set you up for life, take care of you.'

'Any more suggestions?'

'We've a very nice mulligatawny soup in. We know you like it hot and spicy, like Miguel's Mexican dishes.'

'We've got? We know? Have you suddenly acquired a partner?'

'Don't be pedantic.'

'My goodness, that's a big word.'

'Don't patronize me, Lacey,' Doris glared. 'We are both shopkeepers and I send you good customers. When did you ever send me a customer?'

It was mortifying. Doris and Mavis were my good friends, strange friends in a way. They had known each other since schooldays and now they had a motherly kind of interest in me that I did not deserve. Not at this moment.

I took one of the bags from Doris. It weighed a ton and was full of baked beans at nine pence a tin. 'I'm sorry, Doris, I'm so sorry, I didn't mean it,' I said. 'That was unforgivable of me. A bad day. I'll do anything. Chalk up a favour from me.'

'It's OK,' said Doris, shifting. 'What you did for Mavis, when she got beaten up and her cafe robbed, is enough for the moment. Though it could be running out,' she added, with a warning look.

'I'm taking that on board,' I said. 'Let me know when I'm out of sorry street.' Shopping: boxes of Belgian chocolates. I knew both Doris and Mavis had a sweet tooth.

Perhaps I ought to throw a party before summer faded into the grim grip of autumn. A barbecue on the beach would be fun in the warm glow of a late summer's evening. I'd have to check the tide timetable. Ankle deep in swirling waves would dampen the spirit. Bring-a-bottle type of party, although I would not say so. Leave it up to individual generosity. I would invite everyone that I had ever known. All my old cases, if I could remember their names. At least I had files. It would be a riot.

'I'm going to have a party, on the beach, a barbecue, before the summer ends,' I said, going straight in for the deep end. 'Can I buy everything from you? You know, sausages, hamburgers, chips, cheese, salad, rolls, fruit, yogurt?'

Doris changed inflexion on the spot. She loved parties; new dress, new hair, new nail extensions. 'Of course, give me a list and a date. I hope I'm invited.'

'Guest of honour,' I said.

'I don't believe that,' she said. 'Fourth on the list maybe, after DI James, DS Evans and the gorgeous Miguel.'

'You're forgetting that they all work evenings, shifts, restaurant.'

'Not that particular evening, I bet. They've got deputies, haven't they, and they'd make arrangements? Besides, we need men to carry things. Chairs, rugs, the barbecue, the booze.'

I could not believe what I was contemplating. I was up to my ears in work and here I was, saying I was throwing an impromptu, late-night party on the beach. There might be a hundred turning up. I was out of my mind. Pass me the Prozac.

'What about the invitations?' Doris went on, streets ahead in the planning stakes. 'Are you getting them printed?'

'Word of mouth,' I said, pure chicken. I hated anything remotely secretarial. Keeping my notes up to date was bad enough. Writing invitations, posting them . . . the thought was enough for a severe attack of writer's cramp.

'Word of mouth could spread like a bush fire,' Doris warned. 'I know you are Latching's most successful PI, but can you afford this party? It'll cost a bomb.'

There was Mr Steel's retainer, not yet earned and burning a blistering hole in my bank account. If I spent some of it, then I'd have to earn the equivalent. The motivation would be there. Another night up a tree.

'Don't worry,' I said. 'I'm sure you'll give me a hefty discount for a bulk order.'

'Ahem. Don't be too sure,' said Doris, shifting bags again from one arm to another. 'This isn't a charity shop.'

'And it's tiresome to talk about money, to earn money and save money. The only thing to do is spend money.'

51

'Save me the lecture. Is it soapbox day?' said Doris. 'You should have warned me.'

She unlocked her shop and we went in with her restocking. I put the baked beans down on the counter. The bag was splitting. Doris must have the muscles of a lorry driver. But not with those nails. Today's extensions were plum coloured.

'So, when may we expect this party of the decade in Latching?' she went on, unpacking her goods.

She was a canny shopper. My mother had been the same. So am I, when I have time. I remembered my mother coming home from the shops, her basket laden, her face flushed with triumph. Shoppers used baskets then instead of plastic bags that don't rot. 'Jordan,' she'd say. Her red hair, in those days, had been pulled back with tortoiseshell combs. 'Look what I've got! All these lovely bargains. I've saved pounds.'

I had been a schoolgirl, doing my homework at the kitchen table. Lack of money didn't mean too much to me then, but now I understood. My parents had not been big earners but they had been so happy together, always smiling at each other, touching hands, kissing. Sometimes I had felt in the way.

They died together. So that had been right. I don't think one would have survived without the other a single day.

'Jordan. You're not listening.' Doris rapped on the counter. 'When is this party?'

'Soon, but let me check my diary first. Before the weather breaks, I promise. It's turning a fraction chilly at night. Autumn is on the way. We'll catch the last of the summer wine.'

'Cool,' said Doris. She'd been watching too much Saturday morning television. All those tattooed teenage compères prancing around.

That night, up a beech tree at Denbury Court, was no party. I had my own tuna sandwiches and small cartons of blackcurrant juice. I was not going to risk dropping a flask again. A cushion from a sunbed supported my back against the trunk of the tree. At least my clothes were dry. This was an improvement.

The moon was in the first quarter, a distant magical orb

shedding silvery beams across the garden. The leaves rustled in a slight southerly breeze, tiny animals and nocturnal nibbling creatures: noises of the night. Trees swayed, including the one I was in, their leaves tipped with silver. I settled into the folds of the night.

Samuel Steel knew I was up his tree, although he was so distressed by his wife's disappearance, I doubted if he was still interested in the damage to his garden. There was no doubt of his devotion to Anne. His face was gaunt and his eyes dulled with lack of sleep. His daughter might be an actress but this man was not.

'Are you sure you'll be all right?' he'd asked, his mind coming back from some deep, dark hole. 'Do you want me to stay up and keep watch with you?'

'No,' I said. 'I have a camera. I'll take shots of whatever happens.'

'I'm very grateful,' he said, his old charm returning for an instant. 'Take care, Jordan. Don't fall out of the tree this time. Hold on tight.'

It was the first time he had used my first name. I smiled back at him. The man had gone through a lot in the last few days. I wanted to help him. I wanted to solve a few problems. Maybe I could find his wife, but that was fraught with black mysteries. Wives disappear for all sorts of reasons, some of which were too awful to contemplate.

Let's hope she was living it up on his credit card in the South of France.

The night was still warm. I concentrated my mind on the coming beach party, whom I would invite and calculating how many sausage rolls to order etc. Beer, wine, a fruity Beaujolais and a chilled Chardonnay, orange juice . . . I had not won the Lotto so that was the extent of the alcohol on offer.

List: Sergeant Rawlings and his wife; my gorgeous friend Leroy Anderson; Cleo and her stepfather; Doris and Mavis; both Mrs Edith Drury, intrepid chairman of Latching's WI, and Mrs Hilary Fenwick, widow of the councillor; and Louis Guilbert, owner of the best store in town, of course (he was my sugar daddy-in-waiting); Jack from the Amusement Arcade; Joshua the amiable sponger . . . The list grew and grew and was becoming a matchmaking exercise. I did not know that I knew so many people.

Then there was Bud Morrison, the dishy firefighter; Miguel, the passionate Mexican restaurateur; DI James; DS Evans; Ellen Peach the police diver; and Joe the greengrocer . . . My mind was spinning. Derek would not get an invitation. I'd had enough of his violence. No more stones through my shop window, thank you, buster.

And my jazz trumpeter. There was no way I could possibly invite him. How could I? I did not know where he lived or what he was doing. He appeared, out of the blue, and blew a few notes that captured my heart and held me captive. Jazz. We must play jazz at my party, all his tapes. He had a new CD out but I did not have a copy. Anyone who did not like the music could go home or retreat along the beach with their glass.

No plastic or polystyrene. Everyone must bring a proper glass-blown glass. I hate parties where the wine is served in plastic. They might as well serve warm water.

I heard a noise in the distance. It was a vehicle coming up the hill, changing down gear with a whine. I looked at my luminous watch. It was 1.30 a.m. What a God-forbidden time. I should be tucked up in my bed, not clinging on to a tree with crumbs down my front.

I was hearing footsteps on the drive. Then they stopped abruptly.

If I took photos, I hoped the flash would not light up the tree and blow the whole scenario. The flash might be mistaken for a shooting star, Samuel walking Jack or Russell with a torch, a distant lighthouse, glow-worms.

Shopping list: check black box container for camera, if available. My shopping lists were getting more and more sophisticated. Tissues were no longer an item.

My hearing went into an unpleasant disturbance of the pressure in my ear. It felt blocked. Perhaps a nocturnal insect had crawled in.

Something was happening in the garden. I heard the crunch of a footstep near. My spine went rigid. I had no idea what I should do apart from taking photographs. Confrontation might result in being sprayed with weedicide. Not my regular perfume.

Six

I t was freeze and wait. The footsteps were crunching along the drive, each step deliberately placed, yet at the same time I felt the owner was trying to minimize the sound. Could it be Anne Steel returning home in the small hours, not wanting a welcome?

The footsteps lurched off on to the lawn and the sound became muted. I peered through the branches, moving the leaves cautiously. He must be somewhere near, below and to my right. The clouds were casting a shadow across the grass and I saw no one moving. He had cut off and gone round the back of the house.

Decision time. Climb down and stalk him or wait till he returned, after he had burnt off some other area of the garden? I listened hard, trying to hear some evidence of damage being committed. The only sound was the trees rustling and a far off owl hooting, haunting and melancholy. Then came the anguished cry of a small hunted creature. I shivered. It was getting cold. The night was very still.

There was the minutest clatter, the lid of something rolling on the patio at the back. I slid down the tree, catching my hair on prickly branches, scratching my hands and face, landing awkwardly on the lawn.

I trod carefully in soft shoes, trying not to damage a single blade of grass. My breath was almost suspended, just soundless open-mouthed swallows of air which I needed, trying to steady my racing pulse, gathering strength for whatever or whoever I was going to face.

It was foolhardy, I knew. I only had a camera with me. I

could hardly say, with menace: 'Stand still or I'll shoot.' Get a head, girl.

I saw a shadowy figure among the foliage of the rose garden. The heady scent of the blooms was being disturbed. Petals fluttered to the ground, insubstantial and blending into the moonlight. Someone was tampering with the door lock of the conservatory at the back of the house. There were plants inside, a variety of fronded palms, evergreens and yuccas. Was he going to axe them or spray them?

The far hills of the South Downs were dark, only dotted by the occasional headlamp of a car taking the downward curves of the road back to Latching. I made no sound. I wanted the reassuring height of Samuel Steel to appear in the doorway. But he was catching up on lost sleep, fuelled by an extra glass or two of whisky.

The last drops of heat from the day had gone, followed by intense cold. I saw a swift movement as the intruder mastered the door lock and it swung open. As he moved, I moved. I steadied the camera, pressed the flash button, and clicked the shutter release. The noise was like rifle shots. He heard it, spun round on his heel, dropped something, and fled out of the conservatory.

I ran after him. He was slim, lithe, clothed in black from head to foot. My hand was on my chest as my cracked rib started to protest. He tripped and I was nearly upon him, but he was up again in a flash, legs scrabbling for purchase. I caught a glimpse of black trainers with red flashes. Then he turned and gave me a violent punch in the stomach. I doubled up in pain, rolled over on the grass, earth in my mouth, gasping.

Somehow I crawled up on to my knees, spitting earth and coughing. I reached out for my camera. It was not damaged. I let the coolness of the night air soothe my airways. He had a head start on me now but his footsteps were no longer controlled. He was sliding over things as if confused by the layout of the garden.

Suddenly I realized that this was not the garden wrecker. He would not have wanted even a slither of moonlight. He would have wanted the darkness before the new moon.

A vehicle started up in a burst of acceleration and screeched off down the hill. That sound was familiar but I can't keep sounds filed. Lights went on in the house and a door opened. I heard a voice calling my name.

'Jordan? What's going on?'

'I'm over here,' I wheezed. 'On the front lawn.'

An earthworm would not have heard me but I was bathed in moonlight and footsteps hurried over. I could hardly bear to look up.

Samuel Steel was kneeling beside me. 'What happened, Jordan? Are you all right?'

'You've had an intruder. Not the lawn wrecker, someone else. A burglar, all in black, trying to get inside the house. Unless he was after your indoor plants.'

He heaved me up on to my feet. 'Can you walk all right?'

'I can walk. Maybe. Just about.'

'I'll phone the police.'

'Oh, wonderful.' My voice lacked conviction. They were the last people I wanted to see.

'Maybe they'll take some interest in my original complaint now,' he went on. 'Someone breaking in . . .'

I did not want to meet DI James or DS Evans. I did not want to see their knowing smiles, endure caustic remarks. Samuel helped me towards the house and indoors and sat me down in the kitchen on a chair. It was a dodgy walk but the kitchen was warm and comforting, the air fragrant with garlic. Hadn't we done all this once before? It was déjà vu. He was making fresh coffee, getting down the Napoleon brandy bottle.

'I'm sorry that I didn't get your wrecker,' I said. I was not going to admit anything about the moon.

'Never mind. If you disturbed a burglar, then your time was well spent. It would have been too horrendous. Anne has some lovely things, especially jewellery. She likes collecting.'

I nodded. My stomach hurt. It was too low down for another cracked rib. Cracked stomach? I hoped the blow had not ruptured anything vital. Where was one's spleen exactly? Somewhere against the lowest ribs? Nobody paid a PI for injury time.

I was starting to feel a degree better. The doctored coffee went down good and hot. My fingers closed round the mug, absorbing the heat. The brandy was physically reviving and soporific at the same time. I was tired and halfway to dropping my head on to the table for a quick snooze.

But I could hear the sirens coming up the hill again. Those noisy police cars. It was a wonder the bandits did not sue for ear damage. I'd had enough of DI James's sarcasm and was not in the mood for DS Evan's overly touchy-touchy concern. I was in Garbo mode. I had come in my own car this time and left it at the bottom of the hill in a leafy lay-by. Time to drive home, have a bath, take a couple of aspirins and call it a night.

Mr Steel was examining the outside door of the conservatory. 'It's definitely been tampered with. There are several marks where he was trying to prise the lock right off the wood. He was probably using a screwdriver. Thank goodness you disturbed him. I can't thank you enough.'

'I'm feeling better now,' I said, getting up awkwardly, holding my stomach like a pregnant mum. 'I think I'll go home. May I use your bathroom before I go? I'd like to clean up.'

'Of course. There's a guest bathroom upstairs. Second door on the right. Towels in the cupboard.'

'Thank you.'

I moved as quickly as I could. I wanted to be out of the house before the police arrived. This was not a good time to be questioned by anyone. Detective Inspector James could beg me on bended knee and I doubted if he had ever been on bended knee to any woman in his entire life.

I don't remember going up the stairs. I held on to the carved oak bannisters and heaved myself up, tread by tread. Blows winding actors on television only seemed to result in temporary indisposition. They were up and acting again in a flash. Let's hope the producers check their facts. Once in the guest bathroom, I sat on the closed toilet lid, rolled over and groaned. It was a classy bathroom but I was past admiring in-depth colour co-ordination.

There was no vomiting so that was a good sign. Or was it? I

was not bleeding from either end. Not a ruptured liver or kidney. Kidneys were at the back, either side. As the brandy took hold, I was not quite sure where any internal organ was.

I hung my head over the basin and splashed cold water on my face and neck. The cold water took my mind off the pain, because coldness itself is numbing. Towels in a cupboard. I wished I had a cupboard solely for guest towels. Where had my life gone wrong? I should be married to a man like Samuel Steel, even if he was a butcher. That might have been a problem. I could have become a closet vegetarian.

It was more comfortable to lie on the floor, curled up in the foetal position. They would find me asleep in the morning, wrapped in a mountain of guest towels. I wondered what was going on downstairs. Doors opened and closed, footsteps went back and forth. Voices hung on the air. I would wait until it quietened down and then slip out by a different door. There must be several outside doors. Note: always check exits.

The floor of the bathroom was polished teak and hard. My hip bone protested but I ignored the discomfort. I heard footsteps coming up the stairs. I reached up on my elbows and locked the door.

'Jordan? Jordan, open the door.'

Detective Inspector James was on the outside, rattling the handle. I could sense his impatience, could imagine his eyes becoming glacial. My hero, such a gentleman.

'Don't be a fool, Jordan. Open the damned door and let me in.'

'I can't.'

'Don't play around with me. Get off your butt and unlock the door.'

'Butt? What sort of expression is that in front of a lady?'

'I'm not in front of a lady. I'm behind a door.'

It hurt too much to laugh. I tried to move but strangely there was little response from my legs. They'd gone somewhere else.

'Jordan, are you all right?' His voice changed to concern. He was using probes on the lock. His keys? Samuel's keys? 'Are you hurt?'

'Only a bit winded . . .'

'How did this happen?'

'He hit me in the stomach.'

'Who hit you?'

'This burglar . . . the intruder, the man who was running away, who got away.'

'Don't move. I'll get the door open. Don't do anything, Jordan. I'm coming in.'

'Hold on. Don't break the door down. This is a Grade II building.'

I shuffled over to the door, reached up and unlocked it. I'm not sure how it happened but then James was on the floor beside me. He was very close. I could smell his closeness and the night air on his clothes. He was on his knees, an arm under my head, his fingers taking my pulse, eyes searching my face. I could smell the essence of him and it was wonderful.

'You look awful,' he said.

'Thanks a lot.'

'Are you sure you are only winded?'

'It was a punch in the stomach. Nothing more.' I started coughing. He looked round the bathroom and spotted a glass. He filled it with water and came back to me. Again he supported me with his arm, tilting the glass to my mouth.

'Drink, baby,' he said. 'But only a sip.'

I could have choked. Baby. He had never called me baby before. No one had ever called me baby, only my jazz musician. I was past remembering. Moments like this only happen once in a lifetime. I snuggled into the circle of his arm so that he could not move. He was trapped.

'Do you think you could stand up?' he said.

'Don't move,' I moaned a little louder.

I drank some more water, making every trickle last. My face was pressed against his chest. I could almost hear his heart beating. If only . . . if only this had been different and I was close in his arms for relaxation not resuscitation.

'Jordan, listen to me. This is important. I have to go back

61

downstairs now that I know you are all right. I thought you had been hurt too.'

'Scene of crime?'

'You're right. It is a scene of crime. Sorry.'

He had gone and it took me a while to take in what he had said. Scene of crime. What crime? Forcing a lock? Hardly major incident. *I thought you had been hurt too* – that implied someone else had been hurt.

I tidied up the towels, splashed water over my face again. It was time to re-enter the world. Still, those moments on the bathroom floor had been magic. Worth a punch in the stomach.

There was a lot of activity going on downstairs. I held on to the bannisters as I went down the stairs. A yellow scene of crime tape was being stretched around the garden. Samuel Steel was sitting on a chair in the conservatory, his head in his hands. I did not speak to him. It was not the right time.

A line of police were searching the grounds. Other uniformed men were searching the house. Something had happened that I knew nothing about. The familiar hollowness took hold of me. It was that bad news feeling.

No one seemed to notice me going into the kitchen. I reheated some coffee and took it out to Mr Steel. He took the mug from me without looking up. I poured coffee into a second mug and took it and myself out into the garden. Someone must tell me what was going on. The caffeine steadied my nerves.

The sky was changing. Was dawn coming already? Streaks of light were fragmenting the clouds, painting pale pinks across the linear dark in feathery strokes. The night had fled. Now we had to face the coming day.

Everyone had forgotten about me which was perfect. I could disappear into the morning mist and make my way back to Latching. But I did not like what I was feeling or smelling. I could smell fear. There was too much activity in the garden and in the house.

I saw the flash of cameras in the half light. I knew what that meant. Figures in overalls. And they were not just taking photographs of burnt grass. I searched for James. He was standing on the fringe of a group, talking on his phone.

'James . . .' I had to know.

'I thought you had gone home.'

'No, I'm still here.'

DI James did not have time for me. He was already walking away, his mobile close to his ear. 'Yes, yes . . .'

'What have they found? You've got to tell me.'

'A pair of gardening shears.'

'Midnight pruning?'

'In the back of a woman's neck, severing the spinal cord.'

My blood chilled. His words, spoken bluntly without emotion, were horrific. I had been in the garden, up a tree, playing mental games, when a woman had died somewhere in the same garden. I remembered a sound, a small cry. I thought it had been a night creature but it could have been a woman.

'I may have heard it,' I said. 'I heard a strange cry. I thought it was an animal.'

'Can you put a time on this sound?'

'It was a long night.'

'Try.' He ended his call and put the phone in his pocket.

I thought hard, trying to put times to my movement. 'I think it was around 2 a.m., something like that. I remember checking the time at 1.30 a.m. It was before the intruder arrived and before I climbed down the tree.'

James ignored the tree bit. 'But the intruder could have already been in the garden?'

'I suppose so. But I thought I heard him arrive.'

'This intruder could have approached from a different direction earlier. Directions are difficult to pinpoint in the dark. Can you describe this man?'

'Black jeans, black ski mask. I've got a photograph.'

DI James turned very slowly and looked at me as if I were from another planet. He passed a hand over his eyes. 'You've got a photograph? Jordan, you tell me this now?'

'What's wrong with now? I took a picture of him in the conservatory. Said cheese. It probably won't come out. I'm not very good at photography. I get the buttons mixed up or forget to wind the film on. My camera is nothing special, one of those disposable things. The kind you get on special offer, three for the price of two.'

'Have you finished?' He could barely contain his impatience. People don't gnash their teeth these days. Dental care is too expensive.

'I was going to tell you.'

'Give me the camera.' No please.

'I can't.'

'Why not?'

'I haven't finished the film.'

'Jordan. This is a murder enquiry. And you're worrying about finishing a film. I want that photograph.'

'I've got shots on that film, too, you know. My evidence. A certain footprint or do you want that, too? I'm working for Mr Steel, remember? My hard work is on that film.'

'I'll get prints made for you.' His voice rose in exasperation. 'How about that? Will that satisfy you?'

I supposed I should have been grateful but I wasn't. My agency ran on a shoestring. A camera was a camera.

'Hand it over, Jordan. I'm warning you.'

I gave DI James the camera without a word. Sometimes the numbing is so complete that I do not feel a thing for him.

'Go home, take an aspirin and go to bed for what's left of the night.'

'Yes, sir. No, sir. Thank you, Dr James.'

James was as frozen as I was. Neither of us moved. Perhaps those moments on the bathroom floor had stirred him too. This was the slowest romance in history. I was 28 now. Maybe we'd get to holding hands by the time I was forty.

'Have you identified the woman?' I asked.

I did not really want to know. Gardening shears. It was going to be bad news and there was enough bad news around. 'Who is she?'

'It's Mrs Anne Steel. The wrong kind of face lift.'

Seven

H ome was good. My two rooms wrapped themselves round me. You know how it feels. We make a cocoon for ourselves, no matter how small or basic, with the familiar. A few pictures on the wall, a bunch of flowers. It could be a cave or a mansion. Even a prison cell. There's no proof but maybe cavewomen picked wild flowers, propped them on a ledge till they dried.

Hopeless dreams invaded my state of dozing, tired legs stretched out. I'd thrown off the rose-patterned duvet. I was drifting like a cloud, looking for someone, a figure that was always out of reach. My body could not sleep at this hour even when I was exhausted.

Yet, I did not want to wake up. Mrs Anne Steel, a woman I had never met, was dead and on her way to the morgue. A woman who was hated by Michelle, her stepdaughter. But Samuel Steel had loved her, doted on her, bought her jewellery and a fast car. I wiped out the agonizing moments when her spinal cord was severed. It did not bear thinking about. I wondered if you could feel it. There'd been a TV programme about the French guillotine and the victim's last moments. Sometimes it hadn't worked.

About 8 a.m. I got up, showered, put on long-line bra, clean jeans and T-shirt, ate a banana, and went to my shop. My stomach felt better. My ribs felt better. First Class Junk deserved my attention. After all, it kept the baying wolves from the door.

On the doorstep was a package. The postmark was smudged. The address was typed on an old-fashioned manual. I hoped it was a sample of some useful washing product.

But it wasn't. It was a scarf. One of those long, wrap-around things in floaty silk, shot with the colours of the rainbow, more like butterfly wings than real material, very beautiful and expensive. I held it against my face and I could smell perfume. Something out of my league . . . Joy or Gucci or Calvin Klein.

I looked inside for a note but there was nothing. No clue to why this had been sent to me. No smart sell with an invoice saying you will be charged a bargain price of £24.95 if you don't send it back within seven days and four of those had already gone.

Yet I could smell perfume. It looked new but it was only almost new. It had been worn before, round a neck or carelessly over a slender shoulder . . . Was someone sending me a message or was it a threat?

A young man came into the shop. He had a rucksack on his back. His face was vaguely familiar. It had a wild, intense look.

'You sold me a chamber pot, last year,' he said. 'Fantastic value. You said you'd save me any that you got.'

I remembered him. Twenty pounds for God Save the King.

'And I didn't forget,' I said. 'Although it has been a long time.'

'I've been abroad. Doing VSO work.'

'Good for you.' I could feel my price going down. I went out the back for the chamber pot that I had saved for him. It would have made an ideal plant pot. A nice strong red-leaved plant called Moses Basket would have been ideal. The china was strewn with violets and rosebuds, the edge delicately fluted so as not to discomfort a feminine posterior.

He went ecstatic, clutching his head. 'Oh my God, it's beautiful. Hand-painted. The workmanship . . . look at this. Victorian, don't you think?'

'Definitely,' I agreed.

'You aren't going to overcharge me, are you?'

'Now, would I? A VSO worker?'

He relaxed. He got out some crumpled notes and tried to

smooth them. I did not know what to charge him. I was not an expert on fluted Victorian female chamber pots.

'Thirty pounds suit you?' he asked hopefully.

'Perfect,' I said.

I wrapped it carefully in tissue paper. The young man was wandering round the shop, peering at everything.

'I like your commemoratives,' he said. I'd put all the mugs and plates in a glass-fronted case. I'd bought the case at a car boot sale. No one wanted to buy Prince Charles and Diana mugs. Even less, the Princess Anne and Capt Mark Philips. The market had been saturated.

'This one at the back,' he went on, peering. 'The Wedgwood. I'm not surprised you are keeping it hidden. May I take a look at it?'

I nodded, containing my expression of prior knowledge. I opened the case and took out the Wedgwood mug. It was a 1964 birthday mug for William Shakespeare, 400 years after the event. Hardly a prime market.

'Do you want to sell it?'

'This *is* a shop.'

'Will thirty pounds do?'

I peeled off the six-pound price label calmly. 'You must look at it first. There's the tiniest chip on the edge.'

'You can't find these anywhere,' he said, crunching around for more notes in his pocket. 'They increase in value virtually overnight.'

It was too late for me to go on an antiques crash course. I smiled a sixty-pound smile and put the money in the cash box drawer. I had not graduated to a till.

'Your lucky day,' I said, handing him his purchases. He was looking well pleased. 'Where are you off to now?'

'The Sudan. People dying in their millions out there in the dust and the heat and the flies.'

I had to do it. I gave him back ten pounds. 'It's not much, I know. Put it towards buying some drugs for them, the medical kind.'

He looked at me straight. 'You're OK, you know.'

*   *   *

My spurt of fast selling put me in the mood for working on the George Hill case. No disguise needed. Shopping list: new disposable camera, book of jokes, skin glitter. I was not sure why the glitter but as I was now edging into show business, it seemed appropriate.

I planned surveillance at Chapel Court, the block behind the edge of Latching's Co-op supermarket. George Hill was frequently out of town, doing nightly shows around the country, he'd told me. It meant a lot of travelling. He had one of those big people carrier type cars so that he could hang up his stage suits. I suspected that he also kipped down in the back. It would be big enough.

It was pleasant walking along the coastal path towards Shoreham, past the fishing boats, mounds of nets and lockers on the beach to my right, landlocked fast cars to my left. The traffic noise was deafening. Time for a £5 congestion toll on these roads, exempt if there were children onboard or elderly in the car. I ought to be on the council.

This was a short cut, quicker than round-abouting all the shops, traffic lights and estate agents. I cut inland to the left.

I checked for his car in the cramped parking space behind the flats. JES1 08 was near enough for a personalized number plate, allowing for the mispelling. And if you were in any doubt, the jokey jester painted on the side door was confirmation. George Hill was at home.

Inside, the car was a mess, so contrary to the man's personal appearance. The silver-painted people carrier was littered with stale fast food containers, burger boxes, crisp bags, chocolate wrappers. Talk about monkey food. Didn't he know how some of this stuff was made?

It was time to sweep the building, trusty clipboard in hand. The front entrance was security dedicated. I waited until an elderly man came out and I slid in past him with a bright 'Hello again! How are you?' as if I lived there. It worked without a hitch. He smiled back, hesitantly. I climbed the stairs, knocking on doors, doing a tenant/owner survey. I made it up as I went along.

As I cruised the floors, no one fitted the description of the Hill stalker. We talked about many aspects of the flats, particularly security. The tenants/owners were pleased that someone was taking an interest in the awful state of their building: rubbish not collected, landings not cleaned, graffiti on the walls. I tut-tutted in a thoroughly reassuring way, made notes.

If there was no answer from a flat, I questioned a friendly neighbour.

'No, she won't be at home, that one's a nurse. Does shift work. About thirty. As thin as a rake.'

'Does this lady have brown hair in a pleat?'

'A pleat? God knows! She doesn't have time to put a comb through it. And she's got two kids.'

A shift work nurse stalker with two kids? Unlikely. A stalker needs time.

As I reached number 17, I barely had a chance to press the bell. George Hill was at the door instantly. He pulled me inside, his handsome face working with emotion.

'Jordan, am I glad to see you! Thank goodness, you're sent from heaven. I'm going insane. Come and see what she has sent me today. What am I going to do with all this stuff?'

I did not feel sent from heaven but I was not going to argue.

He was wearing a black polo-necked jersey, white jeans. Amazingly dishy. He pulled me through to the kitchen so quickly I barely had time to take in the layout of his flat. It was an ordinary box-like flat. It was not a home, more an office and somewhere to hang up his clothes and put his head down.

The kitchen table was piled with offerings from his admirer. Flowers, champagne, Stilton in a jar, Belgian chocolates, silk ties, boxer shorts, towelling bath robe. There were other goodies on top of a refrigerator. These were unopened. Christmas was early.

'There's something in every post,' he groaned. 'She sends me presents every single day. I don't answer the door now. It just piles up outside. My agent is furious. I missed signing a contract in time the other day. If I hadn't read my e-mails, I'd have lost it completely. I have a living to earn.'

'How do you know it's all from the same woman?'

'Look, lady. Who would send a comedian gifts like these? I occasionally get a drink or a bottle of Scotch. That's my top. I'm not in the league for expensive gifts. I crack jokes for a living. I'm not a movie star or football hero.'

'Any letters?'

'No. She doesn't put anything on paper. Too crafty for that. You've got to do something about it. This woman is driving me mad.'

'I haven't managed to see her yet,' I said.

'Are you disbelieving me?' His eyes narrowed. 'Are you calling me a liar? Why should I make it up or send myself presents? I'm not crazy. Perhaps you haven't seen her because you haven't done enough work on my behalf. I'm employing you by the day, remember. I haven't seen you following me.'

For one moment, I disliked him.

'Exactly,' I said quickly. 'That shows how good I am. If you haven't spotted me then she hasn't spotted me. The fact that you are still getting all these gifts shows that she does not know that I am on her track.'

'Are you on her track?'

'I have some definite leads,' I said enigmatically.

'Come with me tonight,' he said, his mood changing, becoming persuasive and urgent. 'I'm doing a revue show in Brighton. I'll pick you up at your shop about six. Sorry about the early start but there's a lot to check on stage before a show.'

I swallowed hard. I did not really want to go along with him but it was almost an order. He was a very dominant man, eyes glittering, and he was employing me. He was probably a bully at school.

'I haven't got a ticket,' I said.

'Bollocks, Jordan. And wear something snazzy. I don't go out with anything drab. Do something with your hair.'

'I've a dress covered in fireworks. Will that do?'

'Perfect. Only don't get too near the lighting,' he chuckled.

As I went to leave, I checked over the gifts, hoping there would be a label. 'Where's the wrapping paper?' I asked.

'Threw it all away.'

'Please keep all future wrapping paper,' I said. 'And the address labels.'

'I think they were mostly delivered by the shops. Computerized labels.'

I picked up the flowers. A lovely bouquet of late summer flowers, chrysanthemums and dahlias. The scent was heavenly. 'I'll take these. I can check with local florists to see if they have a sender's address, or better still, if they were paid for by cheque or credit card.'

'You may as well have them,' he said carelessly.

Snazzy does not describe anything in my wardrobe. I wondered if Nesta would lend me anything. Perhaps not. Leroy Anderson was more my size and she had lent me a dress once before. I did not want to borrow that blue dress again as it had too many James-type dancing on a landing at Cleo's party memories.

'Leroy,' I said, phoning her at the Rustington branch of the estate agents where she now worked. 'It's Jordan Lacey.'

'Jordan. How lovely to hear from you. I was beginning to think you had emigrated or got married.'

'Neither on my schedule,' I said. 'How about you?'

'As busy as usual. Mad social round. Nothing too outrageous.' I knew she had not had an easy time last year and did not want to stir up the sad vibes.

'This is a begging call,' I began.

'What do you want to borrow?'

'A dress or a fancy top. It's got to look snazzy, whatever that means.'

Leroy suppressed a laugh. 'Not exactly your style, nor mine. But I think I might have just the outfit. I bought it at a sale in a rash moment. I've never worn it. I take it you are working on something?'

'Yes, in Brighton, at some revue show. I've got to look like a comedian's arm candy. Very dishy arm candy. And I'm being picked up from the shop at six.'

Now she could not stop the laughter. 'Cutting it fine, aren't

71

you, but leave it to me. I can fix you up. I'll leave work early and come round to your shop, bring my make-up case too. I know you think a double coat of mascara is the full works.'

'Thanks,' I said, wondering what I had let myself in for. Leroy had good taste in clothes but I did not like the sound of that laughter. It might be innocent fun on her part but I had to work in the damned clothes.

Leroy arrived at my shop a few minutes after five with a suitcase full of clothes, but she already had in mind what she wanted me to wear. The other clothes were in case I put my foot down and refused to go out of the door in her choice.

I put up my CLOSED sign and resigned myself to being made over. Leroy had that look in her eye. She was beautifully turned out, as usual, in a tailored fawn trouser suit and cream silk blouse, her hair shining. She always looked the executive part.

'OK,' I said. 'Do your worst. I am clean. I've had a shower and put on clean undies.'

'You aren't going to need much in the way of undies.'

'Wanna bet?'

'Now look at this, Jordan. This is the works.'

She produced her choice, held it up for me to admire. It was stunning but I could not believe that I was going to wear it. The dress was small and I am a tall woman.

'Call that a dress?'

'It's a mini-dress. You've got decent legs, haven't you? Don't worry, I've brought some strappy shoes. They have elasticated straps and fit most sizes.'

'The whole thing is strappy,' I said, stomach falling as I turned the garment this way and that in my hand. 'There's not much of it, is there? It's nothing but an arrangement of straps. Look, it's only got crisscross straps lacing across the back. Nothing to hold it up.'

'You did say snazzy. Show business arm candy? Brother, this is the goods. You'll be a star.'

'I don't want to be a star.'

'Look upon it as a lifetime experience. You're being paid for this, aren't you? Well then, stop grumbling and get into it, girl. I've still got your face to do.'

I had to admit that Leroy knew what she was doing. The dress fitted like a glove, even though I could hardly bear to look at myself. The impossibly heeled sandals fitted but I doubted if I could walk two steps in them. She worked wonders with my hair and my face. I did not recognize myself. Glitter? It was dabbed everywhere. In my hair, on my eyelids, on my cheeks, my lips, my bare shoulders. Call me Glitter Queen of Latching. I was shedding it all over the floor.

'Isn't this a bit over the top?'

'I've brought a boa to cover your shoulders if you are that embarrassed. It's only feathers but I know they help.'

'Where do I put my notebook, my mobile, my keys?'

'Girls these days don't carry anything. Maybe a lipgloss and a credit card. You could pin your keys inside the top.'

'Leroy, I must have paper and a pen.'

'Put them in your knickers.'

Leroy had gone, still laughing, and I was waiting to be picked up. I could not sit down because the sequins would stick into the back of my legs. I waited, standing up, calling myself the biggest fool under the sun.

The doorbell rang and I went and opened the shop door. It was ten to six. George Hill was early. But he wasn't. It was DI James, hovering on the doorstep, tall and dark and intense. His jaw almost dropped with surprise. He stared at me.

'Jordan? Is that really you?'

'It's me.'

'Where are you going?'

'To some theatre revue show in Brighton. It's OK, I'm working. This is gear. Borrowed.'

'Have you seen yourself?'

'I know. It's not me at all. I'll be all right.'

James paused, wondering whether to say anything or ignore

my appearance and simply carry on as if I was in my usual jeans and T-shirt. He cleared his throat.

'Anne Steel,' he said. 'She was almost dead before the gardening shears severed her spinal cord. They have measured the external bleeding. I thought you ought to know if you are working for Mr Steel.'

'Strangulation?'

'Partly. Forensic came up with all the normal evidence. She may not have been completely dead but she was nearly dead. The shears were final.'

'I don't know why you are telling me this,' I said. I did not want to think about Anne Steel.

James gave a deep groan. 'I never know why I tell you anything.' He looked at me again. 'You've done something different to your hair.'

'You are so observant. No wonder you are a policeman. You'd be wasted in any other profession.'

'I suppose these things are called Jennifer Lopez curls.'

'How should I know? Leroy used tongs.'

James did not answer. He did not want to know what Leroy did with tongs. I could almost read his face. He was gathering his thoughts together and it was as if he was about to say something quite sensational. I waited hopefully.

But as he took a breath before speaking, a silver-painted people carrier drew up, flashy jester flashing on the nearside door. George Hill leaped out of the car and came up the steps. I pulled in my stomach and tried to look as if the dress was normal evening wear.

George looked at the flame-red mini-dress covered in shimmering sequins, the long tanned bare legs, the strappy sandals on spiky heels, the mass of flamboyant corkscrew curls. Then he looked at DI James and he did not like the warning he saw in the detective's eyes.

He turned to me as if I were his sole property.

'Get in, gorgeous,' said George, grinning. 'The night is young and the night is ours.'

Eight

S itting in that tight red dress was not easy. It rode up and the edges of the sequins dug into the soft back of my legs. The big car had roomy, upright seats and I was able to drape the boa over my knees for modesty. Jack's flashy Jaguar would have been impossible.

'You look great,' said George Hill with an admiring nod. 'No one would guess you were a PI. You look like a bimbo.'

I swallowed the two-handed compliment. 'I hope I can act like one,' I said. 'Tell me, what do bimbos drink?'

'Vodka and champagne.'

'Both at once?'

He laughed and showed off his nice teeth. I think he'd had that whitening procedure. I suppose if you were in show business you could put it against tax.

'I've got you a seat right in the front row. I want you to be seen and heard. Make a point of coming backstage and being all lovey-dovey, all over me. I don't mind what you do or say as long as she sees us carrying on.'

'Are you certain she will be there?' I was not sure I could be all over him. I thought he was very good-looking but I did not know if I liked him.

'She's always there.'

We were on the A27 to Brighton, travelling through the brightly lit tunnel that cut under the South Downs. Swiss engineering at its best, or had it been British?

'I checked the local florist shops and found the one that sent the bouquet. They've no name or any record of the woman, except that it was a woman and she paid cash. They remembered her because she said the flowers were for an anniversary, a very special anniversary.'

George groaned. 'Anniversary of the day she started stalking me? I told you she was off her rocker.'

The evening air was cool now that the sun had gone down. I wanted to wrap the feather boa round me like a scarf and snuggle down. I was not used to wearing half a dress.

'Would you like the heater on?'

'Please . . . thank you.' That was nice.

'You shivered. I'll put a jersey in the back so that you can wear it for the journey home. It won't matter then what you look like.'

'Thank you. Will it be very late? I'm a working girl.'

'Depends whether we get asked on to a party. One eyeful of you in that red dress and we'll be bombarded with party invites. I'm at my best at two in the morning.'

I hoped not. I'm at my worst at two in the morning. The plastic bits were already making me itch. The time could not come soon enough when I could take the dress off and have a good scratch. And my cool, cool sheets would be bliss.

'I'm first class at that time, too, but especially when I'm up a tree,' I rabbited on. 'You wouldn't know. That's my other case. Classified.'

'What a girl,' said George, only half-listening, tapping the wheel. He was tensing up. Perhaps it was pre-show nerves. The temperamental star under pressure. 'We'll have a great time and you'll solve the mystery identity of the stalker.'

'I'm definitely going to win,' I agreed. It was easier to say what he wanted to hear. 'It's in the stars. Tell me a joke.'

'Wait for the show.'

The Regal Theatre in Brighton was old fashioned, cosy, with red plush upholstery, masses of gilt paint, but packed to the ceiling with punters. The revue was obviously popular. I did not recognize the star names on the billboards, only George the Jester. George ploughed through his fans, laughing and joking, taking me backstage to his dressing room. He was besieged on all sides by people wanting to speak to him. He was incredibly efficient in the way he dealt with stage crew and the problems. He was not just a walking joke book.

'Good house?' he asked.

'Yeah. We're full. Big coach party from Blackpool.'

'Thanks. I'll work in a Blackpool joke. Got a couple.'

He slipped his arm round my waist and gave it a squeeze. 'This is my dressing room. Make yourself comfortable. Be an angel and mix me a G and T, ice, lemon, a double. There's ice in the fridge. Have what you want yourself, darling, then come out and impress the natives. Act the part.'

The dressing room was cell-sized but well appointed with make-up unit and mirrors, armchair, shower and lavatory, wardrobe and shelves. His stage jacket was hanging on a preformed stand. It matched my dress . . . almost. It was covered in sequins, only these were jet black. The lapels were smooth black silk. George would look magnificent.

I found clean glasses and mixed his G and T. I took a tonic and ice for myself. There was no lemon. They looked exactly the same. His drink was in my left hand. Mine in my right.

It was interesting wandering about backstage. I had only experience of front-of-house work in my voluntary capacity at Latching's theatre. George was on stage, checking the line of the spots. He was particular about the lighting.

'Darling,' he exclaimed, planting a kiss on my curls. 'My G and T. Just as you know how to make it. Delicious. Mmm, you're an expert . . . at everything.' His hand wound itself round my waist again and squeezed the flesh. 'Time to change. Thirty minutes plus. You make a good G and T.' His face was controlled, almost a mask.

'You've drunk mine by mistake,' I said. 'It was a straight tonic.'

'Then I'd better drink mine before I dehydrate,' he said, taking the second glass. 'Smile, darling. Dazzle with the teeth. She's over there and watching.'

I wanted to turn round and look but he had a tight hold on

77

me. George was nuzzling my hair. I could smell his aftershave, Aramis. Heady stuff.

'Can't wait for tonight's show,' I gushed. I was out of my depth with girly small talk. 'You'll be marvellous, as usual, you hunky man, I know.' I leaned closer in what I hoped was a provocative manner, nudging him with my bare shoulder.

'Love it. Love it, more, more. Every word will be for you, darling,' he murmured, practically eating my ear. 'And I can't wait till afterwards. You and I together, alone . . . it'll be bliss.'

I wanted to go home. What was he paying me? It wasn't enough for this garbage.

'Darling, angel, sweetiepie,' I replied, thinking big Goldie Hawn smile. 'It'll be wonderful.'

I heard high heels clattering down the passageway, breaking into a run. Then a door slammed. She had gone out of the rear stagedoor. George let his hand drop and straightened up. He need not have been quite so fast about removing his hand.

'I'll go and find my seat,' I said. 'You probably have a load of things to do.'

He nodded. 'I get wound up before a show. I need to relax, get myself together. Shower and change. Don't wish me luck.'

'Break a leg,' I said.

'Both legs.'

A stagehand took me through a side door, along some musty back corridors, through another door that led into the main foyer. The manager knew all about my ticket and showed me to a seat in the centre of Row A. I sat down slowly, taking time to glance along the row both ways. I was looking for a smartly dressed forty-year-old woman. It was not easy. There was a whole row of smartly dressed women of that age and half of them were looking at me. Perhaps George had a surfeit of stalkers.

It was a long time since I'd been to a live theatre, sitting in the audience, not just selling ice creams in the interval. Big band jazz is the love of my life. Films come a close second, but I don't get to many these days. This was going to be fun. I relaxed and forgot about the sequins and abbreviated dress. It would have been even nicer if James had been sitting beside me, though I'm not sure if he would have enjoyed the first half of pop groups and the big ballad singers belting their hearts out.

The magician was amazing. His name was Max. He was tall and thin and his tricks were truly baffling. He roamed across the stage, shedding doves. I couldn't see where he hid anything. His hands were elegant and feminine, coaxing his magic. I half hoped he might be at one of these promised after-show parties, and I could probe him for a few secrets.

In the interval I cruised the bar, smiling and nodding, as if I was a regular part of the scene. Several people smiled and nodded back. I was taking in the smartly dressed etc, filing their faces, distinguishing features, identifiable differences. One woman caught my eye.

There was something about her. My sixth sense was in gear. She was a well-preserved forty but it looked like hours of hard work. Her make-up was painstakingly applied, as if it had been preceded by plant facials and face masks and an apricot scrub. I throw mine on. I can wash, dress and be out in three minutes plus. She probably allotted a couple of hours and that didn't include wardrobe time.

She was also wary. She did not meet my eyes. Her dress was champagne-flowered chiffon, draped over a well-upholstered bust and rounded hips. The shoes were expensive, intricate straps holding her small feet together by a miracle.

But her hands were a giveaway. They did not stop moving. She was holding a glass of white wine but there was constant interaction. Her nails were painted gold and she began a slight, nervous washing movement when she put down the glass. Washing hands syndrome was significant, I knew. I ought to take a course in human psychology.

George Hill was the star of the show. He got top billing. The whole of the second half apparently – apart from a spectacular dance finale – was his alone. I was impressed. I must remember to ask him if he had been on television. I could imagine him with his own show on a Saturday night. Those good looks could go a long way.

The second half began with a great fanfare of trumpets and a walk on for George, trailing a mike, singing a standard Sinatra song. I didn't know George could sing. The black sequins on his jacket glistened like rain. His make-up was discreet but I could see it from Row A. His long legs were encased in hugging black silk trousers. He was all man. And he did not need a nose job.

I enjoyed about ten minutes of his scripted act. Then I started to get uneasy, looking at my feet. Strange how you get that feeling. The jokes were funny, at first. Then I stopped laughing. Everyone else was still laughing and clapping. I looked round cautiously. It must be me.

Sophistication is weird. It means different things to different people. Some people were holding their sides with laughter; others were laughing politely, not wanting to be seen out of stride. I was cold. I could see nothing funny in what he was saying.

The jokes got bluer and coarser until my spirit became bruised with distress. I'm no prude. I've worked in the police force where jokes were navy hued. But these jokes were beyond the pall. I could hardly believe that this good-looking, out-wardly pleasant man, could have such vile and obscene thoughts about the church, women, even animals, lodged in his head. Let alone put them into words for a mixed audience. Perhaps they could have passed for a private stag night. But this was mixed and public.

I sat there, the edge of the seat biting into the back of my knees. I sat there because I was polite and he was paying me. I tried to shut my ears to the torrent of filth but I grew sick and longed for the performance to end. With concentration, I managed to imagine the sea pounding in my ears, giving some solace. Latching sunsets soared through my mind with their pink-edged clouds and shots of silver on the surface of the sea. They were so beautiful. They were infinitely more enduring than the heap of smut which filled the inside of this man's mind.

I did not join in the explosion of clapping which ended George the Jester's half of the show. The spectacular finale that followed went by unheeded in a climax of musical noise, dancers and clapping. I was longing for the clean night air.

There was no way I could hang about. Job or no job, I was going home. Where was the nearest taxi rank?

I was halfway out into the street when George caught me up. I was wrenched round to face him. The cool air hit my bare shoulders. I forced myself to meet his eyes.

'What the hell are you doing? Where are you going?' George shouted. 'Come backstage. I need you. She's there. For God's sake, please Jordan, help me.'

This was a different man. He was two people wearing the same skin. This one was vulnerable, scared, almost panicking. His hollowed face was no mask. He was truly frightened out of his wits.

'OK,' I said. 'I needed some air. It was hot in the theatre. Take me where you want me to be. Don't worry. I can cope with anything.'

He pushed through the crowds, half laughing and thanking people, the other part of him taut with fear.

'Why don't we just leave?' I said. 'That would be simple. Why do you have to go back? Nothing says you have to be part of this aftershow circus.'

'I have to show her that I'm not scared of her. That she is nothing. That she's zero. Don't you understand, Jordan? Women like her think they are controlling your life. If I ran away, then that would be proving what they think.'

'I think I saw her,' I said.

'Good. Then you know there is something weird about her. She's not normal. She's a goddamned freak.'

I hung on to his arm. He was walking so fast I could barely keep up with him on Leroy's sandals. I felt very tall. The backstage was crowded, many still in their stage costumes. Stagehands milling about, getting in everyone's way. Cleaners trying to cope with the surge of debris. One of my scrappy straps broke but no one seemed to notice. I draped the boa over the flying end.

My head was starting to ache. No aspirins. George put a glass of chilled wine into my hand and I drank it without thinking. I needed the liquid but not a cheap white. Hadn't anyone heard of water?

'Stay here, Jordan. I've got to see someone. Talk to Max. Hi, Max, talk to my girlfriend for a minute. But don't chat her up. She's mine.'

'As if I would,' Max laughed. It was Max the Magician, the clever young man whose act had held me enthralled. He hovered, attentively, his dark clothes sculptured to his body. His face was handsome in a boyish way with perfect features and a good skin.

'You were really excellent,' I began. 'I couldn't see how you did anything.'

'You're not supposed to,' he smiled. 'Tommy Cooper was the only one who did that and it was his trademark.'

'How did you learn how to do all these tricks?'

'Illusions, please.' He laughed again. 'It was a schoolboy thing. I was not popular at school. They used to bully me because I wasn't any good at sport. Two left feet. So I decided I'd better be clever at something and make them like me. My grandfather showed me a sleight of hand trick with cards and I was hooked.'

'Hey, I think I know that one. You have three cards, face down and you move them about . . . Is that the one?'

Max nodded. I noticed he was drinking orange juice and ice. 'That's the one. I found I was quite good at magic and suddenly I was popular at school. I gave shows in the lunch break to the bully boys. It saved my life really. I had to practise for hours. Now it's my profession. I'm booked on a P & O cruise next month.'

'Wonderful. I hope you don't get any rough weather. It might spoil your illusions.'

'It could be a problem but we'll face it then. Will you excuse me? I have to rescue some equipment from the stage before it disappears. Sorry, that wasn't supposed to be a joke. It's been nice talking to you.'

Max smiled and nodded. I smiled back. I liked him but he left me, stranded in the milling crowd. More people had arrived and the room was spinning. My asthma did not like the massed perfume, deodorants and hair lacquer. People merged too close and intruded on my space. I tried to shrink into being a small person.

'So who are you?' The voice was demanding and low, very female. I knew who it was without moving. Her face was bright and tanned, eyes enamel blue as if enhanced with tinted lenses. The lashes were spiked with mascara, harsh brown hair done up in a turban. Her mouth etched with strawberry gloss. The perfume was hard to place. Then it came to me. Poison by Dior, the purple bottle.

'I beg your pardon?'

'George Hill. What are you to him? You've been hanging on his arm all evening. I've seen you.'

'Hanging on his arm? Hardly.' I tried a surprised look. 'He's been on stage for the last hour.'

'I don't know what you are playing at but you had better leave him alone. George belongs to me. He's been mine for years and anyone who gets in the way is going to regret it. I burn babies like you for breakfast.' She was looking at me with loathing, her eyes narrowed, her hands beginning to wash.

Although George Hill was nothing to me beyond a paying customer, I did not like this talk. I grabbed a soda syphon from the bar and filled my glass. This was what I needed. I drank the fizzy water but held on to the syphon. I might need some more, pretty soon.

'Now, I don't know your name or who you are but I do know that I don't like your attitude,' I said firmly. 'George Hill is a star in his own right, and he needs his privacy whether you like his act or not. He has done no harm to anyone and you are nothing to him but a pain in the arse. He does not belong to me and certainly not to you. His patience is exhausted. Either you leave him alone or I'll put detailed documentation of your activities in the hands of the Sussex Police.'

This was a pretty good speech for someone who only wanted to go home. For a moment she looked shocked, then she recovered.

'Aren't we the smart talking girlie! Documentation, indeed! What rubbish does that mean? You clear off before I do something really nasty to your baby face. Quite by accident, you understand.'

'Threats, is it now? There's something seriously wrong with you. I suggest you go and see your doctor. And I suggest you leave George Hill alone. You obviously need professional help before it's too late.'

I turned to move away from her. I'd had enough. George Hill had disappeared somewhere. He was big enough to deal with her himself. I was still carrying the soda syphon but I could not face trying to return it through the crush to the bar.

I had not found out the woman's identity but I might have scared her off. No one had confronted her before. She had been stalking George, undetected, for months. Then it occurred to me . . . this woman might not be the stalker but another demented fan. The real stalker could be watching him right now.

There was time to make a quick survey of the remaining crowd before I left for good. I tucked the end of the broken strap down the bodice of the dress. No need to look dishevelled.

As I went back into the foyer, the same woman cannoned into me. It was like being hit by a soft brick wall. Her chiffon-covered bosom was heaving, her eyes glinting.

'No, you don't go back to him,' she spat at me. 'He's mine, do you understand? He's mine for ever.'

Her gold painted nails flew up to my face, nicking my nose.

It was purely involuntary. Totally unplanned. A reflex action. I pressed the syphon handle/lever.

A stream of soda water sprayed straight at her chest. She gasped at the coldness and at the wetness as it spread over her bust and started to run down the front of her dress.

'My dress,' she screamed. 'You've ruined it. You tart! You trollop!'

'Sorry,' I said sweetly. 'Quite by accident, you understand?'

Nine

Ace. The woman gasped with shock as the cold spray hit her skin. I made a swift move to depart, feeling good. George Hill was hyped-up, keen to go to his aftershow parties. I begged to be excused, usual hormonal headache, and offered to take a taxi. George insisted on paying. The wet witch disappeared fast, to wherever her home or coven was. He was feeling relaxed now.

'The show went really well. You were the ticket,' he said, stuffing several folded fivers into my hand. 'She's cleared off, hopefully for good. Are you sure you don't want to come? It'll be fun. OK, I'll see you tomorrow. We'll talk.'

'Sure.'

He planted a warm kiss on my cheek. 'Great dress,' he added with a saucy wink. 'My scarlet woman.'

The kiss was unexpected. My clients don't usually kiss me. Still, my clients don't usually earn a living telling blue jokes either.

'Interesting evening,' I added. Interesting covered a minefield. 'Enjoy your party, George.'

A late night taxi in Brighton is hard to find. Impossible, in fact. The clubs had emptied out and syphoned off anything on wheels. I did not want a mini-cab. The last train had already gone. It was a depressingly long walk. I should have come in the ladybird. Note: always have own transport. I wondered where I could spend the rest of the night before the first train was timetabled to leave for Littlehampton. Fortunately there was little of the night left. About four and a bit hours. I had three choices:

a. Spend them in a hotel bar
b. Walk to Hove actually railway station
c. Stay within the safety of the police station as guest of HM The Queen and talk shop.

Hove actually is a joke. People are always saying, 'Oh, I live in Hove actually.'

I chose the bar. Call me an alky. It was in one of the grand old hotels along the sea front, a cosy bar all done up in apricot velvet and gold lamps, bottles of unblended malt whisky and old brandies glistening in mellow rows behind the counter. They even had Glenfiddich which was James's favourite whisky.

I could not afford to stay or drink in a five-star for long. There were a few customers still drinking and the barman was pleased to have someone to talk to. He did not mind that I only drank juice. I did explain the circumstances. By three a.m. I was swimming in Vitamin C. The barman took pity on me and let me doze off in a corner armchair.

'What time do you want your wake-up call?' he asked.

'Five a.m.?'

'OK. I'll be closing the bar before then anyway.'

It was still dark at ten to five. He woke me with a cup of coffee and a fawn raincoat draped over his arm. I could hear the rain drumming on the windows, could feel the chill of early morning coming off the sodden beach.

'I'm afraid I'll have to ask you to leave now, miss. I'm closing up before the cleaners arrive.'

'You've been very kind,' I said, trying to unwind my stiff legs from the chair. My neck was cricked. Like overnight flying in economy without the jet lag.

'You'll need this,' he said, offering the raincoat. 'A lady guest left it behind ages ago. I don't think she's coming back for it now.' He looked at a tagged label on the sleeve. 'March 10 last year.'

'Thank you, that's kind,' I said. 'It sounds as if I shall need it.' The raincoat was a pale pinky fawn, light and silky. I bet it had another label on it somewhere, maybe a very expensive Molton Street address.

I tucked one of George's fivers under my empty glass and left. Outside the pavement was wet and shimmering with rain. My shoes were not made for walking. I should have gone to those aftershow parties and sat in a corner.

The first train left Brighton at 5.23 a.m. I made it with seconds to spare. A few early workers stumbled aboard, stretching their faces. The sky was leaking light, pink rays streaking the horizon with a faint amateur wash. The gulls were flirting with the new day, swooping and squabbling, combing the beach for fish heads.

This time I did get a taxi at Latching. It was still drizzling within a grey and forlorn mist. A private taxi was waiting outside the station, windscreen fogged with raindrops. I went up to the driver.

'Can you take me home, please?'

'You're in luck, miss. I was waiting to pick up a doctor due at the hospital. A consultant coming down from London. But the train is half an hour late. I've got time if you don't want to go too far.'

I gave him my address. The roads were empty and we were there in less than five minutes. I handed over another of George's fivers and told him to keep the change. He did not merit such a big tip but what could I do?

The taxi driver looked surprised. 'Thanks a lot, miss. Flag me down anytime. I owe you another trip.' As if I would remember him. He hardly had a face.

'I'll take you up on that,' I said.

I stripped off in my bedroom, hung up Leroy's dress. Most of the sequins had survived the night. The water was not hot because I had switched off the immersion heater before leaving, but it was warm enough to wash off grime and stress and residue make-up. My hair had disintegrated long ago and reverted to mop status.

I slept, wrapped in a sheet, for three hours. After a ripe banana, oats and bran crisp breakfast, I went into domestic mode for ten minutes, i.e. I cleaned the bathroom. Sometimes I am such a slut.

The only way to put those obscene jokes out of my head was to work and forget them. Distasteful memories can be damped down with sheer hard work. I could hardly rinse out my brain. Instead I decided to check out Samuel Steel's property chain. I had his former address. Samuel and Anne had moved from a house in West Goring to Updown Hill.

The Steels' former home was in a high profile avenue, graceful lime trees planted along a central path that divided the wide road. Their old house was a corner site with garden on three sides behind a cobbled Sussex wall. Quite a lot of garden. The house was stuccoed white and substantial. Denbury Court was in a different class. Denbury Court was old quality. They had moved upmarket. This house was solid post-war money.

I parked the ladybird in the next road and walked back to the corner house. As I might have guessed it was called The Corner House. Bingo. I opened the gate and walked up to the porch. It was gabled with grey tiles and a couple of imitation Grecian pillars. The potted flowers were mostly tired geraniums, exhausted by the summer. An uncomplicated buzzer rang as I pressed the bell. No chimes, no sing-song, no football anthem.

'Yes?'

He was not a yes-type man. He was large, pot-bellied over a tight trouser belt at hip level, greasy scrapes of hair combed across a nearly bald head, faded blue eyes, full-lipped and same lips edged with a froth of beer.

'Yes?' he said again, more impatiently. Perhaps I'd woken him up.

'Mr Arnold? I'm Jordan Lacey. I'm a private investigator and hope you can help me with my present investigation. Strangely enough, it's about a garden. Your garden looks . . . very nice.'

'A detective investigating gardens? That's a bit ripe, isn't it?'

'I know. It sounds weird, but I can explain.'

'Got a card?'

I fished out my business card and gave it to him.

'Want a beer?'

'Great.'

Tim Arnold was hospitable. He guided me towards a fairly new Victorian-style conservatory which had been built on to the back of the house. A low pine table was already littered with glasses, beer cans, crisp packets and bowls of nuts, newspapers. He nodded towards the selection. I went straight for the nuts, selected a palmful of cashews, then sat down in a cane chair with cushioned seat. My day's ration of essential nut oil.

'So you are a detective. Well, well, well. I never thought I'd meet a real detective.' Mr Arnold pulled on a ring can of beer and handed it to me. His faded blue eyes twinkled in a tired way. 'Get this down you, then ask your questions. I've only asked you in because I'm slowly dying of boredom in this house. It's suffocating me. You are a welcome intrusion.'

There did not seem to be a Mrs Arnold around. No smell of lunch cooking. Perhaps that's why he was dying of boredom. Tim Arnold was big and bulky but not intimidating. I could cope with him. He seemed lonely. Careful, Jordan. You have enough lame ducks on your Christmas list. Give him a bottle of anti-dandruff shampoo.

I sipped the beer. 'I have to explain that my investigations concern Mr Steel's garden at Denbury Court, Updown Hill. I wondered if anything unusual had been happening in your garden? This is the house where Mr Steel used to live, and maybe you are also experiencing something strange?'

Tim Arnold took a big gulp of beer. 'No, not now, no more. I'm not experiencing anything unusual in my garden now. But, Miss Lacey, it all happened before I moved in. They took everything from the garden. Every bush, shrub, plant, bulb. Now that's unusual, isn't it? It was a terrible shock.'

It was not the answer I expected. Every bush, every shrub? But who would want them? Second-hand bushes do not have a market value. Or had I missed something?

'Who took them?'

'The former owners, of course, the Steels. They moved

everything movable from the garden. It was a lovely garden and that was one of the reasons that I bought the house. It was a picture, put thousands on the place. But when I moved in, I could not believe my eyes. Everything had gone. It was a desert, a wasteland, completely derelict. It's a wonder that they left the grass.'

'Did you ask Mr Steel what had happened to the plants?'

'Yes, of course. I phoned him. He said they were not included in the sale and that they were plants that Mrs Steel was very fond of. Tell me, Miss Lacey, how does one become fond of a plant?'

'A little odd,' I agreed.

'I was devastated. The garden was a moonscape, just holes. They'd taken the lot. I've planted shrubs and flowers since, but it's not the same. They took mature, well-established growth. They ransacked the garden. It's taking years to replace it all and I'm not as fit as I was. I've got diabetes.'

'Does your anger go as far as ruining their present garden with, say, something like weedkiller? Retaliation perhaps. Forgive me for asking, although somehow, I don't think you're that kind of person, Mr Arnold.'

'No, Miss Lacey. I would not know how to go about it, even if the anger was in my heart. I bought this house because of the beautiful garden and some personal associations, but they dug up the the plants, taking them to their new property. I'll never forgive them.' He looked morose, as if remembering the glory of the former garden.

'Have you thought of suing them?'

'Don't believe in suing. Money in the lawyers' pockets.'

'And you spoke to Mr Steel?'

'Frequently. But it was no use. He insisted that the plants were not included in the sale. I eventually gave up. I hope he's enjoying his beautiful garden.'

'Not at the moment,' I said, coughing on the cold beer. 'Their garden has been vandalized. Someone has been spraying it to death with weedkiller. Everything is dying.'

Mr Arnold looked genuinely amazed. The amazement

reached his receding hairline. He shook his head. Then he grinned, puckering his eyebrows.

'Serves them right. They deserve it. Well, I didn't do it though I've got plenty of motive. And I've got enough weedkiller. It's in the shed, Miss Lacey, save you looking for it.' He drank back his beer. 'Want another?'

'Er, no, thank you.' It was my turn to be amazed. If Mr Arnold had done it, then he was putting on a pretty good act for an amateur. I don't have a portable lie-detector but I felt he was telling the truth.

'Have you ever visited the Steels at Updown Hill?'

'Never. I don't even know where it is.'

I wrote my mobile number on my card. 'If you think of anything, however small or insignificant, please let me know.'

'Sure, Miss Lacey. I know the Steels must be devastated but I can't help feeling that they deserved it. Life works in mysterious ways. I'll let you know if anything happens here.'

'Thank you. And thank you for the beer.'

'Come round anytime. There's always plenty of beer. I see you've finished my cashews.'

'Sorry. I needed the protein.'

Who else should I visit chainwise? The people who left Denbury Court and sold it on to Samuel Steel. They might be harbouring bad karma. They might be feeling that they were forced out of Denbury Court or sold it undervalued. I'm not surprised at anything these days.

Samuel Steel had given me their address, too. Mr and Mrs Carlton, St John's Court. I found the place. It was out at Sompting and quite something. I stood looking at the building before knocking on the heavy oak door in the oval porch and introducing myself. I don't often go to church.

'Please come in,' said Mrs Carlton. 'If you will excuse my husband. He has to rest quite a lot.'

The Carltons lived in a converted former chapel. It was quite extraordinary. The building still had its original ecclesiastical

windows, door surrounds and wooden ceiling. I was relieved I
was not asked to sit in a pew.

The ground floor was one vast room with random sofas and
desks and bookcases, polished black tiles strewn with worn
rugs. All very homely. The rugs worried me in case they were
placed over flagstones of ancient graves but I could hardly ask.
Mrs Carlton made a pot of tea in a flowered teapot and
produced hefty wedges of chocolate cake with soft butter icing.

'This is quite different to Denbury Court,' I began, trying to
take my eyes off the cake.

'We were relieved to leave Denbury Court,' said Mrs Carlton, pouring. 'It was a drain on our resources and took a lot of
upkeep. This is quite big enough. Milk, sugar?'

She was a comely woman, once a beauty, eyes like green
globes. Time had taken its usual devastating price on her skin
and hair. I wondered what I would look like at her age. I was
glad it was a long way off.

'Weak tea, please. Milk. Thank you.'

'Denbury Court had become a financial burden. We couldn't
cope with the house or the garden. My husband is retired and
his pension is not generous. But we are very happy here. There's
a new kitchen out the back in what used to be the chapel study,
and two bedrooms upstairs reached by a spiral staircase behind
the organ screen.'

'It's been cleverly converted,' I said, sipping my tea. Beer,
now tea. I was awash with liquid. Any minute now I would have
to ask if there was a bathroom. It would be stacked with old
hymn books and parish magazines.

A tremor of old fear gripped my guts. I was remembering the
hermit's cell, the smell of damp decay. A killer had trapped me
in the cell with only hymn books for company. DI James had
found me but I could have died. I had not seen James for days.
An ache flooded my bones. How could he detach himself so
completely from me? Sometimes I felt we were joined at the hip
but that he hadn't noticed it.

'Did you mind leaving the garden?' I asked.

'Not really. It was too much work. My husband . . . he's not

92

that well and we couldn't employ anyone on a regular basis. At first we had a gardener, Bert his name was, but then we had to let him go. He never seemed to achieve much. Every time I took out his coffee, he was smoking in the shed.'

'Shed? Is there a shed?'

'Not now. It got burnt down. It was quite scary. All those flames licking the wood.'

'How did the fire start?'

'A cigarette end, I expect. There were always a lot of oily rags about to clean the lawnmower and old newspapers that Bert used for starting bonfires. It's a wonder it didn't burn down before.'

'Do you know where this Bert works now?'

'No, I'm sorry. I've no idea. We knew very little about him. I think he answered an advertisement we put in a village shop.'

'Can you describe Bert?'

'Not very well. Big, bony, red hands. Tallish, stocky. I'm sorry. I can only remember his hands.'

I could not resist the chocolate cake. I knew it was laden with calories but my food chain was in a twist. I was not eating sensibly. These last few days had been chaos for my digestion. Shopping list: carrots, iceberg lettuce, mushrooms, radishes, cottage cheese and celery.

Chocolate cake, properly made with dark chocolate, is perfection. I'm not talking about factory line cakes, full of air and sugar and synthetic flavouring. This cake was the real rich chocolate taste.

'Mrs Carlton,' I said, my mouth full. 'This cake is wonderful. Where did you get the recipe?'

'It's mine. I used to be on television. I had my own show, *Sandra Carlton Cooks*,' she said, smiling. 'A long time ago. Before your time, before the cult of Delia Smith and years before Nigella Lawson. You soon get forgotten.'

'Did you commercialize this cake? Did you market it as Carlton's Succulent Real Chocolate Cake?'

'We didn't do that sort of thing in those days. We hoped to encourage people to cook at home but we didn't do spin-offs. It was simply a love of cooking.' Mrs Carlton was still smiling to herself. 'People watch cooking programmes these days but it doesn't mean that they cook. They still go out to the super-market and buy ready-made dinners and bags of pre-shredded lettuce.'

She was right, of course. I dragged my mind back to gardens. 'When you left Denbury Court, the garden was in good con-dition?'

She look surprised. 'Yes, as far as I am aware. My husband was already unwell. A few weeds, perhaps. The Steels were very taken with the garden. They loved it.'

'And your garden here?'

She laughed. 'What garden?'

It was true. The former chapel was fringed with overgrown trees and shrubs. Their garden was no more than a few flower beds flanking the steps to the front porch and some hanging baskets full of nasturtiums.

'Thank you, Mrs Carlton. I'm sorry to have taken your time but not sorry to have eaten your cake. It is truly perfection.'

'I'll wrap up some slices in cling film for you to take home. You look as if you need feeding up. Please come back, Miss Lacey, if you ever have time. It's nice to have someone to talk to.'

So many lonely people. Mrs Carlton with a husband who was unwell. Tim Arnold, as lonely as hell. Not her type, of course, but one of the many, linked by a property chain. There was nothing I could do. No point in throwing a tupperware party.

But I remembered my beach BBQ party, no exact date yet, but in the planning channel. I could do something.

I thanked Mrs Carlton for the wrapped slices and left. It was more than I deserved. I'd even looked under a rug while she was in the kitchen. No gravestones. There had been no sign of Mr Carlton, still resting somewhere. I drove home, my phone on the passenger seat. It began to ring.

I pulled over in a lay-by. There's a law about driving and phoning. Not many people know that yet. I didn't want a £30 fine slapped on me.

'Yes?'

'Jordan? Where are you?'

'On the road coming back from Sompting. Not driving. You can't get me. I've pulled over.' I knew the voice just from four words. 'And I'm working.'

'Can you come back to the station? Right away.' It was DI James. As usual, his voice was impatient and without any civilized consideration for my work. 'It's important. Something has happened and I think you were there at the time.'

'I don't know what you mean.'

'You'll soon find out.'

'Oh yes, I know what you're talking about,' I said with enthusiasm. 'You're talking about the time you asked me out to dinner, wining and dining. I was definitely there at the time.'

He took no notice as I knew he would. But I enjoyed saying it. I liked winding him up.

'I'll wait here for half an hour,' he said. 'But that's all. I've got some questions to ask you.'

That was ominous. I didn't like the sound of it. I never enjoy being asked questions.

Ten

T he journey was only short but it seemed one of the longest drives in my life. I did not want bad news. I was starting to sweat. I knew from James's voice that I would not like what had happened. He had a way of telling me things without telling me.

And I was there, he'd said. Where had I been? To a revue in Brighton. A cold thought struck me. The woman was suing me for spraying her with soda water. Her dress was ruined. Humiliation in front of her friends.

That was it. I was in the sin bin again. Pass me the bread and water. Stale bread. Make it granary.

My phone rang again. I pulled over and switched it on. The lay-bys were beginning to know me.

'I'm coming,' I said quickly.

'Sorry. You're coming where?' It was Samuel Steel. He sounded agitated. 'What do you mean?'

'Sorry. I thought you were someone else,' I said. 'It was an urgent call that I was expecting.'

'This is an urgent call,' said Mr Steel. 'Can you come and see me now, right away? It's about my wife, Anne. I have found some information I want you to have. It's really important.'

'Can't you tell me over the phone?'

'No. You have to see these things. Please say you can come, Jordan. I believe you are still working for me . . .'

'Yes, of course, Mr Steel. I'm still on your case and I think I have a lead. A slender one but something to follow. I'll be with you in ten minutes.'

I turned the car but did not phone DI James to explain. My work came first. He didn't employ me. I had done nothing wrong in my scale of ethics. What's a drop of clean water?

Everything was changing. I could feel it in the air. The year was dying. Its hot bloom was over. Leaves were sucking the last sap from the branches before they withered and fell. I felt the same kind of falling. Birds were singing flat notes. Something was amiss and I was acutely aware of the change. It was intangible, like a cobweb brushing against a face.

The garden at Denbury Court was looking awful. Millions of blades of grass were curling brown with decay, leaves rotting. I could understand Mr Steel's agitation and now his wife had died in tragic circumstances. But she was not my case. DI James was in charge of homicide investigations.

I stopped in the drive, trying to think when I had last been here. The last few days were a fog. This was a severe case of work overload.

But it was a fading late summer, the moment before autumn returned. A hint of warmth lingered in the air, like a woman's touch. Any minute now a chilling easterly wind would remind us that winter was round the corner. And Latching could be cold.

Samuel Steel did not come out to meet me. This was different. He had usually been waiting in the porch, always a welcoming host. My welcome was on hold.

The front door was ajar so I pushed it open and went inside Denbury Court. I knew my way around now. Samuel Steel was in his study. He was poring over paperwork, a tumbler of a golden brown malt at his elbow. He looked up, his face gaunt with worry.

'Jordan, thank goodness. Thank goodness you have come. I don't understand what is happening. You have got to help me. I'm at my wit's end.'

'I'll try. Tell me what has been happening.'

'Come in, sit down. I just don't understand anything any more. Why should someone kill my Anne? My sweetest and dearest wife. She's done nothing to anyone. The garden is beyond help. I don't care about it any more. But Anne . . .'

'It's one of the cruelties of life. Sometimes there's no answer and no reason. Are you thinking there is a connection?'

'I don't know what to think.'

'Try to tell me from the beginning. Take your time. I want to know what you have discovered.' I could not get any sense out of the man. Then he made a great effort and seemed to calm down. I hoped it was my presence.

Samuel Steel sat in a chair, reaching for his glass of malted comfort. His hand was trembling. 'I've found all this stuff in Anne's bedroom. I can't believe it. I'm not showing any of it to the police. They don't have to know, do they?'

'It depends. They are investigating Anne's death.' It was hard to say the word. 'If so, then you should turn over anything that's relevant to them. It might contain clues.'

'No way, Jordan, I refuse. No one is going to see any of this. It's strictly private. I'm adamant. You are the only person that I can trust. You promise me, now?'

Samuel was losing weight. The days had etched sorrow on to his face. He was quite different from the debonair man who had first met me, concerned about a few plants withering. His shirt was crumpled and there was a cuff button missing.

'I am so sorry about your wife,' I said. 'Have they given you any news?'

'No. Nothing yet. I was expecting something from the post-mortem. Not that I want to know any details about her death, really. It's all too awful.'

His voice quivered as he said the word. It is never a nice thought. It is hard to separate the spirit from the body, the body of a loved one. His wife had gone, to wherever one chose to believe. The husk left behind could reveal clues as to what had happened. And it would be wrong to ignore those possible clues.

He reached down to the floor beside his desk and lifted up a briefcase. It was a smart black leather case with digital locking device. Surely not the kind of briefcase used by a butcher, even a millionaire wholesale butcher?

'This is Anne's. I found it in her bedroom at the back of a

wardrobe. I didn't know she had a briefcase. I've never seen it before. She's not a businesswoman. Her life was bridge, shopping, coffee mornings, yoga. And she liked cooking and gardening. She was a wonderful cook. Her curries were perfection.'

He pushed the briefcase towards me. I pulled it across the desk. I did not have the right to look into it. Anne Steel had been murdered. I was not a police officer.

'I want you to look in it,' he said, sensing my reticence. 'I'm giving you permission.'

'It needs a 4-digit code punching into the lock.'

'I've found the code.' He smiled for the first time. 'It didn't take long to work out. She used something simple, so simple. It's her birthday and month. The nineteenth of October. 1910.'

I punched in the number and the catch on the lid released. I opened the lid. The briefcase was crammed with computer spreadsheets, small, used notebooks and a great deal of money, the notes in wads and contained within rubber bands. The money was in notes of twenty and ten denominations, new and used. There were a few other odds and ends. I tried not to touch anything.

'Have you counted this money?' I asked, saying the obvious. It looked counted.

'There's over five thousand pounds.' His voice was hollow. 'Don't ask me what this means or where it came from. I don't know or understand. She had all the money she ever needed from me and she had her own bank account. I gave her everything she wanted. Car, clothes, jewellery. She only had to ask. I've no idea where this money has come from or who it belongs to.'

Prints everywhere. His and others. Some help.

'You could have destroyed all this.' It was a sombre thought.

'Yes, I know. I thought about it, but although I don't want the police to have this evidence, it did make me start thinking that there might be some other reason for Anne's death. Not some mindless killing by a garden maniac.'

'Is that what the police are working on?'

He nodded. 'They think it's connected. Perhaps that Anne

surprised a man with a weedkiller spray and he tried to silence her. That does make a motive.'

I did not touch anything. The briefcase was loaded with prints, including Samuel's. This was going to be difficult. How could I get it dusted for prints without DI James knowing that it had come from Denbury Court?

'Are you asking me to try and trace the money and decipher the contents of the spreadsheets?' I asked. I was seriously out of my depth. I was more a trashed Women's Institute stand type detective. My spreadsheet training was minimal.

'Please, Jordan, will you try? I've no one to turn to. I don't know who to ask to help me. But I do know that I can trust you. This mustn't go to the police until we know what it all means or how Anne was involved.'

How does one bring up the subject of payment when a much beloved wife has died? I could not do it. His retainer covered the garden investigation only. It did not include a homicide investigation. I swallowed my avarice.

A change of tactic might work. 'Did you ever employ a gardener here?' I asked. 'Someone from the village called Bert? He smoked a lot.'

'Yes, we did. He strolled up here one day, saying he used to work at Denbury Court, but couldn't get on with the former owners. He said he loved this garden and would like to work here again. It sounded too good to be true, so yes, we took him on.'

Mr Steel finished his whisky and went for a refill. He poured a generous measure and I feared for his liver. He added a dash of soda and turned round.

'I'm sorry,' he said, ofering the decanter. 'Would you like something to drink? A glass of wine maybe? There's a nice white Chablis cooling.'

I shook my head. 'I'm driving.'

'My good manners seem to have escaped me these days.'

'It's OK,' I said. 'I've a bottle of water. What about Bert?'

'He was not exactly the best gardener in the world but we were grateful, at first. There was an awful lot to do. But he spent more time drinking and eating and smoking than actually working and we had to let him go.'

'Was he annoyed?'

'I've no idea.'

'Annoyed enough to wreak havoc on your garden?'

'I doubt it. I think he was pretty used to being sacked. He just finished his drink, packed his things and left. It was not a big deal.'

'Do you know anything about his family?'

'I should imagine he is a loner.'

Another loner.

'Thank you, Mr Steel. Before I go, how do you get on with the previous owners of Denbury Court?' I pretended to look up their name in my notebook. 'The Carltons. She was Sandra Carlton, the TV cook. She had a programme.'

'All right, I suppose,' he said mildly. The whisky was numbing his brain cells, taking away some of the pain. 'They seemed very nice people. We had no problems, apart from the price. They bumped the price up once they knew we were really interested, not exactly fair trading. But I knew Anne had set her heart on the place, so I didn't argue.'

'And have you seen them at all since?'

'No. I don't even know where they moved to. I doubt if I would recognize them. Everything's done over the phone or through agents these days.'

'What about the people who bought your old house?'

'Our old house?' He looked puzzled.

'The Corner House.'

'Oh, that one. Heavens, I've almost forgotten who bought it. Nice house but no character. It was some man who made a fuss about us taking a few plants. You would have thought it was a crime. Storm in a teacup. I sent him a cheque for the wretched plants and have never heard from him since.'

'You paid him?' This was news.

'I did indeed. I could probably find the payment in some bank statement if you need proof.'

'That's not necessary. I believe you, of course.' I closed the lid of the briefcase using my elbow. I hoped it did not look as awkward as it felt. I was not going to touch anything until I had put on some gloves. My heart lightened. DS Ben Evans would help me. There was no need to tell him more than the bare details. Maybe we hadn't gone on holiday to Cyprus together but he still liked me. He still liked me a lot.

In fact it was more than liking me. Ben had a sort of mega-crush on me. I couldn't think why. It must be the tangled tawny hair. I had not given him that much encouragement apart from normal politeness and a few goodnight kisses. Pleasant enough. Not binding in any way but welcome in a state of siege.

I had not been all that keen on a twosome holiday in Cyprus but somehow I got sweet-talked into it. The security alert in London had saved me. I still hadn't told Ben that I hadn't been at the airport in time. It seemed more gallant to let him do his duty. And we had both been too busy since to make new plans.

I was not proud of making use of Ben Evans. I was not paying with my body, only my lips. Was that two per cent of body surface? DI James still had first call. If ever.

Samuel and I took a walk around the garden. It seemed to help him to see that some paths were untouched and that a few trees and shrubs were still in foliage. There was hope that he could restore part of the garden.

'I was thinking of moving,' he said. 'But I suppose Anne would like it if I got the garden back into shape again.'

I had to say it, get the variance cleared up. 'I'm surprised that your wife liked gardening so much. She seemed a more sophisticated lady, shopping and bridge . . . not exactly wellies and compost.'

Samuel was amused. 'You're quite right, of course. Anne was a sophisticated lady but she loved flowers. She enjoyed taking cuttings and growing things in the greenhouse. Truly, she had green fingers. One day, she said, we were going to grow our own orchids. She had it all planned.'

'Sounds a great idea,' I said. 'Why don't you grow a new orchid?'

'And call it Anne Michelle?'
'Perfect.'

I took the briefcase back to my office, closed the door and put on a pair of surgical gloves. I needed to itemize the contents, selecting some for fingerprinting, see if anything gave any leads. I was not hopeful. Although the money was a mystery, the rest was probably complicated bridge winning formulas.

I laid the contents over my desk, trying only to touch the edges, holding everything very carefully with tongs. There were five small A5 notebooks, each year dated, the last beginning 2004. They were casual diaries, no exact days, but written in coded language, short forms and abbreviations. She was keeping a detailed record of the years. There were sums of money recorded. Was Anne Steel an Avon lady, selling a mountain of moisturizer and anti-wrinkle creams?

The spreadsheets were even less easy to decipher. Payments in and payments out. Also several accounts abroad. Nowhere was there any indication of what it was all about. Each transaction was simply numbered. It didn't say: 20 jars of caviar or 32 bottles of Extra Virgin Olive Oil. The turnover was substantial. Several thousands of pounds a month. Anne Steel was dealing with a turnover of some size. A turnover of what?

I put the money aside in an M & S green plastic bag. I buy my T-shirts there. They wash well. Here was a slight problem. I did not have a safe. Never had anything worth hiding in my shop. Miguel would have a safe and he would not ask questions. His Mexican restaurant would be opening for the evening soon. Problem solved.

The odds and ends were fairly ordinary. A hotel sewing kit. A raft of paracetamol, two tablets punched open and gone. This reminded me of a joke about a parrot who was not allowed in a chemist shop. Because the parrots-eat-em-all. Don't bother to laugh. A clutch of post-it notes with scribbled phone numbers. Should I phone them? A key on a BT ring. A calculator and a credit card. Shopping: buy a computer, hardware and printer;

take Internet course; become computer literate; get highly paid executive job.

It was obvious to me that Mrs Anne Steel had been carrying on a business of some sort without her husband's knowledge. Every time she went shopping or to the hairdressers, she was actually working, and sometimes working late. Well, good for her. Not just a shopping bimbo. But it seemed strange when she had all the money in the world, a beautiful home and a doting husband. It would take me about five and a half seconds to give up working.

Try me, James. Come on, try me. You'd be surprised how fast I could make this transition. Lightning fast. You wouldn't see where you were coming from.

'Ah, my favourite English rose,' said Miguel, sweeping me into his restaurant. The staff were laying up for the evening, putting real flowers into pottery vases, folding bright napkins into fan shapes, making sure the jumbo-sized wine glasses were sparkling. 'You look pale. You need a glass of my best Chilean. I have a new one. It will bring a bloom to your cheeks.'

'I've come to ask you a favour.'

'I cannot refuse you anything.'

Miguel was always like this. It broke my heart. He filled a wine glass with the wine and handed it to me, his velvety brown eyes twinkling, wanting me to stay and keep him company. 'What do you think of this, my beautiful Jordan?'

It was an elixir produced by an alchemist, designed to prolong my life, turn metal into gold, suggest a prolonged affair with Miguel. 'You like it, yes?'

I nodded as the crimson nectar warmed my throat, reminding me of blackberries and cinnamon. It was hard to find the right word. Hand me a thesaurus. 'It's delicious, perfection, wonderful.'

'I knew you would like it,' he said, with satisfaction. 'So, you will eat with me tonight, a special meal, after I have granted this favour?'

Now there was a loaded question. The favour was being bought with my company. It could be worse.

'I admit I haven't eaten well recently. I've almost forgotten food.'

'Then I will be your guide and choose the menu. Not too hot and spicy in case you cough with your asthma. See, I remember your asthma. But the taste buds will explode with amazing pleasure and the good wine will soften your heart.'

'Soften my heart? Do you think I'm hard-hearted?'

Miguel put on a sad face. 'Yes, because you think I am too old for you. Middle-aged, past the romance of life. A dinosaur who should chase the elderly widows who dine in my restaurant. But Jordan, I would ask nothing from you, only the pleasure of seeing your face across a table. And if you asked for more, then we would pleasure each other.'

I was defeated by his words and tried to smile at him. His words threw me. I could read his expressive eyes. They said try a breakfast table. He was not too old, never, but I was not ready. I might never be ready.

'And the favour?' he asked. 'Tell me.'

I put down the wine glass and produced the green plastic M&S bag. 'Could I put this bag in your safe for a few hours? I don't think I should leave it in my shop.'

'*Encantado! Si*. No problem. Give it to me.'

'*Muchas gracias*.'

'Jordan! You speak Spanish! *Me gusta*. It pleases me. *Me encanta*. I love it.'

'I only know two words.'

'It is a beginning. Life is too serious to be taken too seriously.'

Eleven

D etective Sergeant Ben Evans was more than averagely pleased to see me. He came striding out of the police station, his clean-cut face alight. It made me feel about two inches high. I had let him down over the Cyprus holiday and then ignored him for weeks. How low could I get? I developed a shell.

'Hi, Jordan. You look great. I hope this a social visit.'

'Partly,' I said, falling into step beside him. Height ratiowise we were perfect. I was reminded of his physique, his good looks and impeccable dressing. He used a trouser press. He was going towards a patrol car. 'I need a fingerprint check.'

'You know I can't do that.'

'I know you can't but I was wondering if you could tell me how to get round the red tape. Is that too much to ask? It is important for one of my cases.'

'Which case?'

I could lie. But it would not help if Ben found out that I had lied. What I said was almost the truth. 'The garden on Updown Hill that's being vandalized. You know all about it.'

'You've found a fingerprint on a blade of grass?'

'Ha, ha. Not quite, but near.'

'You want me to put this blade of grass through the system?'

'Sort of. It's a couple of sheets of paper which were found in the vicinity.'

I did not tell him it was about twenty spreadsheets. The A5 notebooks could wait. The five thousand pounds in tenners and twenties would have dozens of prints. But how many people would handle a spreadsheet? Maybe two or three.

106

'What do you want me to do? Run off the prints or try to match them up? You need to be a bit more specific.'

I was asking him to risk his job so I got devious. 'Perhaps we could talk about it over a glass of wine?'

I cringed at my deceit. Lacey, you are on the road to perdition. St Peter is not going to be there to greet you. Don't expect him to be hanging around with a cheerleader.

Ben grinned. 'Good idea, Jordan. Give me half an hour. I'll pick you up at your shop.'

I rushed back to First Class Junk, threw tepid water all over myself, found some clean jeans and a black T-shirt, tied my hair back with the floating silk scarf that had mysteriously arrived. It was this month's uniform. The kohl pencil broke and I had to make do with smudged charcoal shadow. It was a cool but mysterious look. Shopping list: pencil sharpener.

His car was waiting outside, engine ticking over. I slid a couple of spreadsheets into a brown envelope, checked everything, locked up and went out smiling to my fate.

'You look very happy, Jordan,' he said, taking in my appearance.

'It's seeing my favourite Detective Sergeant,' I said. Cringe galore time. I would not be able to keep this up. I could act, but not non-stop cringe acting with this really nice man.

'Where do you want to go?'

'The Gun?' I suggested.

'The Gun it is.'

I knew this was his favourite pub. The Bear and Bait was mine, but mainly for the jazz. Red wine varies in every pub from the red vinegar out of a box to the smoothest bliss from sun-drenched vineyards. It was hard to keep track. We talked about a lot of things on the drive.

The alert in London had been a false one, thank goodness, but for a moment it had looked really nasty, he told me. He parked near The Gun, turned off the ignition and sat back.

'I'm glad you are in Sussex,' said Ben. 'You're relatively safe here. Rural and coastal. No way bomb fodder.'

'Relatively?'

'I hardly think that Latching pier is much of a target or your beloved Bear and Bait. Mind you, missiles sometimes go off-course.'

'I don't want to know.'

'None of us do. But it has to be faced these days. We do not live in easy times, Jordan.' Ben turned to me, his eyes softening. 'That's why we have to make the most of life. Enjoy ourselves, not be too serious, have another drink or two.'

'We haven't had the first drink yet,' I said, getting out of the car. I could see an intense embrace coming on. I needed a couple of glasses of wine inside me before I could respond. If only he was DI James, I would be so content. Why couldn't James be like this, sweet and concerned and cruising my wavelength?

We went through into the smoky atmosphere of the saloon bar and sat in a two-seater panelled cubby hole. It was secluded and the pictures above us were old and brown. Faded prints of bewhiskered customers from the past sat outside the pub with their brimming tankards.

'The usual?'

'Please, Ben.'

I liked looking at his back standing at the bar. Taller, better built, better dressed than anyone else present. No one would mess with him. He returned with two glasses. He only drank shandy when he was driving.

'So tell me what you have been doing,' he said, his arm sliding casually along the back of the bench, his finger touching a tendril of hair on my neck. A shiver went down my back. 'I want to know everything.'

Talking shop was my second favourite occupation so I told him about my two cases. Don't ask about the first favourite. He wasn't there.

'Stalking is the devil to catch,' said Ben. 'Have you got a camera? Is there any firm evidence like things coming through the post and telephone calls?'

'Plenty, but it's not confirmed. It's only what I am told or shown. But I think I have met the woman.'

'And what happened?'

'She threatened me. It was pretty unpleasant. She's a very possessive lady.'

'And what did you do?'

'Unfortunately I sprayed her with soda water. It was purely accidental.'

'So now she might be stalking you as well. Not nice. Stalkers can be vindictive. Make sure your car is always locked and check day and night whether anyone is following you.'

'I hadn't thought of that. Maybe I ought to be more vigilant.' I remember my odd feelings of fear. Perhaps she was following me, harbouring malicious thoughts.

'And the rustic vandalism is still continuing,' he asked, 'even after Samuel Steel's wife's death?'

Ah, the conversation was going in the right direction.

'Yes, they've been there again. Early one morning. I missed it. I should have been up a tree but I wasn't. They took a saw to some bushes. Mr Steel is distraught. He thinks his wife's death and the wrecking are connected. He thinks that she disturbed the perpetrators and got killed for her trouble. He's wondering if these spreadsheets are linked to Mrs Steel in any way.' Deviously planted herring of pinkish hue.

'Have you heard the autopsy report?'

'No, of course I haven't.' I held my breath. His glass was half empty. 'Was it interesting?'

'It confirmed what we thought. She was not killed by the garden shears. They were not the primary source of homicide.'

'How did she die then?'

'She stopped breathing.'

I could have hit him. These CID police officers think they own the world. But he was grinning at me. It was a joke which I did not appreciate. Death is no joke.

'Don't ask me to come to your funeral,' I said.

He covered my hand with his in a firm grip. His skin was warm and dry. 'You are the only person that I'd want there,' he said intently.

A tremor of fear ran down my spine. There was always

danger around the corner. The newspapers ran stories every day. A druggie who took out a knife; domestic violence when the husband brandished an old hand gun; car crashes chasing a drunk driver.

I shivered. 'Please don't talk like that,' I said. My parents had died in a car crash. The pain was never far away. When I wore the black leather jacket they gave me for my twenty-first birthday, I could hear their voices and their laughter. I look a lot like my mother, all this unruly tawny hair. She had tried to tame it into a chignon or a bun without success. 'You've got straggles,' I used to say when I was young. 'I'm a straggly lady,' she'd laugh.

'Don't look so sad,' said Ben. 'What's the matter?'

'I was thinking about my parents. Sometimes it comes back to me like it was yesterday.'

'Then I am here to change all that,' he said very firmly. 'I believe this life is good despite the crime and violence. And I believe that every minute is for living.'

He took my hand to his lips. My bones melted a fraction. He was so sensitive, good-looking and streets ahead of any man who had courted me in the past. And so persuasive. Yet I did not love him. Something was wrong with me. My head needed testing.

'Ben . . .' I said. I could only say his name.

'I'm not rushing you,' he said.

'I know, I know.'

'I know where you live, a couple of bedsits over a shop. But you don't know where I live. Why don't you come and see? I'd like to show you.'

Red alert. Danger! Danger! My pulse escalated.

'I don't know . . .'

'I promise to take you home the moment that you say you want to go. Does that make it easier to say yes?'

I hesitated. 'Yes, all right.'

He finished his glass of shandy and stood up. 'Let's get going then. It's not far from here. The Gun is my local.'

He led me out to his car. My heart was thumping. I wanted to run away but my legs would not obey. It was too dark now to see where he was driving me. I hoped I could walk back if things went seriously wrong. It would be a long walk.

The trees entwined overhead in a gloomy canopy as we drove along a winding country lane, always climbing. His headlights caught the eyes of some small creature on the green bank. A rabbit? Where did Ben live? In a derelict barn? Then we began to climb a bumpy track. I hung on to the seat belt. I think I knew where we were heading. Hadn't I walked this track, a long time ago, before my PI work took over my time and my feet?

'Where are we?'

'You'll soon see,' he said mysteriously.

He took a sharp right and we were bumping up another track. The sacrum and coccyx regions of my spine were protesting. A round building loomed ahead, its crenellated roof etched against the sky. I knew where we were. It was Marchmont Tower, the local folly.

'This is the folly, the one on the Downs,' I said, intrigued. 'I didn't know anyone lived in it. I thought it was derelict.'

'Marchmont Tower,' said Ben, sitting back and enjoying my look of surprise. 'It was built in 1841 by a Lord Marchmont. He wanted to block the view of his neighbour, a local farmer who refused to sell him some land.'

'How weird. But then I suppose all follies have an eccentric history. But do you live here?'

'Sure. The tower was converted into a home probably ten years ago and mostly it's let out. It's all stairs. I hope you don't get vertigo. Four rooms, one on top of each other. The views are quite magnificent over the Downs. You can even see the sea on a clear day.'

My curiosity overtook any caution. I followed Ben into the tower. It was built of stone with Sussex pebble ornamentation round the door and windows. The ground floor was a big kitchen. A bachelor kitchen. I itched to get going on the pile of washing up in the sink. The scrubbed oak table in the centre had the remains of several meals, with sauce bottles and newspapers.

'Sorry,' he said. 'It's always a rush, getting called out at odd times. We never manage to catch up. This is the only floor with water. The bathroom was built on and is out the back. The sitting room is on the first floor with two bedrooms above. Want to come up? I can offer you a nightcap.'

A nightcap. I hoped this did not imply a cosy twosome with strings. I was definitely not staying.

'I can't stay long,' I said breathlessly, following him up the narrow spiral stone stairs. It was pretty difficult, keeping a safe distance. 'I've things to do. People to see.'

The sitting room was octagonal which was unusual for a start with windows on four of the walls. It was furnished with two well-upholstered, comfortable sofas, odd low tables and rugs, television and video, radio and CD player. Books and newspapers littered the floor. They were catching dust but I liked the room. Nothing matched, which was part of its charm. It looked lived in even if the occupants had no time for housework. Occupants? Ben had said 'we' or had I imagined it? Perhaps there was a lodger or a partner. He had never mentioned a partner.

Ben put on a disc, smooth jazz, my kind of music. Early Ella Fitzgerald. I was impressed. He had been doing his homework. Then, from a cupboard in one of the wall angles, he produced a bottle of wine. Wow. I could read the label. 2000 Marques de Casa Concha, Cabernet Sauvignon, from Chile. I thought: classic blackcurrants. It tastes like a £20 wine but cost £7 from Safeways.

'I'm not staying,' I said again. It sounded feeble. I was feeble. This was a Grade A seduction technique. I should lie back and enjoy it.

'Tell me about the fingerprinting you want done,' he said, leading me to a sofa. This was not fair. It was one of those deep sofas that you sink into like gravity collapsing. When I had sunk about two feet into the cushions Ben brought over a large glass of wine. The 250 ml pub line was infinitely lost. 'Taste that,' he said. 'Tell me what you think of it.'

'It's delicious,' I said, after a taste.

Now this I could get used to. The stunning wine, the big kitchen, the homely but comfortable sitting room with two huge sofas. I thought of my upright moral chair that discouraged amorous advances, and my minuscule kitchen counter where slicing a tomato meant bumping elbows. Folly, this might be, but it had immense potential.

And the views. I had not seen the views yet but I could imagine them. I'm a sucker for views; solace for the soul. The rolling Downs speckled with sheep, dotted ancient woodlands, sweeping fields of corn and rape seed, glimpses of the sea as the sun disappeared beyond the horizon. The tower might have a roof. I would not ask.

'Has the tower got a roof?' I asked.

'Crenellated. Perfect for topless sunbathing,' he said, nodding with approval.

'I'm more into sunsets,' I said.

'Topless sunsets,' he grinned, sitting down beside me. Not too near, but I could smell his lemony aftershave. He was drinking wine now. He was off duty. His shift had ended. He was all mine if I wanted him. But did I? That was the million-dollar question.

'I'd like the fingerprints off a few spreadsheets,' I said, tapping my bag. 'There are about twenty spreadsheets, but I'm fairly sure they are all pretty similar. The same people would have touched them so you need only scan a few.'

'What's this got to do with the vandalized garden?'

'You will recall that Anne Steel was murdered in her garden.' This was deep water.

'And these are her spreadsheets?'

'They were found thereabouts . . .' I was floundering.

'Now Jordan, you know that if they are something to do with Mrs Steel, then the spreadsheets are part of our investigation. What's the content of the spreadsheets?'

'No idea. Mr Steel gave them to me. They are connected to the garden investigation in some way. Just a few accounts, I believe, nothing special.' That was a close call.

Detective Sergeant Ben Evans leaned over towards me,

putting his glass down on a table in the same movement. 'I don't believe a word you are saying,' he murmured with a wicked smile, his eyes bright with amusement. 'You're not telling me the whole story. Now I don't do anything for young ladies who harbour secrets.'

I am not quite sure how it happened. But my glass was swiftly removed from my hand and Ben slid over and began kissing me very thoroughly. I did not move. They were wonderful kisses, soft and probing and the kind that made my stomach churn with feeling. He certainly knew how to kiss.

A lot of men don't. They are all slobbering lips and eating flesh. Women put up with them, thought of England, made shopping lists. Although I had never been married, I had read Relate reports and attended enough domestic violence in my WPC days. If only men could learn how to kiss properly. It ought to be an A level option.

DS Evans was no amateur. His kisses were made in heaven. I lost count of how many times he kissed me, moistening my lips, tasting my mouth. I lost count of everything. Yet his hands never strayed. A gentlemanly kisser? He was a complete rarity. He would be wonderful in bed, gentle and considerate. I knew that. Maybe I ought to find out?

He pulled the scarf out of my hair and let it fall around my shoulders. 'Such beautiful hair,' he murmured, letting the strands run through his fingers. 'So fiery, so silky. Don't ever have it cut off, Jordan.'

'What about split ends?' I don't know what made me say it. I had to break the spell before I found myself climbing another flight of vertiginous stairs to the room above. We would not be admiring the magnificent views once there.

'Another of my many talents,' said Ben, laughing to himself. 'Split ends are a doddle. Snip, snip.'

Was he trying to tell me something? Snip, snip had another meaning. I hoped not. He was too young for such a drastic procedure. Supposing he wanted to get married and start a family? Supposing he . . . we . . . Ben had not exactly said anything, but those kisses had been full of feeling. I remembered other kisses when men had been using me. Joshua and Derek among the few. They all wanted something that I was not prepared to give. Joshua wanted big dinners and shirts ironed. Derek wanted to own everything on the cheap, preferably with me paying. What did Ben want?

'I only want to love you,' he said softly.

'Love me? Are you sure?' He had me confused now. I could feel his warm breath tickling my ear. I had completely forgotten the purpose of our meeting.

'Of course, I love you, darling. How many times do I have to tell you?'

It was easy to forget everything when Ben was kissing me.

It was easy not to hear things, like a car stopping outside the tower and footsteps coming up the first flight of stairs. But it was never going to be easy to forget what happened next.

Someone came into the sitting room.

I knew instantly who was standing there. My head was obscured by Ben's shoulder; his face buried in my neck. My legs were draped across his lap. Fortunately I was still wearing all my clothes.

'Jordan? This *is* a surprise.' The voice was cool and blunt. I could imagine his face.

'Hello,' I said weakly. 'What are you doing here?' I struggled to sit up, pushing back my hair.

'What am *I* doing here?' he enquired, strolling over to the player and switching off the music. 'Making myself at home. Not difficult, Jordan. After all, this is my home.'

'This is your home, James?'

'Your hearing is excellent. Marchmont Tower is my home.'

Twelve

B en and I somehow managed to extricate ourselves from each ther and get off the sofa with a shred of dignity left. He offered to drive me home. He also kept the spreadsheets and half promised to do what he could about them.

The narrow stairs were hard to walk down, especially when I could not focus properly. The treads seemed to come up at me. I went into the automatic tea-making routine, the solace for all suffering. And I was suffering. I found three mugs, the biscuit tin, sugar. I could not remember who took sugar and who didn't.

I looked round for a tray but abandoned the idea of carrying a tray up those stairs. I called out instead.

'Tea's ready. Come and get it.'

My voice was weird. It did not sound like me. I was emotionally blunted. It was strangled and strange, like an echo down a tunnel. Perhaps I was in a tunnel. Maybe this tower of a folly was inbuilt with a device that changed vocal vibrations. Folly of all follies. Oh yes, this was my folly.

I poured out a mug of weak tea for myself, spooned in extra honey. I needed the sucrose.

'If you stir that tea any more, Jordan, you'll take the colour off the mug,' said James as he came down the stairs and into the kitchen. There was no expression on his face. He looked his usual remote, immovable self. The scene into which he had walked did not seem to have disturbed him one iota. I suppose I ought not to be surprised.

'You make the perfect cuppa,' said Ben, also totally composed as if James's presence was expected and normal.

'I didn't know you lived here,' I said, trying to sound normal. 'And with Ben. How long have you two been living together?'

It came out sounding all wrong. That wasn't what I meant. Every word I said made everything worse.

'Ben has been here three days,' said James, coolly. 'His digs at Portslade were appalling and he had to move out. I offered him a room.'

'It's only temporary until I find my own place,' said Ben, dunking his biscuit. 'But I like it here. It's pretty cool.'

I swallowed hard. 'So Marchmont Tower is actually your home?' I said. James nodded. 'I didn't know.'

'You never asked.'

'I thought you rented a room somewhere.' I was flailing about, out of my depth, wondering if I looked flushed and as thoroughly kissed as I was.

'I thought it was time I had a more permanent place,' he said, taking his tea outside. 'You can't live out of a suitcase for ever. 'By the way, you never came by the station. I had some questions to ask you.'

'They can wait,' I said.

Ben took me back to my bedsits. I thanked him before getting out of the car. He leaned across to open the door, kissing my cheek on the way.

'Don't worry about James,' he said. 'He's not shockable. He's seen it all before.'

What did that mean? Seen it all before? I imagined a procession of women climbing the narrow stairs to the folly's sitting room and accommodating sofa. But in three days? That was some schedule.

It was a relief to get back to my uncomplicated bedsits, despite the minimal space and moral chair. There was only one way to get my mind off the embarrassing scene I had escaped from so recently. Unpuzzle a puzzle.

I took out the rest of the spreadsheets and laid them on the floor. I work better on the floor. Anne Steel was no Avon lady. These were not orders for moisturers and bath foam. I put them in date order. I also ate Mrs Carlton's delicious chocolate cake with a cup of black coffee. Comfort eating. It was understandable.

The amounts gave no clues. Everything was a number slashed with a further number: 1952/33. It meant nothing to me. Unless it was a code. I went into code-mode without success. The dates covered the last three months. No wonder Samuel Steel had passed them over to me.

The number 1952 came up several times. Perhaps it was a customer number or product identity, whatever it was she might be selling. Spreadsheets meant selling something usually.

It took a long time to go through the small A5 notebooks. They were filled with a neat handwriting which I presumed was Mrs Steel's script. I had forgotten to check. But most of it was a personal sort of speedwriting. Words that were not whole words. I ought to be able to make sense of it if I concentrated. Hs was easy = has. Hd = had. Bn = been. Some of her abbreviations were more difficult, even impossible. It was like a sort of diary, covering several years. Was she writing a book? This was giving me a headache.

I sank back on to a pair of cushions, wishing I had some sort of insight into the woman's mind. But she was dead. A pair of shears plunged into the neck. I had never met her and yet I seemed to know the woman. Her presence was everywhere in the beautiful house. There must be some reason for this murder and it might be nothing to do with the garden.

These notebooks had the clue. But I could not see what it was. I put everything tidily away into a box and marked it STEEL/2. The box marked STEEL/1 was the garden. It was time to go to sleep and forget the day.

But I did not get a chance. My phone rang as I was getting out of the bath. I wrapped myself in a big towel and staggered to my mobile, thrown carelessly on the bed.

'Hello?'

'Jordan?'

'Yes, I think it is. But I'm not sure who I am as I am halfway to bed. Do you know what time it is?'

'I asked you to contact me earlier and you didn't. You obviously had other things on your mind.' Nasty barb.

'I had two calls to make re my Updown Hill garden case. At the time, they were more important.'

DI James and I were talking to each other like strangers.

'Can I come round?'

'What? Now? It's late. What will the neighbours think?'

'You haven't got any neighbours. Don't worry, I have nothing on my mind except work.'

'Give me ten minutes to get respectable,' I groaned.

Those ten minutes were spent flinging on a light tracksuit, doing the washing up, hoovering the carpet, throwing out newspapers and rubbish, finally putting a brush through my hair. When the doorbell rang, I had twenty seconds to spare.

'This had better be quick. Sorry, there's no soup,' I said.

'Pity,' said James. 'I may have a home at last but alas no one knows how to cook.'

'I'll buy you a cook book.'

'I only read short words.'

It was the first halfway humorous thing he had said for weeks. I could not remember when we had last been on speaking terms, that is, friendly speaking terms. Things had been going wrong for a long time. There was a ritual that Red Indians did in that situation but I could not recall what it was. Something about dream catchers, something with feathers hung over your bed.

I'm sure it would be helpful if I knew what it was.

'Come in,' I said, leading the way upstairs, barefooted. 'You know the way.'

I was reminding him of our soup and salad days. Before he got so uppity and before I gave up waiting for him to make a move.

'I could throw together a sandwich,' I offered.

'That's food, and I call that nearly cooking,' he said, stretching himself out on my moral chair without an invitation. He put his head back and closed his eyes. He had dark lashes, too long and too dark. He looked ready to doze off.

I made him a sandwich of Dagwood proportions. Two slices of granary bread consumed a generous amount of tuna, sweet-corn, cos lettuce, honey and mustard relish. I made one for myself too, scaled down. Hunger had returned.

I sat on the floor, my back against the radiator, plate balanced on my knees. The radiator had the faintest residue of warmth, not enough to ease my bones but comforting. Summer was not quite over but I had partially turned on my heating at night.

'Wake up,' I said.

It was the first time that we had looked straight at each other. His blue eyes were questioning.

'So?' I asked.

'So, Jordan,' said James. 'Firstly, I am not surprised that you and Ben are becoming an item. But I wish it had not happened under my roof. It makes me a little touchy.'

'We are not an item and nothing happened. It's not my fault that you have such a comfortable sofa and Ben has a high libido. He likes kissing me. It was also a fatigue syndrome. Surely you must have experienced something similar? When you are so tired that anyone will do as long as you can sleep.'

James laughed. It was an invigorating sound. His teeth were strong and white. How had he changed sides so quickly? I edged nearer to him. He was still draped over my moral chair, utterly relaxed. I could have touched his ankles, tenderly stroked the bare skin above his black socks. There were dark hairs on his skin that sent me wild.

Then the truth dawned on me. If I was going around with Ben Evans in a serious sort of way, then I was no longer interested in him. He didn't want me becoming a complication or emotional baggage. I had given him back his freedom and that's what he really wanted. Freedom from me, freedom from any women. The woman who had hurt him so much had made it impossible for him to trust any other. So he did not want a relationship. He did not want my adoration, my care and devotion. He wanted to be free.

Now he thought he had got it and that made him happier.

'Like another sandwich?' I asked, letting the reality sink in.

'I could do with some of your good coffee.'

'Sure.'

I was none too steady, making the coffee. I did not know if I could cope. The knowledge that James did not want me – ever, in any capacity – was unnerving. But the aroma soothed my nerves. He took a mug of coffee from me.

'This is a strictly work call now,' he said, breathing in the pure infusion. 'I have to ask you some questions.'

'I knew there would be a flip side.'

'You know I never stop work.'

'Carry on,' I said, not caring, flinging caution to the elements. I might say anything. 'I've always co-operated.'

'George Hill. How well do you know him? You were seen with him in Brighton, at the revue theatre.'

This was the last thing I expected James to ask me. I nearly had a nasty accident with my coffee.

'And you saw me being picked up by him. Remember, the red dress?'

'Oh yes, you were almost wearing a dress. So that was George Hill?'

'George Hill is a new client,' I said. 'I'm working on a case for him.'

'What sort of case?'

'James, you know better than to ask me that.'

'What sort of case?' he repeated. 'I have every right to ask you. I'm the one investigating a homicide.'

'Mrs Steel? Heavens, what has she got to do with George Hill?'

'I didn't say she had anything to do with George Hill. Tell me what you know about him, please. Where's this famous co-operation gone?'

I took a sip of my coffee. It was cooling. 'I'll tell you what I know about him but nothing about the case. He's a very pleasant man, charming, articulate, clever, quite successful as a stand-up comedian around the coastal theatre circuit. Name in lights. But his humour on stage is so far below the belt, you could trip over it. I mean, I'm not straight-laced or a Victorian prude but his jokes were unacceptable. He was coarse, vile, lewd and disgusting. I was his guest so I couldn't walk out.'

'So you didn't like his show?'

'No, it was rotten to the core.'

'Did you tell him?'

'Of course not. I said it was great. I lied. Off-stage he's really quite ordinary,' I said. 'I didn't want to hurt his feelings.'

'Have you been to his home?'

'I know where it is,' I began carefully. 'He has a flat in a block at the back of Latching. It's just an office, a pied-à-terre. He doesn't actually live there. He flies in and out, on the circuit. It's just a place to change his shirt.'

'What about enemies?'

'Enemies? I've no idea. How would I know?' I'd no idea if a stalker was classed as an enemy. Tricky one.

'Tell me about the revue again. You say it did not appeal to you.'

'No.'

'But everyone else liked it?'

'Yes, I'm a freak.'

'Not necessarily, Jordan. Perhaps there were others who did not like it either but were not brave enough to say so. There's always the herd instinct. People often go along with the majority because it's easier. It takes guts to be different.'

He was looking at me with a kind of benevolent uncle approval. I am not used to his approval. It made me feel like a little girl. Any moment now he was going to pat my head and give me a sweetie.

'And did you go to any aftershow parties with George?'

'No, I didn't want to go. I'd had enough. George had lots of invitations and he wanted to go, but I didn't. I wanted to come home.'

'And did you come home?'

'Not straightaway, it was too late. I walked around for a bit looking for a taxi. The last train had already gone. I had to wait for the first train at 5.23 a.m.'

'And where did you wait?'

'Hey, what's all this? What's it to you where I waited? You asked me what I know about George Hill and I've told you everything, which is not much.'

'Between the end of the show and dawn, can you tell me where you were?' The nice uncle had gone, replaced by the granite-faced detective inspector. His eyes were clipped ice.

'I don't see why I have to tell you, but yes, I was in a hotel bar, chatting up the barman, drinking juice, if you must know.'

'Can you prove that? Which hotel?'

I couldn't remember the name of the hotel. Grand, Glorious, Excelsior? I had walked in without looking, drawn by the soft lights and luxurious interior. I could describe the decor of the bar in detail but little else. Even the barman had no obvious face despite his kindness.

'Do you have an alibi?'

'A what?'

'Would the people in this mythical hotel bar vouch for your presence?'

'It's not mythical and I have absolutely no idea which hotel it was. And why are you asking me all this? If I can find it, of course the barman would remember me, if the same one is on duty. It's of no importance to you what I did that night. I sat in a bar drinking orange juice till it was time to catch the first train. At one point, I fell asleep. Anything else?'

'It's not enough. I need more exact details.'

I suddenly remembered. 'Hold on! I've got a label!'

It was still in the wicker wastebin in my bedroom. The label I'd cut from the pink silk raincoat. There it was, printed clearly. The Majestic Hotel, Brighton, with a March date. I went back, flourishing the label. 'The Majestic Hotel,' I said. 'That's where I was.'

'Jordan, you've been very helpful.' He closed his notebook. 'Though it would be even more helpful if you could tell me why he was employing you. Had he lost a beloved pet, maybe a tortoise?'

The old tortoise wind-up. No one would forget when I was

hired to find a lost tortoise. I solved the case. But not without the help of Latching police who had found the tortoise wandering along the A27. They fed it on canteen salad till I returned it to its rightful owner.

'My lips are sealed,' I said.

'They weren't sealed on the sofa.'

That was a knife in the ribs.

I did not offer James a second cup of coffee. The sooner he left the better. I wanted to go to bed and forget the whole day. A small part of me was glad that DI James had found himself somewhere decent to live and that it was fun and interesting. It had always been a mystery where he hung his socks. He never said, never explained, and never seemed happy.

But Marchmont Tower was ideal for him. He'd find it difficult to conform to a flat. It was not his style. The tower was more than four rooms built on top of each other and linked by a treacherous stairway. It was the expression of an eccentric personality from an earlier age.

'So why the third degree?' I asked, escorting him downstairs and showing him the door. A cool westerly wind blew in. 'At this time of night?'

'Go in, Jordan. It's turning cold.'

'I want to know.'

James turned back, jangling his car keys. His face was grave.

'I said I was investigating a homicide. I didn't mean the Anne Steel case. I meant George Hill. He was found hanging from a hook on the back of his dressing-room door. Your phone number was in his pocket.'

Thirteen

It is never possible to be immune to death. The police find many situations difficult to grasp. The shock was obvious on my face. DI James watched my reaction with surprise. Had he forgotten that I had feelings?

'Are you all right?' He looked concerned.

I leaned against the doorway. 'George Hill? I can't believe it. He can't be dead. I mean, I saw him only Saturday evening. He was fine then, on top form. He was elated because he thought the show had gone well and he had several parties to go on to. No way would he want to commit suicide.'

'I didn't say it was suicide. I said it was homicide. Yes, he was hanging from a hook on the back of his dressing-room door, but he was pumped full of a street drug, a derivative of Methylenedioxy Amphetamine.'

'Ecstasy.'

'He wouldn't have known the time of day.'

'He could have taken it himself.'

'No one takes the equivalent of four tablets. One keeps you going all night.'

'So who pumped him?' I said, shaking my head, trying to take in the options. 'When I left him, he was bright and breezy. Not a sign of drugs or alcohol, I'm sure of that. He'd drunk nothing more lethal than pints of black coffee and a gin and tonic before the show and I made that myself.'

'Are your gin and tonics lethal?'

'Not several hours later.'

'Do you still have a George Hill case?'

'No, not now, I suppose. It's down the drain. D'you know

anyone who wants a cleaner or shelves stacked? No one stalks a dead man.'

'So stalking came into it? Is that right? That was his case you were working on?'

I was starting to get cold. A sneaky wind was cooling my skin. Vicious whips of air attacked any bare skin allowed out. I was sinking into disbelief and shock. I did not even want James around.

'Stalking, did you say, Jordan?' he persisted. 'Have you identified the stalker?'

'Sorry, James, this is not the time for swopping intimate confidences. The man's dead. Would you mind going home, please,' I said. 'I don't want to talk any more.'

'OK, but I'll want to talk to you again. I haven't finished.'

I closed the door and leaned against it. James was still outside. I could hear his breathing. He changed weight from one foot to another. There was still time for me to reopen the door and invite him in. But I was not in the mood to be helpful. It was time to sleep.

Sleep did not come easily to me. Instead I sweated and twisted and turned, images flashing across my mind. Camera shots of George Hill on stage, smooth, successful, sophisticated, the sequins glistening. The flavour of the jokes was fading fast. I could not remember a single line.

At dawn I slid my legs over the side of the bed and hung my head. I needed to walk and breathe fresh air. I pulled on a thin tracksuit and trainers, drank some water and let myself out. The sky was a clear, pure passing summer vista. Cloudless and washed with lightning blue. Latching has such beautiful skies. Nothing had changed in that department.

Few cars were out on the sea road. Most of the early workers were using the bypass on their way to Brighton, or Chichester in the other direction. The quietness was soothing, only the waves talking and whispering to each other as the incoming tide spread over the untouched grey sands. The gulls were wheeling and dealing, waiting for the local fishing boats to reach the shore. They knew there would be plenty of fish heads and tails thrown out for a cafeteria style breakfast. No queueing. Swoop and grab.

One brown-feathered juvenile gull was having a bad time on the sand. The older birds were dragging him away by the leg. It was cruel. I clapped my hands and made them all fly off. He might have a better chance somewhere else.

The empty beach stretched ahead, distant rollers freckled with mist and smudging the horizon. I saw very little as I walked, concentrating on my feet and my breathing as if they might both desert me. The path was cracked in places. It needed resurfacing. The council had forgotten the sea road, far too busy pulling down elegant Georgian mansions for mammoth four-storey car parks. I had that sour grapes taste.

Distances were guesswork. I am always meaning to cap the miles when driving along frequently walked routes but usually forget. The one statistic that stays permanent is that it takes me eight minutes to walk the pier. I need one of those surveyor's things on wheels to push along ahead of me. Shopping list: buy secondhand surveyor's thing on wheels for surveillance. Not urgent as no imminent surveillance case at present.

They were renewing a stretch of decking on the pier. The old blackened timber was piled up against the wire railing that stopped inattentive pedestrians from falling down the hole. I leaned over, interested in seeing a view of the underside of the pier that I had not seen before. The decking was supported by sturdy cross-timbers, which in turn were latched to iron girders.

Latched. Latching must get its name from some piece of similar joinery, way back in distant medieval times. Medieval conversation: 'Eh, lad, that's a fine bit of latching.'

'Found them timbers washed up where there's a bit o' fishing off the beach.'

'That's the place for latching then, lad. We'll reckon on more timber when tide comes in.'

It was my first flippant thought of the day. My spirits were recovering. I took the road to the back of Latching, deliberately going towards George Hill's flat in Chapel Court. It might even be open. He had died in Brighton. His pied-à-terre for a couple of shirts and spare razor might not be of interest to the police yet.

Yet.

The postman and the milkman were on their rounds. It was easy to slip in as they keyed the entry system.

'Morning,' I said brightly, working the arms. 'Summer is still with us then.' I hoped I looked like a new tenant out for a run.

'Morning, miss. The lift's out as usual.'

'I prefer walking,' I grinned. 'Good for the tummy.' I patted said area and both men agreed. 'I'll take the mail for number 17, George Hill, if you like. He doesn't have milk, does he?'

'Never there,' said the milkman, shaking his head.

'Nor picks up his mail. Sometimes I have to leave it in a pile outside the door, there's so much. Can't blame him. Most of it is junk.'

'Perhaps his lady friend collects it,' I said casually.

'Oh, that one. She's not his lady friend,' said the postman, shedding elastic bands on the floor. 'More of a nuisance friend. Never leaves him alone. Always watching for him coming in or out. Got ears like a hawk. She can hear his key turning from two floors down.'

I could not believe what I was hearing. If this was the same woman, if this was his stalker . . . and she lived in the same block of flats? On the ground floor? Call me lucky.

'Is that the woman in number three or number five?' I asked.

'Number four,' said the postman. 'Mrs Lechlade. Spends the rest of her time shopping, judging by all the catalogues. She ought to get a job. Keep her out of mischief. Well, I'd better get on.'

I held out my hand. 'Number 17. Shall I take it up for you, if it's a help?'

'Thanks, mate. Save me doing the top floor. I've got nothing else for up there.'

I staggered under the stack of mail he offloaded on to me. If Mrs Lechlade had been shopping again, who was going to return all this stuff? Not me, I wasn't paid in a secretarial capacity. Come to think of it, I had not been paid at all. Sum total of payment was the small amount I had left over from the money George gave me to get a taxi home.

I remembered where George kept his key, on top of the fire extinguisher outside the lift. It was still there. Thank you, George. Handy place. Lucky I spotted you automatically checking.

No yellow tape across the door. This was not scene of crime. I opened the door carefully. It looked pretty much the same. I did not think anyone had been in. Stale air. Perhaps he had a London address as well and this was a secret escape hole.

Never any letters from his stalker, George had said, but non-stop gifts. If his stalker was not yet aware that George had died, then Christmas would still be flowing to his door. It was. I did not open the packages, but from the store's addresses, I guessed there was more Stilton, some CDs, and the long, flat packet from Harrods could only be a tie. Silk, of course. There was a lot of financial mail, items from several banks, building societies, heavy annual reports from companies. The joke business obviously paid well. I didn't open them.

Time for a quick search of the flat. Along the tops of shelves and under shelves, under seat cushions, behind furniture. All the usual hiding places. Nothing but dust. I was very thorough. But there was something strange about the kitchen and I could not work it out. I stood, looking at the walls.

'Dear George,' I said aloud to the empty atmosphere. 'Would you mind very much if I took the Stilton? It's criminal to waste it and it'll start to run in this heat. And the Belgian chocolates?'

I had a feeling he would understand. I relocked the door and was about to put the key back on the fire extinguisher, but then I didn't. I kept it. No one knew it had been there anyway. He didn't need it anymore.

On my way home I passed Gracie, Latching's bag lady, with a convoy of heavily laden shopping trolleys on the way to her current beach shelter. I gave her the box of Belgian chocolates. She said nothing. Sometimes I think she has forgotten how to talk.

*   *   *

Leroy had said that the sequins would not stand up to dry cleaning so not to bother. They'd probably melt. I returned the dress to her at the estate agents in Rustington with my thanks and a flowering azalea plant. She wondered why I was a bit subdued but thought that the evening had not gone well.

'But he liked the dress?' she said.

'It was perfect, Leroy. Quite brilliant. He loved it.'

'But the evening didn't work out?'

'It . . . the end was a bit unexpected.' There was no way I could tell Leroy that he had died. It sounded like my fault.

'And one day you will tell me what happened?'

'You'll read it in the newspapers, only too soon. It was awful, but thank you again for the dress.'

'Thank you for the lovely plant.'

'Keep it out of direct sunlight.'

I stepped out on to the pavement.

A large lady was speeding by on a motorized scooter. I recognized her and waved. She did an immediate u-turn in the road and came up alongside me, her face all smiles.

'Jordan, lovely to see you. I've been meaning to thank you for the invitation to your BBQ on the beach. I'm coming, of course, when you let me know the date. But do give me plenty of notice. I'm terribly busy these days.'

It was Mrs Edith Drury, chairman of Latching Women's Institute. I smiled at her enthusiasm. I did not know I had even sent out invitations. It must have been by word of mouth. Doris was making sure it happened.

'I'm glad you're coming,' I said. 'It'll be fun but don't expect the kind of food your clever members cook.'

'My dear, we've had twelve activity courses this year and none of them have had anything to do with cooking. I've been driving a tank.'

'A tank?' I was full of admiration, but come to think of it Mrs Drury had driven her old car a bit like a tank.

'A group of us had a day at an Army track and drove a 13-tonne armoured tank and a Rapier support vehicle. We even had to drive them up and over a very steep hill. It's called the knife-edge and the drop was hair-raising, I can tell you.'

'Wow, that took some nerve. What are you going to do next?'

'Hot-air ballooning, then gliding and canoeing.'

'Sounds wonderful. When can I join?' It was wishful thinking. I would never have time, but I liked the idea.

'Anytime, my dear. You'll be welcome. Must fly. Going to a meeting.'

My shop opened willingly. It was feeling neglected. I went through the post, mostly junk. Then I got a shock.

There was a jiffy bag addressed to me. It was not big enough to be a bomb but I opened it gingerly.

Some words were scrawled on the back of a shiny George the Jester theatre flyer:

> Hi, Jordan,
> I forgot to tell you I'm booked on a cruise ship for the next two weeks, so IOU several days' pay. This is all the cash I have on me. Enclosed is a cheque. Carry on the good work. Come for a drink when I get back. Wear snazzy red dress. George xxx

It was a voice from the mortuary freezer and the cash he had on him was two hundred and ten pounds. The cheque was made out for five hundred pounds, that was ten days' work. Moral dilemma: take the money and run. Take the money and find stalker. Take the money, find stalker and killer and present cheque to closed account?

I read the letter again. It hardly sounded like a man about to commit suicide.

I drove to Updown Hill, hoping to see Samuel Steel on his own, but his daughter, Michelle, came to the door. Her designer-faded jeans were as tight as ever, her face delicately made up, hair immaculate and glossy. She was not exactly grieving over the death of her stepmother. No dark glasses.

'I'm very sorry about your stepmother,' I said. 'It must have been a shock.'

'Well, I'm not sorry. She got what she deserved. Conniving bitch.'

Michelle was keeping her voice down as if she did not want her father to hear what she said. She had some human feelings for him at least.

'Michelle, I don't understand what you mean by that,' I said. 'It seems an extreme thing to say about your stepmother. After all, how long had they been married? So Anne Steel must have looked after you at one time, didn't she, before you left home to work in the theatre?'

She didn't exactly answer. 'Father married her eight years ago. The wedding was nauseating. You've never seen such an elaborate extravagance and waste of money. I refused to be in any of the photographs. Father was annoyed, of course, but I told him I was feeling sick.'

'Very diplomatic.'

'You never met her, did you?' Michelle tossed her head, her hand on her hip, eyes narrowed.

'I never had that pleasure.'

'Hardly a pleasure. She was two-faced, you know. Sweet as sugar to my father and anyone she wanted to butter up or get something from. But rub her up the wrong way and she was out for your guts. I still have the scars.'

'Not physical scars?' I hoped I was not actually hearing this.

'Emotional, mental. She didn't beat me up but she tried to wreck my theatrical career at one point, spreading vile and evil rumours about me. She taped a personal conversation and threatened to use it. It worked at first. I couldn't get any work for months but I never gave in to her. It was always a fight between us. Father never knew, of course. She kept it from him.'

Michelle's face was screwed up with bitterness, remembering the past. She was near to tears, but the tears were of rage and anguish. Her make-up was beginning to streak.

'Michelle, you should really be careful what you say. This is a homicide case. You don't want to find yourself the chief suspect.'

'I don't care,' she said defiantly. 'I'd have killed her if I'd had the chance.'

'Now that's a very stupid thing to say,' I said firmly, suddenly being the elder sister. Michelle was childish beyond belief. 'Take my advice and keep your animosity to yourself. Don't broadcast it around. Police cells are no fun, even as temporary accommodation. They are minus any stars whatsoever and the food is terrible. And if you value the luxury of constant hot water and modern sanitation, keep your mouth shut.'

'I'm sure you mean well, Miss Lacey, but I don't need your advice,' said Michelle, flicking back her hair. 'Why don't you direct your energies to finding the person who vandalized my father's garden. That's why you are employed.'

'Your father has also employed me to make some enquiries into your stepmother's death. I hope I'm not going to find leads that point straight to you.' My patience was thinning. This was unbelievable.

Michelle looked at me with disdain. 'I doubt if you are capable of finding leads of any sort. Your success gardenwise is minimal. Perhaps my father should be employing someone more successful, with proven experience in the field of private investigating.'

I swallowed my distaste for this unpleasant young woman. Her genes were in a nasty twist. I had to remember that she was not my problem.

'I find your attitude extraordinary,' I said. 'This isn't the way to make friends and influence people. I like the red slashed sneakers, by the way. New, are they?'

It was obvious that they were not new and I suddenly remembered where I had seen them before. It had been a fleeting glance. Surely not? Not Michelle. It didn't add up. Why would she be in her father's garden, late at night, dressed up in black, trying to break into the conservatory? But the punch was pure Michelle. It had been below the belt and spiteful. It did not hurt anymore but the intention had not been friendly.

And I remembered the noisy car engine starting up, a lot like a little yellow roadster. Note: start noise index, if possible.

'I don't remember,' she said sniffily.

She began to close the door but I put my foot in the way. 'I've come to see your father,' I said firmly. 'He has excellent manners and is always pleased to see me.'

'Don't let him ply you with brandy,' she said. 'His manners might deteriorate.'

Fourteen

S amuel Steel came through from the kitchen with a blue striped butcher's apron tied round his waist. He looked one degree less depressed than when I had last seen him. Perhaps his daughter's company was good for his morale.

'Hello, Jordan. You're bright and early. I'm just making breakfast. Would you like some?'

A man cooking me breakfast? It was almost immoral as if we had just showered together after a long, hot, passionate night. But what would I know about long and passionate nights? In your dreams, Jordan.

I could smell the bacon, succulent home-cured rashers with no injected water. 'A proper English breakfast would be wonderful,' I said, moistening my lips and walking straight past Michelle. Shock can do strange things to people. I gave her the benefit. She may not have known what she was saying.

'I always cook plenty,' he said. 'Michelle only has half a crispbread and a segment of grapefruit.'

Mushrooms, tomatoes, fried bread and scrambled eggs served on a big oval plate. I declined the bacon. A breakfast fit for a starving PI. Every mouthful was delicious.

'You certainly can cook,' I said, when I had scraped up the last morsel of glistening egg. 'Gold star.'

'I made the scrambled eggs,' said Michelle, crumbling a crispbread. 'In the microwave.'

'Good for you. I'm impressed.'

'She's not just a pretty face,' said Samuel, ruffling his daughter's hair. 'Michelle doesn't have much time to come home when she's in a show. She's incredibly busy.'

'I bet she is,' I said, helping to stack the plates in the dishwasher. 'All those rehearsals. I would never be able to remember lines.'

'It's a gift.' Samuel was clearly besotted with her talent.

'I wonder if you would mind if I had a quick look at your wife's bedroom,' I asked, choosing a good moment when Michelle had disappeared outside. 'I promise not to disturb anything. Sometimes I can spot something which the police may have overlooked.'

I could not think of a single instance when I had done this but the odds were that there must have been one. But yes, at the Beeches. The dead nun case. Nearly a success story.

'Of course,' he said. He hesitated as if it was an afterthought. 'I haven't been in there since she died. I simply couldn't bring myself . . . all her things. I'm not sure what I'm going to do with her clothes but I suppose I've got to do something. But if you see anything, anything that you like . . . please feel free to take whatever you can use. Don't be at all embarrassed.'

'That's very kind,' I said awkwardly.

It was a strange feeling at the door to Anne's bedroom, actually walking in, like invading her privacy. I don't know what I expected to find. The acres of white pile carpet and cream satin bed quilting were a surprise. I expected a decor more floral and Laura Ashley. This was pure Rita Hayworth in the Thirties. Glass lampshades clouding delicate porcelain stands. Gilded mirrors everywhere. The room had been polished, vacuumed and tidied up since the police had scoured the premises; even sprayed with a lilac air freshener as if her death had polluted the atmosphere. Or perhaps the uniformed mob had brought in an unwelcome whiff of the law.

She had a dressing room adjoining the bedroom with wall-to-wall fitted wardrobes, full of clothes. I opened the doors. The quality was staggering even for a successful butcher's wife. It was all top designer labels with not a single Marks & Spencer garment in sight. Even the pink bomber jacket was Armani. The shoes had been made by that Jimmy Choo designer, dozens of pairs. Handbags by Gucci, mountains of frothy undies from

Janet Reger. The cosmetics on her dressing table were the costliest paint pots from international beauty names. A staggered row of perfume bottles displayed a range of fragrances to suit any mood. Anne must have spent a fortune on her skin and face.

There was a photograph of her on the dressing table, taken at some dinner party. She was quite beautiful, blonde and cool, very Grace Kelly.

But even my maths told me that this Mrs Steel was living way beyond her husband's means unless he had won the Lotto. Denbury Court was lovely. The garden, before the vandalism, was beautiful. Her car was expensive. But these clothes were not normal High Street shopping and did not reflect posh country living, even on Updown Hill.

I began an inch-by-inch search of the drawers in the dressing room. There must be something which was the tiniest bit out of character. I did not know what I was looking for. A letter? A phone number? A pawn ticket?

It was all so damned clean. The smallest money spider did not stand a chance. I took to going through the jacket pockets like a suspicious wife. She liked polo mints so we had something in common. Then I found an appointment card for a Harley Street clinic. She was booked in for Botox, laser skin surfing, collagen implants, hyaluronic acid gel. You name it, she'd booked it. I was beginning to see a vulnerable lady, determined not to lose the fight against time.

Her bathroom was luxurious. Ivory marble, gold taps, fluffy towels and a thick, toe-kissing carpet. I went through the medication in the mirrored wall cabinet. The usual aspirin and paracetamol, antiseptic, plasters. No prescribed sleeping tablets. I expected a few exotic items. Then I struck gold. Behind a bottle of witch hazel (spots), I found a disk, a three-and-a-half-inch floppy disk. It was hidden inside a packet of support tights. I doubted if she wore support tights or shopped a lot in Superdrug. No one keeps tights in a bathroom cabinet. The police had not noticed this inconsistency.

Then I went back into the bedroom and saw a membership

card. It had been used as a prop under a lamp, to stop it wobbling as one does. Surely no one would notice if I took it. My palm closed over it like a pickpocket in flight. I closed the door as if not to disturb her slumbers and walked downstairs. The air seemed very peaceful. It was a curious feeling. Perhaps she had wanted me to find these clues. Her killer had not been kind.

Michelle was standing outside. 'So you have been nosing around my stepmother's room. What did you think of her clothes?'

'Pretty fancy,' I said.

'They cost a fortune.'

'They look it. Maybe a little too fancy for around here,' I suggested, throwing the bait. 'The countryside and all that.'

'She wasn't always around here,' said Michelle with a sniff. 'This was slumming. The slums of Latching, she called it.'

I was puzzled. Latching is hardly slummy, despite some of the monstrous council building. Its gardens and walks are a pleasure, the Georgian houses an architectural delight. I had a feeling that Anne might have been deliberately provoking Michelle. She had liked gardening.

'If Latching wasn't her scene, I wonder why she decided to marry your father. I presume you all lived together in The Corner House when they first married.'

'They fell in love,' said Michelle with a cynical sneer. 'All that old-fashioned lovey-dovey stuff. But really it was rampant hormones. They couldn't keep their hands off each other.'

'Your father is a very nice man, a gentleman,' I said hurriedly.

'She wouldn't have known a gentleman if it had been tattooed on his . . . forehead.' She had almost said something else.

I decided to leave. There was only so much of this vitriolic young lady I could stand at any one time. She'd be the one needing the Botox if she continued ruining her face every time she thought of her stepmother.

'Thank you,' I said to Samuel. He was out in the garden now, pulling up dead plants and throwing them on to a wheelbarrow.

'I suppose it's too late to find out anything about this now?' he said, waving his arm towards the garden.

'Maybe, probably. But don't give up hope. You never know, the unexpected could happen.'

I drove home, wondering where to go and what to do with my finds. There was a chill in the air, a breeze disturbing the trees with feathered fingers. Summer was definitely over. I could not remember where I had put my two vests. In two bedsits, it's essential to keep the current clothes at hand and hide the rest. There was a batch of bin bags tossed behind my moral chair. Another month and I might be needing one of them.

There was a message on my answerphone.

'Jordan, I want to see you right away.' No name, no pack drill, but I knew who it was. I doubted if it was an urgent lunch date or he was gasping for a pint at the Bear and Bait. No need to dress up. I'd go as I was.

DI James had either spotted my arrival from his office window or had been waiting for me downstairs. He grabbed my arm the moment I came through the doors of the station. They had recently installed automatic entry doors. They thought it would ease in any reluctant visitors, especially those handcuffed to an officer.

He marched me upstairs to his office, propelling me towards the inquisition chair. I sat down opposite his desk, out of breath from the rough handling. The surface was piled with files as usual. On top was a copy of the *Sussex Record*.

He picked the newspaper up and shook it in my face. I flinched back. This was not in the least like the normal remote and cool DI James. He was spitting mad, like a bull in a ring.

'And what do you mean by this, Jordan? Tell me. I want to know and I'd prefer an intelligent answer.'

'I don't know what you mean,' I said faintly. 'What do I mean by what? I can't give you an answer when I don't know what you are talking about.'

'Don't go all fragile on me, young woman,' he snapped.

'Read this.' He thrust the newspaper at me. 'Front page. Read it, damn you.'

I did not care to argue with language like that. I took the newspaper and read the front page. It was obvious why I was not the flavour of the month.

VITAL POLICE DOCUMENTS GO MISSING
LOCAL PI LOSES EVIDENCE

The enquiry into the murder of Mrs Anne Steel, wife of well-known local butcher, ground to a halt yesterday when it was discovered that valuable evidence has gone missing. The police will not disclose exactly what is this evidence but our sources say that it was in the hands of local private investigator, Jordan Lacey, when it went missing. Miss Lacey was unavailable for comment.

The story went on to describe the discovery of Mrs Steel in the garden and the vandalized lawn and shrubs.

I calmly folded the newspaper and handed it back to him.

'I have no idea what they are on about,' I said. 'It sounds like a load of rubbish to me. I haven't spoken to any reporters and I don't have any vital evidence. Of course I wasn't available for comment. I don't know anything about this.'

'So what's this then?' said James. 'What do you call these?' He produced three A4 sheets. They looked horribly familiar. 'You asked DS Evans to get these dusted for you. Didn't you realize what they were?'

I was one hundred per cent confused. No, I did not know what they were. No, I did not know that I had lost anything. I did not know that I had anything in my possession which could be lost. My main concern at that moment was that Ben Evans might be in trouble.

'The dusting was just between friends,' I said, trying to cover him. 'Nothing heavy.'

'I am not the slightest bit interested in who is friends with whom in this station,' James said. 'But I do want to know where the rest of the spreadsheets are. Where are they, Jordan?'

'Ground,' I repeated. 'They put *ground* in the story. That wasn't a very nice word to use. Mince and all that. Reporters have no sensitivity.'

DI James's face was packed in ice. His ocean blue eyes had darkened and he was a million miles away. My blood freezes in my veins when he looks like that. I am undone and my head empties. Sometimes I think my fingernails will fall off. I wanted to get out of the room but my escape was blocked.

'Where are the rest?' He was sitting on the edge of his desk, using his height to intimidate me.

'Rest of what?'

'Have you completely lost what little sense you normally have?'

'The rest of the spreadsheets? Is that what you mean? Well, I don't exactly know how many more there were. Can I sue the *Sussex Record*? That story is libellous. I haven't lost vital evidence. This could affect my livelihood. Clients won't come to me if they don't trust me. Confidentiality is prime.'

'You're dead right, Jordan. No one will hire you now. You might as well hang up your shades. First Class Investigations is finished.'

I didn't like what I was hearing. It was starting to sound serious. Where had the *Record* got this story? How many people knew I had the spreadsheets in the first place?

'I've never heard such pessimism. Finished indeed! Of course, FCI isn't finished, because this ridiculous story isn't true. I demand that you issue a denial. And I'm not leaving till I hear you on the phone to the editor saying just that.'

I put a great deal of indignation into that speech. It was Churchillian. On the beaches stuff.

DI James slid off the desk and went to look out of the window. This was a familiar trick when questioning a suspect. The pregnant pause. Let them sweat. Me, a suspect? Suspect of what, I wanted to know.

'I might just do that if you conveniently start remembering where the rest of the spreadsheets are. You do have them, don't you? Your shop is probably wall to wall with spreadsheets.'

'I don't know exactly where they are. DS Evans just took a sample as a favour. I don't even know what they are. Perhaps she was an Avon lady. You know, ding-dong Avon calling.'

'Did you read them?'

'I read some of them. They didn't make sense.'

'And what did you think of them?'

'Someone's buying a lot of lipsticks.'

'To the tune of half a million pounds? If you had done a little research, some adding-up, you might have realized that these ‹preadsheets are big business. Unusual for the wife of a local butcher. We think we have been looking for her for years. We checked Anne Steel's bridge friends. They haven't seen her in months.'

'Half a million pounds?' That's a whole lot of noughts. No wonder her wardrobes were full of designer clothes. 'What sort of business?' I asked faintly. I wondered if there was an opening for me now that Anne Steel had more or less, and against her will, relinquished the job.

'Smuggling, Jordan. We've known for a long time that there's smuggling still going on. Just like in the 18th century. Only now it's not casks of rum and brandy, but cigarettes, laundered currency and hard drugs.'

The list made me feel weak. 'Drugs, here in Latching?'

'Mostly Ecstasy and anything new that is going to sell to the kids on the street.'

'You think Anne was running a drug ring? I can't believe it.'

'I didn't say that. I think she controlled the money side, shipping money out to suppliers and seeing that bills are paid for goods delivered.'

'Like an accountant?' I offered.

'I'm not putting any name on her involvement but I don't think she dirtied her hands any further than dusting her laptop. Those spreadsheets are vital. I must have them, Jordan. I'll apply for a search warrant if I have to. I don't know how the *Record* got that story but it was not from this office.'

'I'll do a deal with you,' I said, my courage returning. 'You get them to print a denial, in big bold letters, on the front page and I'll find the rest of the spreadsheets and let you have them. I'll also let you have something else which I found today, in Anne Steel's bedroom.' I paused for dramatic effect.

'OK,' he groaned. 'I'm asking. Have your pound of flesh. What did you find?'

'A three-and-a-half-inch floppy disk. Funny thing to keep in your bathroom behind a bottle of witch hazel.'

'I want it now,' he said. And he meant it.

As I went out of the door, a thought occurred to me. 'Perhaps whoever pumped George Hill with Ecstasy tablets also told the *Sussex Record*. Perhaps they want to discredit my work. Maybe I'm getting too near the truth.'

'I doubt it, Jordan. You couldn't solve a case even if you took a photo of a man with his hand in the till.'

I walked home via the beach after parking my car behind the shop. I swung the gold trimmed carrier bag in my hand. Samuel had said that I could take anything that I fancied. I had not fancied anything that much. Her clothes were not my style, and anyway, she was dead. I did not want a dead woman's clothes.

But this was different. It was still in the original bag, wrapped in tissue. She had not worn it. The belt was packed separately in a smooth piece of tissue paper. Spare buttons and spare buckle were inside a plastic drawstring pouch.

My conscience was troubled that it was part of her ill-gotten gains. Should it go back to the shop in Moulton Street? Should I hand it over to the police? Did Samuel know what his wife had been doing in her spare time? I didn't think so.

It was a big worry.

Like Scarlett O'Hara, I would decide tomorrow. In the meantime, I thought how warm I would be when winter came and I was wearing a full-length, soft black leather coat with collar turned up against the wind and the belt pulled tightly round my waist. A bit like an olde-tyme smuggler running in the shadows down a twitten.

A glamorous smuggler, of course, nothing remotely shabby.

Fifteen

Almost immediately my conscience went into a double reverse take. I could not keep the coat, even though it was classy, dramatic and teasingly beautiful. The leather was as supple as silk. Unless I kept the coat in lieu of future fees . . . maybe I could live with that.

I would mention it to Samuel Steel at the first moment. Meanwhile, I hung it behind my bedroom door, so that I could admire it on waking. It did not remind me of Anne Steel. She had never worn the coat. I knew I would feel Russian every time I put it on. Perhaps I ought to learn a few words. Slovenavitch – that would do for a start.

· It was time to unlock my shop and start shopkeeping. My last trawl of the charity shops had not yet been unpacked, sorted and washed or dusted.

My answerphone was unblinking and silent. No one had contacted me about anything. None of my various avenues had come back with new information. They had not remembered a single vital fact after I had gone. So much for my investigations. Anyone tapping my phone would be driven to euthanasia.

A woman was peering into the window, showing a passing interest in some miniature china cottages, the kind that people collect. I recognized her instantly. She was smartly dressed in a well-cut trouser suit with a silk scarf thrown over one shoulder. Her brown hair was pulled into a tidy French pleat with a gold comb catching the stray ends. It was the intermittent hand washing that caught my attention.

But would she recognize me? In the seconds before she entered the shop, I ducked under the counter, pulled on a pair of tortoiseshell glasses and tucked my hair into an oversized man's beret.

'Yerse?'

It came out without thinking.

'Those little cottages, they're so very sweet,' she said. She was like a Monet painting. From a distance she looked impressive, but close up she was a mess. She reminded me of pictures of dandies in the late 18th century, their faces encrusted with lead-based cosmetics. And she had Elizabeth Arden on her side.

'Ducky, ain't they?' I said. 'D'yer collect them?'

'Oh yes. I have a big collection but I don't think I have these two. What are they?'

I turned them over. They still had the maker's round gold labels on their undersides. 'The cobbler's cottage and the smithy's.'

She had not recognized me. No snazzy red dress. But I knew her. Every word she spoke confirmed that she was the woman who had gone for me with her nails after the show.

'No, I don't have those,' she said, occasionally rubbing her hands and moulding her fingers. If she used hand and nail lotion at the same time, there might be some point. 'How much are they?'

'Six pounds each.'

She looked taken aback. 'Each?'

I shrugged my shoulders. 'Collector's items, ain't they?'

I wanted her name, her address, her life history, any previous convictions for stalking. But George Hill was dead. He was not bothered by his stalker any more. He was entertaining a new audience and I hoped his jokes were a lot cleaner. St Peter would not be amused.

She obviously wanted them. If she cut down on buying make-up, she could afford them in an instant. 'Do you take plastic?'

'Oh yes,' I said. Then I realized that I didn't. But I took her card all the same and pretended to do some innocuous swiping under the counter. In fact I was noting down her name and account number plus expiry date. I turned it over to look at her signature. It was signed Sheree Lechlade in bold biro.

'I'm afraid yer card isn't being accepted,' I said, straightening up. 'Is it outa date?'

'Nonsense, of course it isn't,' she snapped, taking it back. 'There must be something wrong with your machine.'

I nodded like one of those glass-eyed puppy dogs in the back of a car. 'It's the machine,' I agreed. 'Always playing up. Bubble and squeak.'

'What?'

'Greek to me.'

'Could you put them by for me?' Sheree Lechlade was about to lose her patience. This time there was no handy soda syphon.

'I'll do better than that,' I said. 'Gimme yer address and I'll bring 'em round to yer this evening. These cottages get snapped up pretty quick.'

'Number four Chapel Court,' she said. 'About seven?'

'On the dot,' I said.

'Thank you.'

She swept herself out of my shop Cunard-style and I wondered if she had killed George Hill. It was no fun selling china to a murderer. But George was still paying me (although he did not know it) and I would honour that payment. My word was my bond even to a dead man.

Sheree Lechlade was not exactly a few chips short of a fish dinner but there was something wrong with her. Hand washing was a serious dome doctor problem but I did not know or understand what it meant. Perhaps my good friend, the bottle-collecting retired doctor, would enlighten me. I must ask him sometime.

Number four Chapel Court. As I thought, his stalker lived on his doorstep, foxing his every movement. But no more. She would have to find another victim.

A tinge of fear invaded my thoughts. Who would be her next victim? In a second I had guessed. Who else? It would be Miguel. I had seen her at his restaurant on one of my wine swilling visits. She'd eyed me with seething resentment. It was enough to turn wine sour in the cask.

As soon as she was out of sight, I wiped off the beret and

rumpled my hair to its normal state. I locked up the shop and hurried round to the Mexican restaurant. It was closed, of course. I went round the back of the shops and climbed over a few walls, finding the Mexican more by the spicy smell and delinquent seagulls searching the food bins in the yard.

'Jordan, my beauty, why are you here, climbing like a gazelle over my wall? Is something bad happening?'

Miguel never changed. He was as handsome as Omar Sharif, liquid brown eyes full of messages of love and admiration. He took me through to the kitchen. It was spotless, of course, piled with fresh vegetables, lemons and limes, waiting for the arrival of the evening staff. The restaurant was empty but already laid up for tonight's diners.

One table was strewn with papers and bills. Miguel had been checking his takings and sorting out his accounts. He automatically went for a bottle of wine from behind the bar and poured me one of his full-blown mega-sized glasses.

'It was already open, Jordan, so the flavour will now be perfect.'

It was perfect. Miguel always gave me the best. He was the most generous man on the planet. Correction. Jack was the most generous man ever, especially when he could expect nothing in return. Miguel did get my devoted company on rare occasions.

I sipped the wine. Juice of summer raspberries and a hint of blackberry swam through the grape to the back of my throat. I don't know where I get these fool ideas.

'You like the wine?' he asked, his eyes tasting the pleasure on my face.

'It's lovely,' I said. 'Perfect.'

'Tell me why you are climbing my wall.'

'Do you know a woman called Sheree Lechlade?'

His face lit up with mischief. 'Ah yes, Mrs Lechlade, the lady with the fulsome attributes in front. She eats here often. She would eat my best waiter too, if she had half a chance and less years.'

I tried not to smile. This was serious.

'I have reason to believe that Mrs Lechlade could be a dangerous woman,' I said in my best officer of the law voice. 'You should be very careful, Miguel. Don't give her the slightest encouragement.'

'My little bird, don't you worry,' he laughed. 'Miguel can look after himself. I am, as you say, the dabbed hand, at warding off advances from amorous customers. So sad, when the only lady for my heart makes no advances.'

He put his hand over mine and it was warm and friendly. Nothing to get alarmed about. Only a frisson of regret.

'She might stalk you,' I warned. 'Become a nuisance. Pester you for attention.'

'Waste of time,' he grinned. 'I am too busy for this stalking lark. I work too late and much too long hours. She would soon be home for the cocoa.'

I had to laugh. The thought of Sheree Lechlade with a cup of cocoa was ludicrous. It would definitely be laced with rum or brandy.

'I hope you're right,' I said. 'But if she does start to annoy you, please let me know. I might be able to help.' I did not mention George Hill or his unsolved death.

'Such concern deserves a meal for a queen, Jordan. Come tonight? This would be a kindness to me. I will cook you something special. I have today bought the most succulent fish from the fishermen on the beach. The fruit of the sea.'

My taste buds melted. I almost volunteered to wash up our glasses. Instead I promised to be back at 9 p.m. A bit late but I guessed that Miguel already had a first sitting fully booked. Sometimes he had a waiting list for cancellations.

'Don't forget I have your carrier bag,' he said. 'The bag full of mystery. It is still locked in my safe.'

'Can you keep it for a few more days, please?'

He nodded.

I knew it was not fair. I was leaving him open to danger and he was too nice for that.

'Not much longer though,' I promised. 'I'll take it back soon.'

I drove through Goring, Ferring, and East Preston, then filtered right on to the main A27 to Chichester. The roundabout south of Arundel was choked with traffic. Drivers glared at my ladybird's spots as if an insect had no right to be masquerading as a car and on a main road.

An hour later I was at the boldly designed Chichester Festival Theatre enquiring the whereabouts of Michelle Steel, or Michelle Tapley as she was known in the profession. Or not known, it seemed. No one had heard of her. I enquired backstage and front of house. Unemployed actresses often filled in as ASMs to gain experience and network the producers. Her yellow roadster was not in the theatre car park.

I parked my car and bought a parking ticket. I had a two-hour limit in which to make some enquiries on foot. Chichester is a labyrinth of one-way streets and a nightmare for a visiting driver. It was possible to get stuck on a circular route and never to be seen again in society.

Firstly I made a quick survey from the top of the ancient stone city walls which surround the four main compass pointing streets. The broad ramparts are easy to walk on and give an uninterrupted view of back gardens and lanes and car parks. The spire and detached bell tower of the cathedral dominates the skyline. The medieval market cross in the centre of the town is still a landmark and thriving meeting place.

If I had not been checking for every glimpse of yellow, I would have enjoyed the walk. Other people's back gardens are so interesting and revealing. One slice of back garden was an overgrown tangle of weeds and brambles. It had not been touched for years yet the house was smart enough with fresh paint and neat curtains. Perhaps they were allergic to horticulture.

I descended to street level and checked every pub, restaurant and cafe to see if Michelle was filling in time as a waitress or barmaid. Another blank. The phone book was blank on both names. Yet Samuel Steel seemed pretty sure that Michelle was working in some show. I wondered if Chichester had an underground theatre, some avant-garde company that put on fringe shows in an old warehouse or garage.

Time flew by and I was beginning to tire. I bought a cucumber and cheese sandwich from the last cafe and sat in the Bishop's Garden, catching the last of the summer sun. Some tame starlings watched from nearby, bright-eyed, hopefully waiting for crumbs. Their iridescent black feathers were tinged with glossy green and purple, the marking on their heads like a tiny dusting of gold. We shared the unbuttered and uncheesed crusts. Their idea of gratitude was to fly off immediately it was all finished. Not a single note, scale or song.

As I wandered back to my car, aware that I was late, but too tired to hurry, I saw a petite figure in tight white jeans and red cotton buttoned shirt hurrying out of a shop. She was swinging two carrier bags. They were light enough to swing, but full enough to bulge. I looked up at the name of the shop. Home Based Garden Supplies. Artificial leaves decorated the big windows. A lawnmower stood theatrically posed on a stretch of verdant plastic grass. Jumbo packets of commercial weed-killer were being offered at two for the price of one.

I was going to be late for my date at Miguel's. My bath took longer than expected as I fell asleep. Not the most sensible course of action, or non-action, at that time of the evening. I woke up with a sharp jolt. The water had cooled and I was fast succumbing to hypothermia.

The snazzy dress had gone back to Leroy so I was left to dither between one blue cowboy shirt and another blue cowboy shirt. Then I remembered the black dress from Guilberts and the low-heeled pumps. And I would take the poncho that Miguel had given me in case it turned cold when it was time to walk home.

Miguel liked the black outfit. His eyes said so. He was beaming as he escorted me into the restaurant, his hand lightly under my elbow. He had reserved a table in the corner and there was a single red rose in a vase. The restaurant was full of noise and clatter, waiters bustling about with steaming dishes of spicy Mexican food; the background music a classy, guitar domi-nated low-key jazz.

'You look beautiful,' he said, taking the poncho from me and hanging it up on a row of brass hooks near his desk. 'I'll join you when I have the dish ready for us.'

He lit the candle with a flick of his lighter, poured out some wine for me. I did not need to ask what it was. I knew it would be the best and it was. Don't ask me the price. I would not even look at the wine list.

A girl brought me a starter dish, spicy potato skins, raw veggies and dips, garlic bread. Suddenly I remembered I had not eaten for ages.

I dipped and dunked, relaxing into the atmosphere, letting my thoughts about Michelle, Anne, and Sheree simmer in my mind as Miguel simmered a different set of ingredients. The two deaths were a puzzle and DI James was no nearer solving the murder of Mrs Steel. At least, he was not telling me anything. He was handling it in his usual laid-back manner. He'd said the shears had not been the main cause of death. It was my guess that someone had already tried to throttle her. Maybe they had thought she was dead, then found she wasn't. Or maybe they had suddenly got scared and backed off.

But I remembered the red flash on a pair of trainers, a Penguin bar wrapper on the grass, the look of hatred in Sheree Lechlade's eyes in the foyer of the theatre. Could she have killed George in a moment of passion? A twisted mind could do anything. She was more than a loose cannon. She was a hand grenade with a broken pin.

George was a tall man. There was no way she could have managed to lift him on to the door hook unless she had an accomplice.

Then I remembered that I had forgotten to take the miniature cottages to Mrs Lechlade. I didn't care. I had her address now and that was what really mattered. If she wanted the cottages for her collection she would come back for them.

The street door opened letting in a gust of evening air. It was a faint herald of autumn. A touch of an easterly. I did not look to see who was coming in although normally I can immediately sense his presence. My seventh sense. Perhaps it was the wine or the anticipation of a lovely meal ahead that dulled my senses. I was already feeling hungry, savouring the thought of fish fresh from the sea.

DI James stood by my table. He was dishevelled, mud on his jacket and knees. He looked shaken. His face was gaunt, almost ashen. This was not a social call.

'Jordan,' he said.

'Hello, James,' I said. 'Nice to see you. Would you like a beer or something cold? You look as if you need a drink.'

'Jordan,' he said again, not actually answering me. He was lost for words. I had never seen him lost for words before. A shiver went down my spine as the door opened again. In the doorway was the bulky figure of Sergeant Rawlings in uniform. He was looking straight at me with an expression I could not fathom.

My throat knotted into hardness.

'What's the matter?' I said, standing up awkwardly. I automatically steadied the glass of wine. The tablecloth was a spotless white and I did not want to spill the wine. Somewhere a candle fluttered in the night air. A moth flew in, attracted by the light, like a lost soul.

James tried to find his voice. I was reading his face. All thoughts of a meal with Miguel faded into nothingness. I waited for the worst. I tasted ash and fear.

James made the smallest movement towards me. 'There's been an accident,' he said. 'I think you had better come with me.'

Sixteen

The hours folded into time that had no meaning. DI James and Sergeant Rawlings took me to the station and then to the hospital. People spoke to me but I did not remember their words or faces. I was derailed. One day I would remember the details of that night.

Eventually, a long time later, James offered to drive me home but I asked him to drop me near the pier. I needed to walk.

'Are you going to be all right?' he asked.

'All right? What does all right mean? I don't understand why you even ask. You know that none of us will ever be the same.'

He was swallowing hard. 'One day I will tell you something that I had to live through,' he said. 'But not now, Jordan. This isn't the time.'

'Thank you for finding me,' I said when we reached the pier.

'Doris told me where you were.'

'Doris knows everything. Or she thinks she knows everything.'

I got out of his car and beheld the pier pavilion, white domed and ghostly in the early dawn. The shape was comforting in its familiarity. Streaks of pink light shot the sky. The dawn chorus of seagulls was raucous and vulgar but for once I was not listening.

James put the car into gear and drove away without another word. I couldn't help him and he couldn't help me.

I took off the black shoes and held them loosely. The poncho was over my shoulders and I needed the warmth. I don't remember who put it there. Miguel, I suppose, in that kind way of his. I must go in and thank him for cooking the meal I did not have.

The sand was wet and grey, the tide on its way out. I followed the water out to the furthermost legs of the pier, not caring if the stones cut my feet. I wanted to bleed.

I had no way of dealing with this. There was only walking and pushing my feet into the sand, my head down against the wind. At the station, Sergeant Rawlings had given me a cup of tea. At the hospital, a nurse had given me a cup of tea. What was it with this tea business? My feelings were locked inside a block of stone. No amount of tea was going to help.

Did this mean I was beyond normal feeling? The answers were somewhere but not legible. I could barely see the water although I could hear it. My sight seemed to have gone but not my hearing.

And I kept hearing his voice.

'Hi, Jordan.'

A thin scream sent the seagulls flapping panic-stricken into the air. They wheeled in fright, wings beating the air, no idea of which direction to fly. I could hear their wings disordered and desperate.

I knew I was the one screaming because my throat hurt but I don't remember opening my mouth. My throat felt raw and sore. I was becoming overwhelmingly tired and wanted to sleep but I knew if I lay down on the sand, on the pebbles, here under the legs of the pier, I might never get up.

I threw back my head and screamed again but this time the sound didn't come but welled into a gulf of white pain and my cheeks were streaming with tears. My eyes were screwed up and salted and I staggered about, not caring where I went. The air was tinged with a raw grey. The sky was not talking to me. There was no way of finding the route back to the shore line. They would find me on the beach the next day, some time, somewhere. I didn't care.

I never heard anyone come running over the sand. Hearing, seeing, thinking, were skills I had forgotten. Arms locked round me in a tight grip, almost hoisting me off my feet. I went into another wave of shock.

'Jordan, Jordan, baby. Where the hell are you going? What's

the matter? Wotcha doing out here? Come on back, gal, come on home. This is no place for you in the middle of the night. There's my gal. Come with me.'

He was half carrying me, leading me, lifting me over stones. Tears were running down my cheeks and I had no control over them. He took out a rag and dabbed inefficiently. I could not stop him. The noise I was making was drowning all coherency.

I only knew we were climbing the shingle when the pebbles began to roll beneath my feet. They slithered and clattered as I slid to my knees, my bare feet in agony.

'Come on, Jordan, you can make it. Come on, baby. Don't give up on me now.' He lifted me with ease. I could smell sweat on his T-shirt.

I felt myself being bundled into a car. The leather was sweet. He was putting on my shoes, with difficulty because my feet had swollen. Night-bound, I was being driven along roads. Then the car stopped, the engine died and a door slammed and the driver got out.

'Where's your bloody key?' he said, rapping on the window. Key? What key?

'OK, I'll pick the lock. Gawd, I still know how.'

I was too exhausted to argue. My bag had been mislaid somewhere along the way. Had I left it in the station or at Miguel's? I was hauled up the stairs and propelled into my bedroom and pushed on to my bed. Then a weight was on top of me and it was pure male. Heavy and suffocating, legs wrapped round my thighs. They were like steel.

'Oh Jordan, darlin'. You're wonderful. Dammit, I've dreamed of this moment, being like this together, but don't worry, I'm not staying. Don't cry, darlin'. I'm going now. I just wanted to feel you close for a little while.'

He stayed a moment longer, a rough face against mine, gripping my arms hard.

Then he got off, still shaking, and pulled the duvet over me. I was gasping for breath. 'Get to sleep now. You'll feel better in the morning.'

155

'He's dead,' I wept.

'I know.'

There was no way I could feel better in the morning, although I was grateful to have been brought home in one piece. My rescuer had been Jack, of course, from the Amusement Arcade. I knew who it was now, though I'm not sure if I did then. What he'd been doing on the pier in the early hours of the morning I would never know. Perhaps another night boot sale or betting on the dogs somewhere. I had a feeling he was a betting man. What else would he do with all that money?

The next few days were a haze of work. I had to work. I barely remember washing or dressing though I suppose I did. Eating did not come into it until Mavis practically force-fed an omelette down me. I'd only gone into the cafe for tea.

'I can't eat that,' I said, even though it was glistening with melted cheese, the way I like it.

'Yes, you can, my girl, and you will,' said Mavis. 'I shall sit here until you do.'

'You've a dozen customers.'

'They can wait.'

I put a minuscule morsel on the end of a fork and lifted it to my mouth, pretending to eat it.

'Swallow,' Mavis ordered.

Doris was no better. She practically lived in my shop, bringing goodies daily like the Three Wise Men. She was buying me things she could not afford, like fresh figs and smoked salmon. A tin of lobster soup appeared from nowhere.

'You've got to stop this,' I said desperately.

'Stop what? This is a shop, isn't it? The law says I can come into it.'

'But not bringing me things all the time.'

'Nonsense. I'm expecting several favours in return. Just wait and see.'

Leroy came round with a bunch of spray carnations and put them into my hands without a word. I stood them in a pretty vase in the window of my shop and let the small lemony flowers tell the world of my grief.

I needed James but I knew he would not come. He was using work in the same way as me, as a cushion, a sponge, a blindfold, a gag, morphine, alcohol, a shield, buffer, a prop. As he had once before when it happened to him, he'd said. And one day he would tell me. He'd promised.

The funeral was shattering. Even the weather was grim with a curtain of warm drizzle. All those rows of policemen in well-pressed uniforms, their badges highly polished, shoes like black diamonds. I stood at the back, hidden behind a pillar. I didn't wear black. I don't know what I wore. Francis Guilbert stood beside me. He looked grey and solemn, very much the elder statesman. The last funeral I had gone to had been his son's, Oliver Guilbert. I guess we were both thinking of Oliver as well.

There were people I did not recognize. Relatives and friends, I suppose. He must have had relatives. The service and tributes were moving but I refused to let myself become involved in the words. I pretended it was all about someone else. No way was I going to break down in public. Especially as I did not really know how I felt.

'You're doing fine,' said Francis, handing me an open hymn book. 'Psalm 23. The Lord's My Shepherd. You don't have to sing.'

'You haven't heard me sing,' I said.

It was good that Francis was there because he took care of me, propelled me out of the church and away from the hand-shaking and condolences. He steered me along the blowy sea front and into one of the posh hotels where I sank into an armchair in a lounge the size of the *Titanic* deck. A waiter came over immediately.

'A pot of coffee for two, please,' said Francis. 'And two very large brandies. Could you bring the brandies first, please. We need them.'

'Certainly, sir.'

'I shall get very tight,' I said. 'I'm not eating much.'

'Then I'd better order sandwiches as well.'

Francis followed with another precise order. There was no question of anything being inconvenient or not served in the lounge. The waiter was attentive. Francis Guilbert was Francis Guilbert. I wondered if they would let me sleep in this armchair. It was comfortable.

'So, Jordan,' said Francis, returning his attention to me. 'Tell me about the cases you are working on right now.'

I tried to gather my pale thoughts and put them in order. 'There's a garden on Updown Hill that's being vandalized. Glyphosate on the lawn, weedkiller on the shrubs, plants, everywhere. It's horrendous. And the wife of the owner has recently been m-murdered.' I stumbled over the word. 'Garden shears stabbing her neck but they were not the only cause of death. I haven't seen the post-mortem report, but I think she may have been strangled.'

'Oh Jordan,' said Francis, pushing the glass of brandy towards me. The colour of the liquid in the glass was burnished gold. 'You should not be doing this work.'

'Then I was following a stalker but the poor man who was being stalked has died also. He was found hung on a hook behind his dressing-room door. He was a comedian but there was nothing funny about his death.' The brandy went down my throat as burning liquid fire, but not the Spanish fire water brand. It was not duty free from across the Channel. It was cask mellow and centuries old.

'When am I going to persuade you to give up this awful job and come and work for me at Guilberts?'

'As a store detective?'

Francis hesitated. 'Yes, if that's what you want.' It was not what he wanted, obviously, but I let it pass. 'So your cases have dried up? You're not being paid any more.'

'Yes, I am being paid. Posthumously, in the case of George Hill as he sent me money before he died. And I have been paid a retainer for the vandalized garden which I have not yet worked off.' I did not mention the long black leather coat, straight from Tolstoy and *Anna Karenina*.

'You are too honest.'

A plate of tiny triangular sandwiches arrived, decorated with watercress. No parsley. Francis must have heard I was off parsley. There was egg and cress, cucumber and cream cheese, chicken and bacon. And the tray of coffee with an elegant silver coffee pot, cream and sugar, and two gold-rimmed cups and saucers. I could live like this. I stirred myself to be mother and pour.

'We are not leaving here until everything has been eaten,' said Francis, offering me the plate. 'Don't just take the watercress. You must have lost half a stone.'

'I like watercress. It's full of iron.'

I suppose Francis brought me back to the land of the living. He had been through a dreadful time when his son was murdered on a monster fairground spinning wheel last winter. Yet I had never heard a word of complaint from him or a word of self-pity. He had got on with his work running Guilbert's store, hosting a staff Christmas party, and caring for other people, including me, when his heart must have been breaking.

We talked about a lot of other things. I knew he wanted me around. But there was no way I could be what he wanted. Whatever that was – daughter, mistress, second wife? I could not see myself in any role.

'You must be strong. If you become ill, Jordan, I don't know what I should do,' said Francis, his eyes serious yet twinkling. The man wanted to touch me, take my hand. There was longing written all over him. I could feel my heart crawling the walls. 'I shall have no one left.'

As I walked home, feeling one and a half degrees better, I counted all my good friends. It was humbling. I did not deserve so many. I had done nothing really, apart from being a nuisance and getting into scrapes. James was always hauling me out of one predicament or another. Mavis fed me. Doris kept an eye open for the best chance. Miguel cooked and poured out his best wine. Francis took me under his mature wing. And Jack

. . . my shining knight in amusement arcade stainless-steel, ball-rolling, lights-flashing, hit the buzzer type armour. He was a star.

So I put my mind to my shop and my cases. And I had a party to cancel. This time a red light was flashing on my answerphone. I pressed replay.

'Hello, Miss Lacey. This is Tim Arnold. I'm sorry to disturb you but I have just thought of something. I wonder if you could drop by? I shall be in all day. It's nothing really, but you did say if I thought of anything . . .'

I dialled back. There was no answer, only his gruff answerphone message. He was probably having a nap, enjoying the last of the summer sun in his new conservatory. 'Thank you for the call, Mr Arnold,' I said. 'It's Jordan Lacey. I'll be right round.'

I did not hold out much hope. The importance of what people remembered was variable. The ladybird was glad to have an outing, her engine humming, and we were there in no time.

I stopped along a side road, parking near The Corner House. The garden was looking more colourful. Tim Arnold had bought some new shrubs and plants. He was asleep in his conservatory, head back, a half-drunk beer warming up on the table.

Something made me do it. I switched on my mobile phone and keyed in DI James's number. It was also on answerphone. Does no one answer these days?

'It's Jordan. I thought I'd let you know I'm visiting Tim Arnold at The Corner House, Goring, where the Steels used to live. He left a message for me saying he had thought of something. Since you are investigating Anne Steel's murder, I reckoned you might like to know where I am.'

I let myself into the garden by the front gate and walked round to the conservatory. A bee was buzzing frantically against the glass. It looked hot inside. Tim Arnold looked hot. His face was red and dry looking. Not a sign of sweat. I went to touch the handle of the door and leaped back. It was burning. I breathed on my fingers, trying to cool them with saliva.

Wrapping my hand in the stretched-out hem of my T-shirt, I went for the door again and turned the handle. The door burst open and a blast of heat hit my face. Inside the conservatory was like a furnace.

Tim Arnold was not moving. He was in a coma. He'd passed out with heat stroke. He was being baked to death.

Seventeen

The ambulance arrived quickly, sirens howling. One look at the patient and the paramedics went straight into the kitchen and came back with armfuls of damp towels and tea towels which they wrapped round Tim Arnold. They fixed an oxygen mask over his face, talking as they worked.

'What's his name?'

'Tim. Tim Arnold.'

'Tim, Tim, can you hear me?'

There was no response. He didn't move, his face still red with the heat. They began sponging his face with tepid water.

'Will he survive?' I asked.

'Are you a relative?' they asked back.

'No, a friend. I was calling by. He'd phoned me earlier.' It sounded lame. It was lame.

'You can call the hospital. Do you know if Mr Arnold has any relatives?'

'No. I believe he's a widower.' I needed my notes to check. He must have told me.

They looked at me suspiciously as if I'd turned up the thermostat myself. That's what I guessed had happened. The heating was turned up to full blast. And it was already a sunny day outside. The big panes of glass had kept the heat in, doubling the temperature inside. The back of my T-shirt was wet with sweat even though both doors were open for a through draught.

'I'd better turn the thermostat off,' I said, wondering where it was.

'I shouldn't touch anything until the police have been here,' said one of the paramedics sharply. 'They'll want everything left. They'll need to dust for prints.'

I longed to flash a badge and say, 'But I am the police' like in the movies. They were lifting Tim Arnold on to a stretcher and wheeling him out into the fresh air, talking on a mobile to alert the hospital of his arrival. Then he was moved into the ambulance. I didn't ask to go with him. I wanted to be left in the house. Which I was. Very considerate of them.

The house was quiet. It had no pulse. He obviously had a cleaner. Everywhere was spotless and tidy but without the usual touches of a woman. No flowers. Very little fruit. One wizened orange in a bowl. His freezer was full of single portion microwave meals. The refrigerator held only milk, cans of beer and an opened packet of bacon.

All the downstairs rooms were furnished comfortably but without individuality. It felt like a set-piece show house, not a home. Upstairs was different. Tim Arnold's bedroom looked like a real room. Maybe it was out-of-bounds to his cleaner. The double bed was not made. The furniture was strewn with discarded clothes. Beer cans and newspapers littered both bedside tables. A portable radio stood on the floor, next to a telephone.

No obvious diaries or address books. Several gardening catalogues. No scraps of paper with the magic words: *must tell Jordan Lacey about* . . . Nothing personal at all, apart from crumpled socks and underpants.

I went through his wardrobe. It was not much fun. He had below average clothes sense. The chest of drawers was cluttered with socks and pants and ties and broken cufflinks. He apparently did not keep letters, photographs, receipts or bills in his bedroom.

The other bedrooms were empty apart from a few suitcases. The Corner House was far too large for him. I wondered why he had bought it. He'd said he liked the garden.

I was on the point of leaving when I decided to scan his collection of records in the cabinet downstairs. There was a stack of long-playing 33 r.p.m.'s. I wondered if he liked jazz.

Maybe I would find a rare Stan Kenton with his Big Band. But no, it was fairly predictable, songs from the shows: *My Fair Lady*, *Mary Poppins*, *The King and I*. I could hum along to them on a wet day.

One Barry Manilow sleeve did not contain a record. I took out a slim school-size exercise book into which someone had stuck a variety of photographs using adhesive corners. They were informal photographs of a skinny little girl with fair hair. She was pretty in a feckless way, playing up to the camera with a smile.

Each photograph was dated underneath and named. Annie, aged 4. Annie, aged 7. Annie, aged 9. Annie at her 11th birthday party. Annie at Christmas. And so on, through the teenage years. Till the photographs reached Annie, aged 19, looking grown-up, smooth and glamorous. By then I knew who Annie was. The collection stopped. Lots of empty pages. There were no more photographs of Annie smiling to the camera.

Annie was Mrs Anne Steel.

Was this what Tim Arnold had been going to tell me about, or not? Maybe he was never going to tell me the connection between him and Anne Steel. But I was guessing that she might be his daughter. If she was his daughter, then her death would have been a terrible shock. Perhaps he was responsible for the thermostat mishap. It could be a suicide attempt. Maybe he had forgotten that he had phoned me or had not reckoned on my immediate response. Maybe he wanted me to find him so that his cleaner did not discover him on her next visit. A decomposing body is not a pretty sight.

'What are you doing, Jordan? Not snooping again, I hope?' DI James stood in the doorway, not exactly glowering at me, but finding my presence a surprise. He looked the same. His face had not changed. He was hiding whatever he was feeling.

'I can't resist other people's music,' I said, tapping the Barry Manilow cover. 'Have you come about the accident?'

'If it was an accident,' he said. 'The paramedics were not happy. They called me. And I had time for once.'

'How's Mr Arnold?'

'They are still trying to cool him down. It's touch and go.'

'Poor soul,' I said, turning away and slipping the slim book of photographs under my arm. 'It seems I arrived just in time.'

'What do you mean, just in time? I was going to ask you what you were doing here,' he said, peering into the still baking conservatory. It was a wonder the glass hadn't cracked. 'Phew. I'm not surprised he passed out.' He looked at the thermostat, loosening his collar, sweat running down his face. '140 degrees Fahrenheit. As hot as the desert.'

'Mr Arnold left a message for me on my answerphone, asking me to call round. I think I arrived sooner than he expected. He really wanted me to arrive when it was all over. I was almost a friend, you see. He did not want to be found a week later, which might have happened.'

'You think this is suicide?'

'Could be.'

DI James was on his phone. 'Get the print people over here and a photographer. I'm not sure what it's all about and I don't know if it's homicide or an accident. Well, not yet.'

'It's not homicide. He tried to kill himself,' I said, glad that James was with me, glad that for once he was listening. His attitude seemed to have shifted gear although it was not that obvious. There was the tiniest thaw in Latching's top detective inspector. It might not last long but I had to be grateful for this moment.

'And you know why?'

'I think Mrs Anne Steel was his daughter.'

'His daughter? Interesting. How do you know that?'

'I'm a detective, remember? Denbury Court is my case and I'm employed by Mr Steel.'

'Mrs Steel is a homicide.'

'I know. I'm not trying to solve her murder. That's your case. I know better than to interfere. The garden at Updown is my case. Weedkiller, not garden shears.'

'The shears didn't kill her. They were like the final stab in the back of a bull's neck at a bullfight. She was already dying.'

'From what?'

'They are still making tests.'

'Still? How long does all this take?'

'You know, Jordan, it's never straightforward. Forensic are working on a cadaveric spasm.'

'She had something in her hand. Tightly grasped? It's usually hair or fabric, isn't it?'

'It was a genuine death grasp, not an attempt to fool us with fake evidence. I can't tell you what it was.'

'Maybe a button. If someone is trying to kill you, then you grab at anything. I'd grab hard,' I said. 'Really hard. I'm not a Crab sign for nothing.'

'You'd fight tooth and nail, wouldn't you? Tell me, Jordan, you would fight, wouldn't you?'

James was staring at me intently as if willing me into some action. There was something in his eyes that made my body go cold. I could not believe what was happening. James had kept a distance from me all the time that I had known him. I was used to it. I expected nothing else. But now he was looking at me differently.

'Are you trying to warn me about something?' I said suddenly.

'I think so,' said James. 'You could be getting too near for comfort. I'd rather you dropped your present cases. Can you do that?'

'No, of course I can't. My work is important, you know that. People rely on me.'

'George Hill is not relying on you any more. You can drop that one. He won't mind. Could you go away?'

'George Hill has paid me, in full. I can't give him the money back. I've got to find out all I can.'

James moved closer. I could smell his aftershave. It was something very subtle. I could not name it. Whatever was happening was so unexpected. My face would not respond. It had frozen into a useless expression.

'Listen, Jordan. You have got to get away. Take a holiday. Go to Cornwall, Jersey, Spain, anywhere. Change your name. If you need the money, I'll lend you enough.'

I could not believe what I was hearing. And that 'holiday' hurt.

'James, you must be joking. I can't go away and I never borrow money. And especially not from you. I'm not in any danger. What do you think is going to happen? Am I going to get sprayed with weedkiller or something?'

I hoped he didn't mean that. It was not a nice thought. So itchy.

'I don't know,' he said wearily. 'Everything smells bad. The whole case.'

'Which case? Denbury Court garden or George the Jester?'

He wasn't going to answer. I could tell that. His stubborn look had reasserted itself. I was going to be left wondering what on earth was going on. The underwater stillness of his face gave my eyes a chance to search the fine lines and hollows. His cropped hair was so dark, the eyebrows matching in severity.

'Jordan . . . why don't you do what you are told, for once? I know I can't make you go. I can only ask you.'

'You weren't asking me, you were telling me, ordering me about,' I said. 'Kindly remember I don't work for Sussex police any more. They thought I was a liability, you know, liable to tell the truth at any instant.'

He swallowed a groan, his fingers combing through what there was of his hair. 'I don't know what to do with you.' He paused, as if making up his mind. 'Would you go and stay with my mother? She lives in the country. She'd enjoy your company for a couple of weeks, longer maybe, until this thing blows over.'

His mother. Now that was a serious offer. It must have cost him.

'That's a very kind offer,' I said, hoping I sounded properly grateful. 'If the going gets tough, I may take you up on it.'

'I don't want you to take me up on it when it's too bloody late. I want you to go now.' He was nearly shouting. Perhaps it was the heat.

'If you don't mind, I think I'll be off. I have quite a lot of work to do. Is it all right if I phone the hospital to find out how Mr Arnold is doing?'

James nodded impatiently. 'Please yourself. But I did warn you. This could turn nasty.'

'I'm aware of that,' I said with some dignity. 'Two murders and one possible suicide are not exactly a quiet life. I actually prefer social security frauds. Cleaner type of living.'

'Your shoulder bag is back at the station. You can collect it when you bring me the rest of those spreadsheets.'

An unmarked police car drew up outside The Corner House and the requested photographer and fingerprint man were getting out with their cases of equipment. James turned away from me abruptly and went out to meet them. He wanted the scene of the accident recorded in detail.

I drove back to the shop, wondering if I would find burning rags stuffed through the letterbox. I hoped not. My insurance did not cover everything. Only the contents up to a certain value. The premiums were beyond my budget. Maybe I ought to disappear for a while or take on another identity. James's warning had unsettled me. I was starting to get nervous.

Then I thought of George Hill's empty flat and the key in my filing cabinet. No one would think of looking for me there. It was ideal. Only an idiot would hide away in the home of a murdered man. I could take on a new identity with ease. It was my trade mark. A different person every day.

Sister, girlfriend, scriptwriter, publicist, secretary, producer . . . the choice was endless. I could be anybody I liked. I might even solve things.

I went round to Doris to stock up on essentials. George Hill's flat probably contained little in the food line. I bought rather more than usual. Doris surveyed the pile of tins and packets on her counter, tapping the tuna with her long nails.

'What do you call this, a siege?' she asked.

'Sort of. I may not be around for a few days.'

'Jordan, that's not good enough,' said Doris. 'How can I keep an eye on your shop, if I don't know where you are or what you are doing?'

'You know more about me than I know about me,' I said morosely. 'I'm going to ground. I've been ordered.'

'Ah . . .' she nodded knowingly. 'DI James. He was around here, wanting to know where you were. Seemed quite concerned. Take hope, Jordan. The man is not all stone and cement.'

'Let me know when there's a crack,' I said, paying for my stock of food out of the money in my back pocket. I hadn't gone for my bag. Luckily I had spare keys. 'I want to be around when it happens.'

'And I want to know where you are going.' Doris stopped filing her nails which was a sign of concentration. 'You've got to tell me.'

'I can't,' I said, touched by her concern. 'But I tell you what, howabout I phone you at the same time every day? Would that put your mind at rest?'

'You taking your mobile?'

'Of course.'

'Have you charged up the battery?'

'Just about to do it.'

'Mind you do or I'll have the police out looking for you.'

She pursed her lips which meant she was seriously worried. I couldn't put her mind at rest. It was a rule that my friends were never involved.

'It'll be all right,' I said, packing the food into a large brown paper bag. 'And it's only for a few days.'

'I don't want them to find you floating off the end of the pier,' was her parting shot.

'They won't. I can swim.'

George Hill's flat was a cheerless place to live. No pictures, no cushions, no home comforts. Just the basics. Thankfully I had taken along a radio cassette player and could play jazz tapes. I'd also brought paper and card indexes. It was time I had another go at my game. Write everything I know down on different cards, place on floor and switch them around till a new picture emerges.

Supper was a tin of tomato soup with ready-made croutons. This gastronomic wonder sent me into a superflow of energy and I wrote up Mr Arnold's notes. I'm not sure why. He was not a case. He was only on the fringe of a case.

An idea crept into my mind. Could he have committed suicide because he knew he was going to be found out? Had he been vandalizing the Denbury Court garden at night? He had a motive. Had he by some awful mischance played a part in the killing of his daughter? The dark thoughts tumbled around and I did not like the answers that were appearing.

Man. Murder. Daughter. Weedkiller. Revenge. Shears. Plants. Shrubs. Night. Danger. Car. Car . . . car. I had not looked at Mr Arnold's car. Cadaveric spasm. Maybe Anne Steel had gripped his coat or his hair. I needed to look at his car. I might find a lot of answers.

There was a knocking on the door. 'George? George, I know you're there. Open the door. I've something for you.'

It was a woman's voice, urgent and demanding.

Eighteen

I froze. Without making a single sound, I carefully shifted a heavy chair and put it against the door, so that it would not open if anyone happened to have a key. The strength came to me from nowhere.

'Don't be stupid, George. I've made something really nice for you.' It was the voice of Mrs Lechlade, the lady I had syphoned. 'I made it myself. Your favourite.'

I was not tempted. I sat on the chair, adding my weight for security. The woman was still rapping on the door as if there was an emergency.

'Look, I know you're there, George. I saw you less than an hour ago. Don't think you can walk right past me and pretend not to see me. I saw you on the stairs.'

I was starting not to enjoy this conversation. An hour ago and she saw him on the stairs? I had been in the flat about half an hour. Time to heat a tin of soup, play around with my index cards. And she sounded almost friendly. An almost friendly stalker?

'I shall be back,' she said, annoyed. 'You can bank on that.'

She flounced away, heel-tapping footsteps receding down to her flat on the ground floor, taking the something really nice with her, unless it had been left outside the door. I had no intention of trying to find out. A home-made Victoria sponge with butter icing? I eased off my trainers and walked around in bare feet. The wood floor was cold. This flat had no carpeting. My choice of hide-out was not comfortable. I was beginning to regret it. I had a feeling I would not be staying long.

But I was in need of a stimulant to support my courage.

Something a little Dutch. Unusual for me. I'm a social wine drinker. George must have a basic supply of alcohol somewhere. He liked a strong gin and tonic. It wasn't stealing. I would pay him for it, if possible, somehow. It was well hidden. I could not find a drop, not even a miniature bottle removed from a hotel room bar.

The refrigerator. Look for the ice and the gin could not be far away. The refrigerator was in the kitchen. I was getting warm. The cupboard had a glass. It fitted my hand. I was halfway there. The taste was already swimming in my mouth.

It was a small refrigerator tucked under the working top. The door would not open. It was jammed shut. I wrestled with the handle. It didn't move. Had George locked it? Do people lock their fridges these days? Perhaps burglars make a beeline for refreshment before trashing a place.

Something was not right. I could smell the wrongness. I remembered feeling the same way before in the kitchen. It was the size somehow. The wall of cabinets and cupboards, the refrigerator and sink, encroached over the left side of the window frame. No one fits a kitchen like that, even a small kitchen.

I went back to the refrigerator. It was an inspired move and I was desperate for a drink, anything would do. I got hold of the door handle and gave it a good shake.

'Come on, drat you,' I said, still shaking. 'Open up.'

I heard a click and the door swung slowly open. There was nothing inside. No ice. Nor was there a back to the cabinet. It led to a dark space. Show me a refrigerator without a back and I have to crawl through. This was Jordan in Wonderland, almost.

I stood up on the other side and found myself in a narrow room. It was the other third of the kitchen. No window. I felt for a light switch. The room was suddenly very brightly lit.

There was a big photocopying machine. A top-of-the-art photocopying machine. It could do everything except make tea. Colour, photo images, enlarge, decrease. The display manual was like a computer. The digital lights twinkled. I could have produced my fingerprints on it.

172

On a table stood a high quality computer, scanner and printer. Inks, paper, more equipment I did not understand. There was a pile of passports. They came from Britain, Belarus, Estonia, Lithuania, the Russian Federation and Uzbekistan. It took me a few minutes to work out what was happening here.

This was a passport factory, making forgeries from six different countries. They were helping illegal immigrants come into the UK with passports, driving licences and National Insurance cards.

There was a box full of standard passport size photos, faces of all ages and ethnic races, both sexes. Were the photos for new customers? I was not sure how a passport factory functioned. DI James would like to know about this. Perhaps I was about to enter his good books.

This lot were going to prison for a very long time if they were caught. George Hill was dead. So who were the others, the ones using his flat? Who were the rest of the gang? I was not waiting to find out. I got a horrid thought that I was in the wrong place. This flat had that inside-out feeling.

My breathing was not going so well. I phoned Doris on my mobile as I bundled all the stuff back into the canvas bag. 'Can you phone the police station and tell DI James that I'm coming round to see him right away,' I said quickly.

'Where are you?' she asked. 'What's happening?'

'At George Hill's place.'

'A brilliant hideaway,' she said. 'A dead man's flat. You chose well, Jordan.'

'I'm leaving now.'

'And about time. You seriously need your head testing.'

I was out of the flat in seconds, locking it behind me, keeping the key again. My brain was not functioning well. Any escape route was too open. Even an air rifle could be a lethal weapon in the wrong hands.

I hurried to the ground floor and flat number four. I knew Mrs Lechlade was in, pressed the buzzer. She opened it immediately, a half smile of welcome on her glossed lips.

'Hello,' I said brightly. 'I've come to apologize for not bringing round those dear little cottages that you liked so much. I haven't got them with me now, as I was not sure if you still wanted them. Can I come in?'

'The cottages?' She clearly did not recognize me without the glasses and headgear. And in my haste, I'd forgotten the different voice. There was no way she would associate me with the girl in the snazzy red number. I was strictly low key.

'May I come in and see your collection?' I asked, pushing past her and managing to close the door at the same time. Tricky manoeuvre. Mrs Lechlade was speechless for once. I went into raptures at the display of cuddly little cottages in a glass-fronted cabinet in her lounge.

'Oh, the darlings,' I beamed. 'What a fantastic collection! I've never seen so many cottages!'

Mrs Lechlade thawed half a degree. 'Yes, they are lovely, aren't they?' She almost began a purr.

'And oh, what a lovely cake,' I enthused, spotting a big chocolate gateau on her dining table. I could see myself making a living doing television ads. The enthusiasm is so genuine. 'It's a dream and smells divine.'

'It's a Sandra Carlton recipe.'

'Sandra Carlton! Heavens!' My voice went up another notch. 'Sandra is a friend of mine. She lives out Sompting way. I saw her only last week.'

'You know her?' Mrs Lechlade's eyes opened wide. 'I've always been a great fan. It was awful when they axed her programme.'

'She was very hurt,' I said. 'But she'll be pleased to know her recipes are still being used.'

'Will you tell her? I'd really like that. I made this cake for a friend,' she went on.

'Lucky friend!'

'You didn't see him, did you, as you came in? He's tall, dark and very handsome.'

I went cold. 'No, I didn't see him and I would certainly have spotted someone of that description. Few and far between, these days.' I did a merry laugh.

'I saw him a few minutes ago and then he disappeared.'

Time for me to disappear, rapidly. I was starting to feel unnerved.

'I've got some cash now, for those cottages,' said Mrs Lechlade. 'I'll go and get my handbag.' She went into her bedroom.

But I was out of the front door in a flash. Second time I've missed a sale for those cottages. I made straight for the super-market opposite, feeling a certain safety among the crowds cruising the aisles for special offers.

This supermarket had decent lavatories. It was time to go into the baby-changing room and alter my appearance. The scarf went turban-wise. I even used two free disposable nappies to change my bust size. I came out older but not wiser.

There were often taxis cruising the store, picking up custo-mers who had bought more than they could carry.

I used a faltering step and a taxi driver put his head out of the window. 'Where to, lady?' he asked, guessing geriatric.

'Do you know Marchmont Tower, the folly? It's up some winding lane near Cissbury Ring.'

'Hop in. I'll find it.'

I felt reasonably safe in the taxi and no one was following us. I checked several times. The driver was a decent sort and did not mind wandering about lanes looking for this folly. The clock was ticking up the miles. I could not remember any precise directions but I did try to amuse him with the story of why the folly was built.

He found it eventually. The tower looked impressively ab-surd. I had just enough money to pay the fare. I was grateful although the tip was pathetic.

'I'm sorry,' I said. 'I'll give you a proper tip the next time I see you.'

'Don't worry, lady,' he said, grinning. One of my busts had slipped. 'It's been a pleasure. This is all new to me. I ain't never seen these lanes before.'

He drove off. I stood outside Marchmont Tower, wondering how to get in, remembering the last time I had been there was when Detective Sergeant Ben Evans and I had been caught kissing on the sofa. Dear Ben. It all seemed so long ago. I had to smile at the sweetness of the memory. Call Me Irresponsible. And I had not seen my jazz trumpeter for weeks. At this rate, I might forget him. He was probably across the pond, making a fortune.

The folly was locked, of course. DI James did not leave his fortress open to intruders. I looked under a few stones, dislodged a brick. No key. I didn't fancy breaking in. I wandered round, hoping he had left a window open. No luck. He'd probably got security cameras trained on me at this very moment. I nodded and waved to the air, just in case.

I had to get in. I wriggled out of the second bust and wrapped my hands in the nappies. Any moment now I was going to have to break glass.

DI James found me asleep in the downstairs bathroom. In the bath. Wrapped in a large dark brown towel. The tap had dripped and my feet were damp.

'I saw you on camera. There's a relay to my office,' he said.

I sat up awkwardly. Later I would tell him that I had forced open the bathroom window with a metal nail file.

'I'm doing what you said, following your advice. You said I had to go into hiding. And I'm doing just that.'

'In my bath?'

'Last place anyone would look for me, eh?'

'If you say so. Get up. Dry your feet. I'll make you some coffee. By the way, here's your bag you left behind.'

'Thank you,' I said, taking it. 'Can you?'

'What?'

'Make coffee.'

'Instant, but it passes. There's dry towels in the cupboard. Your jeans are wet too. I'd better find you something to wear.'

'I don't want anything.' I panicked. 'It's only the hem. I don't mind.'

James was making coffee in sturdy blue mugs. He stirred in the granules. At least the label on the jar was gold. 'Milk? Sugar?'

'Neither, thank you. You know that.'

He did not mention dry clothes again. The wet ends clung clammily round my ankles. This was weird. I was sitting with James in his kitchen, drinking his coffee. For months he had lived in one awful bedsit after another but at last he seemed to have settled down and I was glad.

'So . . .' he said at last. 'To what do I owe the pleasure? You don't usually take my advice.'

'I've found a passport factory. And a man who is supposed to be dead doesn't seem to be very dead any more. In fact, he's been seen and seen by quite a normal woman. If you can call a stalker normal.'

James did not say anything for several moments. He was digesting the information. He looked into his coffee as if reading tea leaves.

'Interesting amalgam of items. I suggest you start at the beginning, Jordan. I am a little confused. But you have all my attention. I'm going to take notes.'

It was so strange, this moment out of time, drinking coffee (if you could call it coffee) which James had made for me, and he was listening to me. So, I rambled a bit. But the novelty was stimulating. I came to life. It was like being on stage with an audience of one.

I did not know where to start but James kept bringing me back on track. He made copious notes. Once he stopped me and made a phone call. I could not hear what he was saying.

'So where is this passport factory?'

'In George Hill's flat. I'm not surprised you didn't find it. The kitchen is the wrong size, you see. The other room is full of high-tech equipment, a computer, laminator, copier and a scanner.'

'How do you get to this other room?'

'You go through the refrigerator.'

His face was blank. 'Explain.'

'You crawl through the refrigerator to the other side.'

'Why did you go to George Hill's flat?'

'I thought it would be a good place to lay low. No one would think of looking for me there.' He didn't ask how I got in. 'You never told me why I had to disappear. I want to know.'

'It was those spreadsheets. They tie in with some others that have turned up in Brighton. We thought it was smuggling but it could be forged passports. Both equally dangerous crimes.'

'But the spreadsheets were from Anne Steel's briefcase,' I said without thinking. 'She's nothing to do with George Hill.'

James made no comment. I gave him the collection of forged documents to distract his thoughts. His face changed again.

He went through every document that I had taken from George Hill's flat, scrutinizing item after item. He strew them all over the table. I could see his interest rising. His eyes gleamed with Icelandic tenacity. They were almost the purest blue. He made another phone call but this one was on the long side.

'Carry on, Jordan, I'm listening. Did you know that these blanks from Greece, Belgium and Holland have a street value of £1,500 each? And these doctored British passports change hands at about £600?'

'No idea,' I said. 'Or I would have sold them myself. Set up a street market stall.'

'You've got a shop. I shall have to search it.'

He was only joking, I hoped.

This was the most of his time that I had ever had. It was extraordinary. He was actually listening as if I was someone of consequence. I doubted if I would ever get over it.

'And what about George Hill?'

'Mrs Lechlade in flat number four said she saw him on the stairs. And she had made him a cake. Now she wouldn't make him a cake if he was dead, would she?'

I got up and looked in his refrigerator to see if there was anything to eat. Half a packet of dried-up bacon and a lump of Cheddar cheese. There was nothing gastronomical I could make out of that.

'Don't you ever cook a meal?' I said, closing the door.

'Rarely. I eat at Maeve's cafe mostly.'

'Too much fried fat.'

'But delicious. Would you deny me one of the pleasures of life?'

I would deny him nothing. But James did not know it or care. I wonder if he would ever know how much he meant to me. Especially now, after that late night chase and car crash. And the youngsters had got away scot-free. They had walked away from their stolen vehicle, laughing, still high on drugs and alcohol. They had not even bothered to see if Ben was all right.

'You could phone for a pizza,' I suggested.

'It would be cold by the time it arrived here.'

'We could go out to a pub.'

'You are in hiding.'

He'd got all the answers. And he was hiding a smile. It was a pleasurable moment. He came over to me and pulled me to my feet. For one sublime instant I thought he was going to kiss me but he didn't. I almost closed my eyes.

'I have to go,' he said. 'Work calls. Thank you for all the leads. Eat anything you like. Open a tin of something. Go upstairs, take off those wet jeans and sleep in my bed. I won't disturb you. Make sure that everything is locked up and don't answer the door or answer the phone. And I will secure the bathroom window that you forced open. I was watching you. Neat job with a nail file.'

'You're going to leave me . . .' I could not believe it.

'Yes, I have work to do. But, of course, you don't know what it's like to be married to a policeman.'

In my dreams.

James finished his coffee and left. I washed up. The tin of something was sausages in baked beans. I left it on the shelf. I found an apple which he had forgotten and ate that with the hard cheese. It was so hard I had to suck it. I locked up the fortress and went upstairs but I did not go into his bedroom. That was sacrosanct. One day, perhaps, if I was lucky.

I slept instead in Ben's bed. It was odd really, somehow

feeling as if he was there, beside me. I had the strangest dream of his arms around me and he was saying the sweetest things. And he kissed me warmly. I could have sworn he was really there but I did not want to destroy the dream.

Perhaps he came back to me for a moment to say goodbye. I did not doubt the strength of his feelings. Maybe they had been strong enough to travel a million miles, a million light years from eternity. Whatever that is.

Nineteen

I slept for a long time. I knew it was unhygienic in a dead bed. No one had changed the sheets or tidied Ben's room. His possessions were strewn around as if he was coming back any moment. Books, letters and clothes lay in happy disarray. Perhaps it was something I should do when the time was right.

There was no DI James around when I got up. I trailed downstairs wrapped in a sheet, just in case, but the kitchen was empty and so was the bathroom. The water was hot. He had left the immersion heater on. Thank you, James. And there was a selection of cereal packets for breakfast with a bowl of fruit. I had a bath, washed my hair using his shampoo (note brand for future reference), then trailed upstairs to dress.

It was so odd, being here in James's home. I felt like a thin, opportunist cat, seeing something I was not supposed to see. But James did not seem to mind leaving me in charge. I didn't sneak a look into his bedroom. An array of intimate family photographs would have spiralled me into a tunnel of despair. I still didn't know what had happened to his family. Family? Had there been children? Once he had mentioned children . . . I couldn't remember exactly.

As I munched through a bowl of bran and sultanas with day-old milk, I moved my index cards around on the table. One of them rattled my memory box. I had lifted a plastic membership ID from Anne Steel's bedroom where it had been propping up a lamp. It had seemed out of character and I wanted to follow it up. Rewrite: borrowed, not lifted.

It was in my shoulder bag, right at the bottom, forgotten, a bit of fluff sticking to it. Mrs Anne Steel had paid to be a life member of the Higher Latching Post-mill Society, one of the town's landmarks, standing alone, defying the weather. I knew it well. It was an impressive black timber building with two sixty-foot canvas sails, recently restored, and it ground grain on some days to make bags of flour for the tourists to buy. But I had never been in it. The steep walk up an unmade road always put me off.

But from Marchmont Tower it would be a doddle. The folly was on higher ground than the windmill. It would be downhill all the way. No one would think of looking for me in a windmill. I was not a hiding-away for ever type person even after a serious warning from James.

I washed up, wiped tops, tidied James's kitchen, feeling very housewifely. I even made Ben's bed if pulling up a striped duvet rates points. James wouldn't mind if I took an apple, would he? He'd obviously been to one of those all-night shops and bought some fruit. I took a satsuma as well.

There was another tinge of autumn in the air. It was just around the corner, an untimely frost up its sleeve. I wondered how Mr Arnold was getting on in hospital. He was a lonely soul. Perhaps he might like a visitor. But he might not. He might be appalled that I had arrived too soon and ruined everything.

'No,' I said aloud. 'Have some sense, girl.'

A startled rabbit looked up and scuttled back into the undergrowth.

'Sorry,' I said. I always apologize to animals. You never know if there has been a previous life. This rabbit might have been a Tibetan monk.

It was a good walk to the windmill. I would have enjoyed it if I had not been alert for every sound. But no one came along. Not a car, a bike, nor a cyclist. Not even a dog. There was just me and a disgruntled rabbit.

The windmill stood on its isolated hill, awesome with age and power. It was first built around 1724 and had ground grain for all the local farmers for two hundred years. Then steam power came along and put paid to wind-driven mills. The millers went out of business, found other jobs.

The gate to the grounds was padlocked but that did not stop this intrepid PI from climbing over. I was not breaking and entering. I had Mrs Steel's lifetime membership in my shoulder bag.

The roundhouse had been rebuilt recently and it was a sturdy structure on a brick base. It housed the main oak post and the diagonal quarter bars which took the colossal forty-ton weight.

I remembered reading somewhere that the hurricane of October 1987 had turned the pair of sails for the first time for years, even though the brake was on.

There was a steeply stepped ladder outside going up to the first part of the body of the mill with a handrail and grab ropes. The thought of coming down those steps was pretty scary. Scary alerted me to my exposed position. Anyone could see me. I was a standing target.

I was up those steps faster than Hornblower, praying that the door would be open. It was closed but opened to my touch. There must be some of the volunteers around, doing their volunteering.

It was not very big inside the first floor. I looked at a useful diagram on the wall. This was called the spout floor and the one above was the stone floor, i.e. the grinding stones were there. And the tiny storage area above that was called the bin floor. Now I knew where I was.

It was all beams and pulleys and shutes and moving elements. Fascinating if you were seriously into grinding grain. The windows were tiny. I peered out of them into the surrounding countryside. The dusty glass needed cleaning. At least no one could see me. I decided not to take any chances and closed the door.

The wooden steps up to the next floor were even steeper with a single handrail. I hung on to the rail and ascended crab-wise. Here I recognized two sets of grinding stones and the huge elm and apple wood wheels with 132 teeth that turned them. Both wheels had metal brake shoes fitted. All this information was on another helpful diagram. I didn't understand the tentering system.

It did not smell musty. It smelt wholesome and floury. If I'd had an egg, I could have baked a cake.

Now why would Mrs Anne Steel have paid for a life membership? It might have carried a few perks, like extra visits or open different hours. Or was she genuinely keen on old windmills? There were a lot in the area, at least eight within two miles of Brighton. No way of asking her. I would have to find out. I began a minute search of the building, every nook and cranny. More crannies than nooks. It was instinct.

My hand closed over an odd thing to find in a windmill. A little square card, quite new. There were three cards, close together, each half the size of a normal business card, tucked away, almost out of sight, pinned to the wall behind a pulley.

There was writing on each card. Groups of numbers. This might have something to do with Anne's death. The answer hit me.

It was ingenious. A device from some inspired criminal mind, if Mrs Steel's activities were criminal. I kept my mind on that heavy haul of £5,000 cash and looked more closely.

The windmill was a drop. It was a place where messages could be left. Who would notice small scraps of card pinned to the wood behind intricate unused pulleys? Some of the writing on the cards said a date and a time. But the dates were current and the times unsocial.

This could be a chain of drops. Maybe all the windmills in the area were being used for this purpose. These beautiful old relics from centuries past. No one would think of searching them.

I did not remove the cards but I made a note of the dates and times. Perhaps they would mean something to DI James. They could be totally innocuous, something to do with milling times. But grinding at 3.20 a.m.? You'd have to be a mad miller. Besides, didn't you have to check if it was windy or not?

There was a bit of a wind getting up now. I could hear the sails creaking. I looked out of the window. Fleeced clouds were racing across the sky as if chased by banshees. I did not like the sound of that wind. It was time to go back to the safety of Marchmont Tower.

Just as I turned to go down the steps backwards to the first floor, I heard someone coming up the steep flight from outside into the buck, the body of the mill. I made a beeline for the vertical ladder against a wall that led to the bin floor, a tiny space at the top of the mill where grain was stored in sacks before going down shutes to the stone. I tried not to breathe but it was dusty and I felt a cough coming on. For once I had my Ventolin with me and took a quick inhalation. There was only room for me to crouch on my knees.

The footsteps were heavy enough for a man and they seemed to know where they were going. This was not wandering about like a tourist, reading and peering everywhere. These footsteps came up the second flight of steps to the stone floor.

I held my breath, trying to visualize the tight, complicated layout below me. The footsteps were going straight to where the messages were hidden. I heard a muffled oath. Definitely a man, and an impatient man.

Then he turned and retreated down the steps back to the first floor. The wind had caught the door and it was banging. It was an easterly wind and streaming at a fair rate of knots already.

The door slammed. I peered cautiously down the trap space. There did not seem to be anyone around but I waited a good ten minutes, nursing the cramps, to make sure he had gone.

The bright morning air had disappeared as the clouds filled the sky with turbulence. It was time I went back to the folly. Maybe I could bake DI James a cake. Or scones. Something simple. I did not know how to make scones but it must be dead easy. Throw in a few raisins and stir, or was it sultanas? I hurried down to the spout floor.

The door was not opening. I pulled and tugged and pushed but it would not budge. The man had locked or bolted it on the outside. For a moment I panicked. Millers did not believe in chairs. There was nowhere to sit. I sat on the floor and calmed myself. Perhaps I could climb out somewhere.

The windows did not open and also they were too small even for someone my size. They would not accommodate a body. No sill outside. I would have to drop and it was a long drop. Unless I could slide down the sails.

Drop. I went back up to the hiding place and now there was a fourth card. Tomorrow's date and a time of 1 a.m. These were no grinding times. I had to get out and tell DI James.

I sat for a long time, still thinking. This brain was on overtime. I could think of no way of getting out apart from waiting till some volunteer came along to show a party around. And that might be days ahead.

I ate the apple which I had taken from the folly. I had a small bottle of mineral water in my bag but it would not last long. A few polo mints as usual and the satsuma. Sum total of life-sustaining refreshments.

But I had my mobile. I keyed in DI James's station number. It was on answerphone. He was out.

'James,' I said breathlessly. 'It's me, Jordan. I've found a drop. It's really weird. Tomorrow at 1 a.m. Does this mean anything to you?'

I was just about to add more information when the phone went dead. I shook it and dialled again. Nothing. The screen was blank. The battery needed recharging. I sank back on to my knees and cradled my head. I could never remember to recharge the damned thing. I had told Doris I would and I hadn't.

So I had to get out. I toured the mill for emergency exits. There were none unless you counted the small space in the roof at the top of the bin floor or the trap door through which the grain sacks were hoisted. What comes up, could go down. Seemed perfectly logical to me.

It was a normal sort of pulley with a rope going over a grooved wheel. If I could hold on to both ropes, let myself over the trap, I might be able to slide down to the roundhouse where the sacks were stored. Hopefully there would be a way out from there.

The important thing to remember was to grab both ropes to prevent the pulley mechanism from working. I hoped I was not too heavy. A sack of grain might weigh anything but maybe not my nine stone.

I slung my bag firmly across my shoulders and centred it on my back. Then I sat on the edge of trap space, my legs dangling into nowhere. It looked a horribly long way down. Without changing my weight, I reached for both ropes and pulled them towards me. They were rough. My hands would be no good for washing up for days.

This was no time for a coughing fit. A few deep calming breaths were needed. I could hear the wind and the creaking of the sails. It did not sound too healthy though I am never frightened of the weather.

The moment of launch was tricky. I had to have a good grip on the ropes and balance the mechanism. It could be done, I told myself. This was not a Ye Olde Worlde pulley, but part of the restored machinery and still in use. I could slide down like 007 himself.

Wrong. I judged it badly. My pull was enough for the furthest rope to slide out of my hands and rattle noisily on its way, snaking down to the floor of the roundhouse, dragging the other half with it. The descent stopped when the hoist mechanism caught in the hooks at the end used to grip the sacks, one rope left swinging. I looked up at the jammed hook. There was no way I was going to trust my weight to a hook that size.

I sat back and contemplated the circumstances. This was not the first time I'd had to use my wits to get out of an unacceptable situation. What wits? They had deserted me. Shopping list: ginkgo biloba tablets, 6000 mg size.

The phone was still dead. I searched the mill for spare rope which I could sling over some sturdy beam and shin down. Not an inch. Some tidy person had put it all away.

The wind was gusting up. Tops of nearby trees were lashing about. I could feel the mill starting to sway, not much, but enough for feelings of alarm. It was like being at sea. The windows were taking a battering as well and the creaking noise was becoming quite loud.

Some movement caught my eye. The huge ten-foot diameter brake-wheel was moving slightly, a tapered tooth tenon fitting precisely into a mortice hole. Surely it should not be doing this? I checked the metal brake shoe. It was firmly clamped to the rim of the wheel.

I ate the satsuma slowly. Perhaps the vitamin C would revitalize my ideas. The bottle of water was three-quarters full. I would not be gnawing on wood for quite a while.

I took up watch by a window where I could see the roadway in case there was any passing traffic that I could hail. The sails were straining against the wind. I had no idea what would happen if they started turning.

Nowhere seemed safe. The swaying of the mill was unnerving and I did not like the movement at all. I managed to open a small window but the sudden force of the wind knocked me back and I had to struggle to refasten it.

I could smell something acrid. I could smell burning. I raced up the steps to the next floor. The pressure of the sails turning in the wind was setting up friction against the steel shoe. It was getting hot. Wafts of smoke were already coming from the wheel, little eddies of grey that drifted around. I began to fan the area with my notebook to cool it down. Wrong again, Jordan. A spark ignited the wood and a network of tiny red embers wormed along the grain.

I took off my T-shirt and tried to smother the embers. My shirt curled up into fragments of ash. Panic was making an entrance.

I did not know whether to open the window to let the smoke out or keep it closed. I was beginning to cough. The smoke was finding its own way out through cracks in the structure. I wetted a handkerchief and held it against my nose. Surely there must be a fire extinguisher somewhere? I began a rapid search. Where was it? This was a public place. They had to abide by regulations. Fire equipment is so commonplace, it often goes unnoticed.

The creaking of the sails was now so loud and ominous that I did not hear footsteps coming up the outside steps, the door bursting open, and helmeted firemen pouring into the mill, dragging a hose.

'Anybody inside?' they shouted.

Relief swept through me. I went weak.

'There's me,' I wheezed, peering down through the smoke.

'Where's the fire?'

'Up here. The wheel has caught fire. Friction from the brake shoe, I think.'

'Come on down quick, miss. This is our job.'

'I was doing my best,' I said, shaking an empty bottle of water.

Twenty

M y macho fireman friend, Bud Morrison, was not among the rescuers. Perhaps he had moved on to another station or been promoted. No one carried me over a shoulder, but a burly chap in maroon gear, yellow helmet, guided me down the steep steps outside while the other fire fighters put out the smouldering fire. No one noticed the lack of T-shirt. I couldn't look down. The fresh air was wonderful, exhilarating despite the gale blowing. The creaking of the sails was even louder now as the wind battled for supremacy.

'I'm so glad to see you. How come you are here?' I gasped breathlessly at the bottom of the steps, holding on to the rail to steady myself. My legs were wobbly. Mother Earth never felt so good.

'Someone spotted the smoke and dialled 999.'

'Hurrah! Another historic post-mill saved,' I said, coughing. Water was whooshing down the steps like a garden waterfall.

'Are you all right?' the fireman asked. 'Perhaps you ought to be checked out at the hospital. Smoke inhalation can cause damage to the lungs.'

'No, thank you, I'm fine,' I said, trying to breathe normally. No more hospitals for me. 'If I have any problems I'll go to my own doctor.'

'My sub'll need to make out a report first, then do you want a lift home?'

That was how I got a ride on a fire appliance in the middle of a late summer storm, squashed between two burly firemen and wearing a fire officer's open-necked shirt. A trophy. I knew DI

James would be annoyed that I did not go back to Marchmont Tower but I could not remember his address. The fire fighters might get suspicious if I said I didn't know exactly where I was living at present. They might decide I was an arsonist.

I thanked them for the lift and promised beer and cakes another time. I needed to drink more water and go to my own bathroom. It felt wonderful to be home. My plants were glad to see me holding a watering can. Stateless and homeless does not suit me. I remembered to put my phone on charge. The doors were locked and I propped chairs up against them. It did not seem all that safe. Anyone could get in. Who was after me, anyway? James had not told me that.

'James?' I said on the landline phone, when sufficient water had rendered me vocal again. He knew instantly who it was.

'Yes?' he snapped.

'I've some information for you. Someone or somebodies are using Upper Latching Windmill as a drop.'

'Who are they?'

'How should I know? It came as a surprise. I'm telling you that cryptic little cards are being planted behind a pulley in the mill.'

'What do they say? Read them out to me.'

My note-taking paid off. I read them out to him, including the last one for 1 a.m. tonight.

'Was there anything else on the cards?'

'No.'

'Think hard.'

It was not easy to think hard when the cards were now only a vague memory.

'Yes, I think there was something else. A little scribble, a sort of number. Something like that. I can't quite remember. It didn't seem to mean anything.'

'I think it does mean something. Might it have tied in with the numbers on the spreadsheets? Where are you? My place or your place?'

'My place.'

'Why?'

'I didn't like your choice of cereal.'

I don't know what makes me say these things to him. It wasn't what I meant at all. I meant that I could not trust myself to be so near to him, that one day or night I would go over the top and pin him to a sofa with my legs. It was a deeply sobering thought.

'Don't you have any sense? Don't you realize that you are not safe where they can find you?'

'What on earth have I got that anyone would want? Some bits of information all of which I have passed on to you in the goodness of my heart and in the pursuit of justice.'

'Think, Jordan. What else have you got that someone might go to extremes to get?'

'I really don't know,' I said. 'Tell me.'

'It would be better if I don't tell you. You might say something incriminating. Best to play dumb. You're good at that.'

He rang off.

What a nice man.

Of course, I had the money, a rather large sum of it. Or rather, Miguel had the money. Oh dear.

Or maybe it was the notebooks. Anne's diary-type notebooks. They were under my bed. I think up such brilliant hiding places.

After a fitful night, everything barred and locked like Fort Knox, I was up early to go round to the police station. I did not feel at all safe. I almost wanted them to lock me up and call it police protection. I put on my bag lady outfit, long skirt, old raincoat, pull-on felt hat, grubby trainers. Even Doris did not recognize me.

'Get a move on,' she said when I hovered outside her shop. She was about to open up. 'You'll give me a bad name.'

I picked up a couple of her wastebin bags. They smelt of old fruit. A few flies thought so too.

'OK, you can have those. But the stuff's off.'

I stumbled along the road, trying to look grateful. Something in the bags was squashy too. I did not want to know what had leaked. People moved away when they saw me coming. Some kids threw pebbles at me. They missed.

The station was changing shift. Police officers were leaving in civilian clothes, glad the night was over. They climbed into cars or wheeled out motorbikes, fastening helmets.

'Who's on the desk?' I croaked.

'Sergeant Rawlings.'

'Oh good. He likes me.'

'Don't count on it, not the way you're smelling.'

I went through the new automatic doors, my bags bumping against them. A strong smell of sour yogurt filled the air. Sergeant Rawlings took one look at the ensemble and shook his head.

'Jordan, not again. Will you give up coming in here looking like that? You're putting off the real villains.'

'Sorry, but it was the only safe way of travelling, i.e. incognito, around in Latching this morning. I have a horrid feeling someone is trying to get me out of the way.'

'I'm not surprised, in that outfit. We're trying to clean up the streets.'

'Can I see DI James?'

'Sorry, he's not in yet.'

'Yes, he is,' said James, coming in fast. He was shrugging out of a light jacket. 'This way, Jordan. Shower room first, please.'

I thought for one ecstatic moment that he was planning for us to have a shower together. It was a dizzy thought. But he was pushing me towards the women's showers, bundling a towel and soap into my hands.

'I don't want to see you until you are clean,' he said. 'You smell of smoke.'

'I've been in a fire.'

That shook him. He had not linked the windmill fire with me. Why should he? It was nothing to do with the police. It was not arson. It was the wind driving the sails against the brake. You can't charge a Gale Force 6.

'A fire?'

'Windmill fire, caused by the wind. I haven't any clothes except these,' I added.

'I'll find something for you to wear.'

I had a lukewarm shower, taking as long as possible. I did not want to come out, but I had to eventually, wrapped in a very thin, scratchy, well-laundered towel. Some clothes were laid on the chair in the washroom. A pair of jeans and a shirt that I recognized as belonging to James. The one with the pilot style shoulder tabs. No clean bra or pants. Well, I couldn't expect the moon. I put my own back on. I bundled my bag lady clothes into a plastic bag. No way was anyone throwing them away. Much too valuable.

I wandered along the corridor, trying to dry my hair. It hung down my back in wet straggles. DI James called down from his first-floor office.

'To what do I owe the honour at this time of the morning?'

'I think you are right. I don't think I am safe. I've come for police protection.'

'We don't have the time or the resources,' he began.

I shot him a look of disbelief. 'I'll go and put a stone through Guilbert's shop window. Then you'll find the time and the resources.'

'You're too young for a life of crime. I'll get you a coffee. Come and drink it. I've got ten minutes. What do you want to tell me?'

I told him again about the windmill being a drop. I told him about Anne's annual membership card. He listened carefully. Then I told him about the five thousand pounds.

He did not know what to say for a few seconds. 'This is outrageous, Jordan, withholding police evidence. You could get into serious trouble. You should have known better, you idiot. Surely your WPC days taught you that.'

'I know, I know, but Mr Steel made me promise not to tell anyone. I knew it was wrong but what could I do? He's the one paying me and I did as I was told. The money is in a safe place, at least I'm hoping it's still safe.'

'Where is it?'

'In a friend's safe.'

'Which friend?' He did not look up from his note writing.

'Miguel.'

'The Mexican romeo.'

'He's a dear, sweet, kind man,' I began, knowing it would annoy him. 'And he sends me roses.'

'Does he know that he has all this money in his safe?'

I shook my head. 'It's in a carrier bag.'

James obviously thought there was no point in reprimanding me any further. In one ear, etc. 'We'd better make arrangements to collect the cash. You would not want your dear, sweet, rose-sending friend to be carved up with a kitchen knife.'

'He probably won't give it to you. He's very loyal.'

'Write him a note,' James growled, pushing a pad towards me. 'Authorization for my officer and sign it.'

I thought for a moment, then wrote: 'Dear Miguel, it would be safer if you gave the carrier bag to this police officer. You have my permission. Make sure he doesn't drop it. Thanks, Jordan.'

James read it through without comment, then got up and left the room. It was ages before he came back. I was reduced to trying to read the files on his desk upside down.

'Haven't you gone yet?' he said, returning.

'You promised me a coffee.'

'If I get you a coffee, will you promise me to go back to Marchmont Tower?'

'I'll go back to Marchmont Tower if you promise to tell me something,' I said.

'I haven't got time for games, Jordan.'

'It's about George Hill.'

'What about George Hill?'

'Can I see the body?'

'No.'

'Can I see the autopsy report?'

'No.'

I tried a new tactic. Such sweetness and light. 'I wonder if you could kindly tell me who identified poor George Hill. Someone has to identify a dead person, don't they? It won't be breaking any monumental police investigation law to tell me who identified him, will it now?'

He was obviously weighing up my reasons for wanting this information. So far, he could see no obvious interference on my part, but then he did not know what I knew.

'I suppose there's no harm in telling you, although I can't see what good it'll do you. We had a problem. As far as we could trace, George Hill didn't have any relations. Not a soul. Parents dead, no brother or sister. No aunts or uncles. No regular girlfriend.'

'Only me,' I put in. 'Except I wasn't regular.'

'At that point in the investigation, we had no idea what your involvement was.' James went to fetch coffee from the coffee machine. I followed him out into the corridor.

'So?'

'In the end we had to ask one of the other performers in the theatre to make a formal identification. This man had known George Hill for over a year, toured around in the same show, knew him quite well. He was upset. Suffocation doesn't look nice.'

'Who was it?'

'A chap called Max Cornelius.'

'I know Max,' I said. 'He's the magician.'

James put me in a taxi and gave the driver instructions to take me to Marchmont Tower without delay.

'And keep your head down,' he said, closing the door. I didn't know if he meant literally. I did not fancy going any-where under a blanket.

As soon as we had driven out of sight of the police station, I turned to the driver. 'There's been a change of plan,' I said in an official voice. 'Could you please take me to the Regal Theatre in Brighton, you know the old theatre? I think that's what it's called.'

'I thought he said Marchmont Tower . . . ?'

'That's normal police procedure,' I said. 'In case someone is listening. Bugging, you know. This is undercover police work. I've to check something at the theatre.'

'If you say so, miss. But I'll have to charge them.'

196

'Of course,' I said, settling back. He was taking the scenic route along the coast road. 'No problem.'

I did not have any money on me or my mobile. Bag ladies only carry vital keys and those they pin inside a bra. I always seem to embark on these things without thinking them through first. It would not be easy getting home. Brighton station had those automatic barriers. No slipping through without a ticket. Something might turn up. It often did.

The warmth in the car was making me sleepy. I nearly dozed off. The driver was not chatty. Most taxi drivers chat a lot but this one preferred listening to Radio Two. Suited me.

'Thanks a lot,' I said as we drew up outside the theatre. I recognized the regal exterior. Already a new show was posted up, a stage play, opening soon. 'Hope you get a fare back.'

'I shall charge them both ways,' he said.

'You do that,' I nodded. DI James would kill me. I'd have to offer to pay.

I went round the back and pushed open the stage door. There was no doorkeeper checking but a lot of activity going on as a new set was being built on the stage. I walked confidently towards George Hill's dressing room.

'Hi,' I said to several stagehands.

The scene of crime tape had gone. No point.

It was funny going into his dressing room. It was not locked. It had not been cleared. Unusual. It was still full of his possessions. Perhaps there was some stage superstition about moving an actor's things before he was buried. Stage people are a very superstitious lot.

I remember reading about a famous actor who walked the streets of London every evening before a show, speaking through his entire part. Another who wouldn't wear a certain colour for fear of bad luck. And an actress who must have the same dressing room and everything in exactly the same place or she won't go on.

His black sequinned jacket was still hung on the preformed model. George had changed out of it after the show for casual party gear. I tried not to look at the hook behind the door. I knew I was looking for something but I was not sure what it was. Everybody and every event leaves behind some trace. Something so small and insignificant that it is overlooked. I rummaged through the waste bin and took out a chocolate wrapper. No harm in removing it.

The jacket drew me. George had looked so handsome in it, the sequins glistening like wet water. Now it was not quite so well pressed as if he had flung it off. I peered closer. A couple of sequins were snagged. They needed a stitch.

Then I saw it, something very small and white caught among the sequins. I held my breath in case actual breathing might dislodge it. I had found what I was looking for. I had found the vital difference which might provide a link.

I did not touch it or remove it. The white link had to remain exactly where it was.

The door opened quietly behind me with a small rush of air. For a moment I was not sure if I had heard it open or not. But then I became aware of someone standing behind me.

There was a low chuckle as the door closed. A chuckle that I knew.

'Well, well, well, so here is the intrepid Miss Lacey. Who would have thought it? She has some brain cells that actually work. And we have a lot to talk about.'

I turned very slowly but I already knew who it was.

Twenty-One

I t was George Hill, all six foot one of him alive and well, smiling at me from the doorway. He looked different. He was different. The sleek ponytail had gone and along with it the suave immaculate look. The gear was baggy cargo trousers, heavy belt, overlarge T-shirt and a baseball cap.

'What's this?' I said. 'A fancy dress party?'

I was surprised, yet not surprised. Mrs Lechlade said she was sure she had seen George on the stairs. I'd half thought she was hallucinating.

'So you're not dead?'

He pinched an arm playfully. 'Nope.'

'So who is dead?'

'How should I know? The morgue is full of bodies. People die every day.'

'But not in your dressing room. There's a body in the morgue wearing a George Hill toe tag, but no tattoo.'

'I shall have to get it removed.' The tone of his voice changed. 'And what are you doing in my dressing room?'

'Your dressing room? You're officially dead. I don't believe it's your dressing room any more,' I said. 'I was just looking around for old time's sake.'

I carefully positioned myself so as to block his view of the sequinned jacket. I did not want him to suddenly think of taking it away and disposing of it.

'Strangely enough, I don't believe you,' said George. 'Your brain is twitching. You're poking your nose where you are not wanted.'

'You paid me so I'm still working on the case. I'm tracking your stalker,' I said.

'My stalker!' He began to laugh showing those whiter than white teeth. 'We really hoodwinked you there, didn't we? Sheree isn't a stalker. She's an out-of-work actress. Did pretty well, didn't she? But she was furious about the dress. I didn't know you were into soda syphon tactics.'

'You don't have a stalker . . .?' I asked slowly, the implications unravelling. 'It was all play acting?'

'That's right, I paid Sheree to act the part a couple of times, just to keep you on your toes.'

'On my toes? The stalker case was something to divert me?' It was starting to dawn, like a fog lifting.

'Sure. I wanted to keep you very busy. And I paid you well, don't deny it.'

'And all the gifts?'

'She sent them but I paid for them. I was annoyed about the Stilton.'

'Was she acting the part when she spotted you on the stairs in Chapel Court?'

'No, that was a damned nuisance. I wondered if she had seen me so I got out fast. No, dear Sheree is not yet aware of my sad departure from this world. I'll have to confuse the timing somehow. Send her a farewell suicide note dated today. That might work. She'd never check with the morgue.'

'But you haven't departed, have you? You are very much alive.'

'No one else knows that, Miss Lacey. In fact, you are the only person who knows I'm alive. Isn't that interesting?'

I felt a twinge of apprehension, an edgy sense of danger. It was dangerous to be the only person who knew. I did not like the cool gleam in his eyes.

'You really fooled me,' I said, changing the subject fast. I had to keep him talking. Perhaps someone would come in. 'I was really taken in. A wonderful performance from you in particular. You should be an actor.'

'I think so too. It's time for a career change. I'd make a great James Bond. The height, the looks, the comic timing. They'll be looking for a new one soon. Pierce Brosman can only make a couple more films.'

'So why the elaborate disappearance trick?' I asked, veering away from the body in the morgue. 'What was the reason for it? Why involve me? After all, you don't know me from Adam.' 'But I know an awful lot about you and your other case. Weedkiller, isn't it? One of the six banned chemicals. You see, Jordan, you're the one who has been stalked. I've been watching you for weeks. Pity you fell out of that tree. And what a shame about the unpleasant story in the *Sussex Record*. I wonder who tipped the reporter off with all that garbage? In fact, I had another nice little scandal up my sleeve for the aftershow party, but my new girlfriend departed home to bed before it started.'

I said nothing. He looked malicious, eyes narrowed, and he was sweating. I had to get out. The dressing room was so small. There was no way I could get past him.

'I admit it was a pity about Anne but she was getting a mite too greedy. Always wanting a bigger and better cut. Women are never satisfied. The funny thing about the garden shears is that when forensic get their act together, they are going to find your prints on the handle. Isn't that amazing?'

I was starting to feel sick. Had he killed Anne? Had the cadaveric spasm clutched his ponytail? 'How did you manage that?' I croaked. George laughed again.

'All those lovely cups of coffee you drank in the kitchen at Denbury Court. It only took a pair of free theatre tickets and Joan Broseley removed a couple of mugs after one of your visits. I didn't tell her why. I said it was a silly joke I was going to play on you. She was quite taken in.'

'She would be,' I said faintly. 'She's a very trusting woman.'

'I have friends in the trade who can transfer prints. It's a tricky procedure but it can be done. Cost me a packet.'

'So you know Anne Steel?'

'Known her for years. We go way back. A platonic business arrangement, you understand. I was the brains. She was the accountant.'

'I suppose you're going to tell me now that you have been vandalizing the garden at Denbury Court and somehow incriminating me.'

My voice sounded pathetic. I was really frightened. No one knew I was here except the taxi driver. I put my faith in him. He was going to charge for the double fare. But how long would it take him to claim the money?

'No, I never thought of that. Not into weedkiller, not my style, but sorry about the footprint on the verge. Clumsy of me, wasn't it, ruining your only bit of evidence.'

'I suppose you've got Anne's white car?' I went on prodding, more out of habit. 'It's disappeared.'

'Disappeared under a spray job and rehomed with a family man. It didn't take long and I needed the money. A top-of-the-range car. But I need that cash urgently. Where is it, Jordan?'

'The police confiscated it. It's probably locked in a cell.'

His eyes narrowed with anger. 'Not funny, Jordan.'

'But what about the vandalism at Denbury Court, if it wasn't you and I know it wasn't me.'

'Right under your nose, Jordan. Right under your nose. You're supposed to be a detective. I'm not going to tell you who's been doing it. You should have sussed that out weeks ago.'

He was starting to get restless. I could see this conversation was not going to go on much longer. But I had to keep him talking. He did not seem to know about the diaries.

'I don't understand,' I said wearily. 'Why me? Why this vendetta? You don't know me and I never knew you till you walked into my shop. We've never met before.'

He started rubbing his forehead as if he was getting a migraine. The new hair cut was not a barbershop version and did not suit him. He seemed on the verge of losing control.

'No, I didn't know you but my mother does know you, much to her regret. My mother, a sweet and beautiful woman, is at this moment languishing in a women's prison, wasting her life away working in a laundry and it's all your fault, Jordan Lacey. You could have left her alone to continue her life's work, her vocation, but oh no, you had to interfere.' He was clenching his hands, sweat appeared on his upper lip.

The brain cogs were turning rapidly. A beautiful woman. Her life's work. How many beautiful women did I know who had a vocation? A cog ground to a halt at a file labelled NUN.

'Do you mean Sister Lucinda? From the hospice . . .?'

His mouth was working. Heat crawled from the four small walls. He was beginning to change. His eyes swivelled. My nerve cells were tingling with fear.

'Yes, she was Lucy Grey, the most famous modelling face of the Seventies. The cover of *Vogue*. What a gorgeous woman, stunning. She's my mother.'

I had to tread very carefully. It had been a complicated case, and two other people had originally been charged with man-slaughter of the dead nun found in the derelict hotel, Trenchers, on the seafront at Latching.

'And you think I had something to do with your mother being arrested for the death of Ellen Swantry?'

'I know you did, Jordan. It was entirely your fault and you can't deny it. I heard your name myself in court. The police said they followed a tip-off from a local private investigator, Miss Jordan Lacey. The arresting officer was most particular about giving you due credit.'

James. My James. But that was the kind of thing he would do. Never any credit to my face with a nice thank-you note and a bunch of flowers. But in an impersonal crown court, he would tell the truth.

George was getting more restless. He looked at his watch, tapped his teeth.

'Of course, I had several more fascinating activities planned which were going to backfire on you, but you have ruined those ideas and I'm going to fast forward a few things. I am not an unkind man, so while you are still here, you may use my bathroom. I know the bladder can let one down in moments of stress, and since we are going to be inseparable from now on, I'd rather you paid a visit now.'

I was into the tiny loo in a flash. There was no window. An

internal air extractor fan came on. A frantic search revealed nothing of any obvious use to me. I wrapped a small complementary soap in toilet paper and put it in my pocket. I folded more toilet paper into my bra. Then I used and flushed the loo.

As I came out, George was right behind the door. He snapped a handcuff on to my right wrist and attached the other half to the leather belt of his trousers. Snap, snap.

'I said we were going to be inseparable. Wherever you go, I go now. The nun was found hanging on a hook, wasn't she? I thought you would have made the connection.'

George couldn't use his big carrier car. I was hustled out to a nearby carpark, his arm slung tightly round my waist as if we were buddies. He went to a small Ford and bundled me into it. I refused to hold on to his belt, so my hanging right hand was half wrapped round the gear lever in a most uncomfortable position.

'Where are we going?' I asked. He did not answer.

James might track me to the Regal Theatre but now he had no idea where I would be. My heart sank into despair. I looked out of the window, wondering if I could attract someone's attention. There might be a police officer at a set of traffic lights. But there's never one around when you want one.

'Don't try anything,' George warned as he drove east. 'I should have no compunction about knocking you out.'

'I'm not going to try anything,' I said, muffled in misery.

'I hear you're mad about the sea, always walking the pier and beach. You might like this. I thought we'd go for a little sea trip. Nothing fancy. Just a breath of sea air.'

Newhaven. We were going towards Newhaven. There were cross-Channel ferries at Newhaven.

The handcuffs were rubbing a sore place on my wrist. It hurt a lot. I might never be able to write again.

'Did you write on a card left in my car?' I asked.

'Yes, I know it was a bit childish. Who's next? I couldn't resist it. You were so sure of yourself and everything you did. I had to puncture that confidence. Make you a little nervous.'

'It didn't work,' I said grimly. 'I thought it was some damned fool kid.'

'The scarf worked though, didn't it? You've been wearing one of my mother's scarves. Doesn't that give you a weird feeling now?' He was grinning.

I went cold. I thought the scarf had been a gift from the lady who had been so pleased about finding her mother's umbrella and I'd worn it a lot. My skin cringed.

He was following the signs to Newhaven Harbour. We were going on the ferry. I'm not opposed to a little shopping in a French supermarket, all those lovely cheeses, but I had a feeling that George had different plans.

Assertiveness is a behaviour you can acquire. I remembered this from my training days. Showing too little concern for your captor is as wrong as showing too much. That was captive training. Keep a mental log of everything and everyone, we were told. Construct something positive in your mind. I would try to find out everything about the situation and George Hill's mentality.

'You must have had a lovely childhood with such a beautiful and famous mother,' I began, being assertive and constructive.

'Yes, it was. My parents had a fabulous flat in Bayswater. There were always people coming round. Sunday lunches were wonderful, rich and famous people from the media eating brunch in the garden, lots of laughter and talk and wine flowing. And, of course, everyone used to spoil me. And I could make them laugh. I was born to amuse people.'

'Ah, an infant entertainer?'

'You might say that.'

'And did it continue to be wonderful?' I knew it hadn't.

'Something went wrong. I'm not sure what it was. I was too young at the time.' He was lying. He must have known something. 'My parents split up and there was a scandal. I don't know what it was all about.'

Lucy Grey had been mixed up in some big financial scandal. I didn't know the facts but it had been about then that she had vanished from the modelling scene. Perhaps no one would employ her. It was long before my time too.

'What a shame. But what happened to you, George? You must have been very frightened, only a little boy, and your whole world changing . . .'

'Yes, I was. And no one would explain or tell me anything. I was bundled off to boarding school. My father remarried and I spent some holidays with them. Then my mother suddenly resurfaced and she was a nun in this grey habit and she was still the most beautiful woman I had ever seen . . . her face, her skin. I was enchanted by her.' His voice drifted off as if remembering this vision of goodness.

'Did she encourage your stage career?'

'Yes, she was all for it. She was my mentor, my guiding light, my guardian angel . . . I loved her.'

Oh dear, and I had removed her from the scene. I knew she received a long prison sentence. Time to change the subject.

'The ferries are over there,' I said, being friendly.

'We've made excellent time. You are going to enjoy this, Jordan.'

The ferries ran frequently. We joined an orderly queue of cars and George drove the Ford into the bowels of the ship. There did not seem to be any point in yelling for help at this moment. Too much noise. He dragged me out across the driver's seat, painful manhandling, and walked me on to an upper deck.

'Enjoy the view, Jordan,' he said with relish. 'It's going to be your last.'

My pulse was pounding and I felt sick. I was not enjoying this at all.

He made me lean on the rail in a companionable twosome. I did not have any choice. As the ferry slid away from the dockside and began the tossing and turning required to man-oeuvre a tricky harbour exit, I realized that George was not a good sailor. He did not look well. I took advantage of his preoccupation to find the tablet of stolen soap, transfer some saliva from my mouth to it, and begin the process of saturating the handcuff on my wrist in soapsuds.

It had not taken long to realize that the handcuffs were not regulation Sussex police force issue, but stage, Max Cornelius, fake show handcuffs. They felt different. They felt soft, pliable, light. I didn't know how the stage trick worked but I was determined to find out.

As George sighed and stared out at the watery depths, I smothered the cuff round my wrist with soap and with my free hand, i.e the left, tried to manipulate the catch opening. There had to be one somewhere. I'd seen the show and Max had released the cuffs in seconds.

'Why don't you go and lie down?' I said, helpfully. 'Or have a brandy at the bar? I can hardly escape from you on a ferry in the middle of the English Channel.'

'I know you, slippery as an eel,' he groaned again, white faced. 'I'm not letting you out of my sight.'

The ferry was heading for the open sea and George was regaining his colour although not his stability. We staggered towards the bows of the ship. There were not many people about. It was going to be a rough crossing. Those easterly winds had blown up.

The sea was not in a happy mood. Great waves surged towards the sturdy bows of the ship. She slapped up and down, burrowing a path through the deep troughs of water. The crew had put on waterproofs. Not a good sign.

'I think it's time you and I said goodbye,' said George, the wind whipping his shortened hair all over his face. 'It's getting pretty rough. You won't last long in this.'

From a back pocket he got out a black plastic bin liner and shook it open. This was not an easy manoeuvre. The wind flapped it away, the ferry heaved, I was attached to his belt and I was definitely not going to help.

I was struggling with the handcuffs. There were only seconds left. I had almost felt the notch. George was too preoccupied with the flapping plastic bin liner to notice what I was doing.

At the very moment that George managed to open out the bin liner and drag it over my head, I succeeded in sliding the cuff over my slippery-soaped wrist, find the notch and flip open the handcuffs, all at the same time. This took him completely by surprise as we flew apart and the ship gave a helpful lurch which caught him off balance. He fell hard against the rail, reaching out for a hold.

'Damn and blast!' he howled in pain.

I ran the length of the deck, fighting to throw off the bin liner from my head. I didn't know where to go. I knew I had to find the captain. Did a ferry have a captain?

For a start I slid down steel steps, ran along corridors, put as much distance as possible between us. My breath was rasping. I ran into a women's lavatory and locked the door behind me. This might be the first of places he'd look for me, but it was a breathing space. And I needed to get my thoughts and my breath together.

I was on a ferry going to France. George Hill was trying to kill me, to toss me overboard to the fish. I had no money, no phone, no identification. But I still had some wits.

I slid out of the cloakroom and found myself near the cafeteria kitchen. I had no compunction in borrowing an overall from a hook and a cap-like head covering. Get rid of the hair and I'm a different person. I picked up some menus.

The corridors were uncannily empty. Everyone was drinking duty-free in the bar. I walked down more gangways and found myself in the car hold, among rows and rows of cars. There was a big camper van, the kind with a sleeping area in a humped roof space. They had not locked the side door. I went in, shut and locked the door behind me and climbed up a tiny vertical ladder into the cramped roof space. I had to curl up my legs. I felt like a squirrel. The owners would get a surprise in France.

It seemed as if I was there for hours as the ferry battled the waves and the cross-currents. I hoped George was feeling really ill. I must have dozed off. It was hot in the roof space and I needed a sleep.

Then I awoke with a jolt, heard banging on the side of the camper.

'Jordan! Jordan! I know you're in there. For God's sake, open up before I break the bloody door down.'

It wasn't George. Wrong voice. It couldn't be Ben. It had to be James. I had to trust it was James and not George playing some trick on me. He might be able to do impersonations. I scrambled down and stood with my hand on the door lock, hesitating.

'Who is it?' I said, dredging up the last of my assertiveness.

'Detective Inspector James, you fool. Open this door at once.'

'Prove it.'

'You don't like my choice of cereal.'

I could not open it fast enough and I tumbled out into his arms. James held me very close. I could feel his heart beating steadily, and his solid warmth. It was all I could do to stop myself from breaking into tears.

'He was going to kill me,' I said, choking. 'He was going to throw me overboard in a bin bag.'

'We know, we know,' he said soothingly, patting my back. 'We heard it all.'

I leaned away an inch, but barely an inch, so that I could look at him. I did not want to leave his arms. 'You heard what?'

He tapped my shoulder, half smiling. 'Under the tab on your shirt. A tiny bug. The wonders of modern surveillance equipment. We've been tracking you all the way. But could you please take off that ridiculous hat. It doesn't suit you.'

Twenty-Two

A police helicopter flew James and me back to Shoreham airport. It was a glorious way to travel, despite the noise, watching the waves surging beneath, all shades of green and blue and deepest navy.

They arrested George Hill as he drove off the ferry at Dieppe. He would spend several nights in a French police cell awaiting the process of extradition. I hoped it would be a rough crossing.

'I don't ever want to see him again,' I shuddered.

'I'm afraid you may have to,' said James. 'You'll be a witness in court. Of course you won't have to look at him.'

'Could I have a screen?'

'Come off it, Jordan. You can't be that nervous.'

'I might be, by then.'

His car was parked near the police helicopter hangar at the far end of the airport. He felt under the driver's seat and produced a thermos flask and some wrapped polysterene beakers. 'Pour out some coffee, please, Jordan. Perhaps it'll steady your nerves.'

James noticed my rubbed wrist. 'That looks nasty,' he said. 'You ought to have it dressed. It could get infected. We'll go via A & E.'

'I'm allergic to hospitals,' I said.

'I'm not surprised,' he said. 'You must have been in every hospital in Sussex.'

'What an exaggeration. Not every hospital, but quite a few. It's my newish year resolution. No more hospitals.'

James drained his coffee and turned the ignition key. 'We'll argue about that when we get to Latching.'

210

I kept quiet, did not ask any questions, on my best behaviour. James was amused. I could see it on his face each time I snatched a look at his profile. His nose and chin were etched so finely. It was hard to take my eyes off the shape of his head.

'So, don't you want to ask me what's been going on?'

'Surely if I'm going to be a witness, I'm not supposed to know,' I said carefully.

'When you have almost been thrown overboard and drowned by a killer, I think you are entitled to know why,' he said, the amusement vanishing from his face.

'OK,' I said. 'Entitle me.'

We were on the main road and James kept exactly to the speed limit. The needle on the speedometer never wavered.

'George Hill and Anne Steel ran this false identity passport factory. It was not drugs as we first thought, but still a lucrative business and a complex organization. They made thousands. But you started getting in their way when you took on the Updown Hill garden case. It began to worry them and they realized that they had to distract you.'

'They distracted me with a false stalker.' I could not help interrupting. 'More time-consuming surveillance.'

'When you removed the briefcase, George Hill knew he had to remove you as well. You knew far too much, or he thought you did. You had all the incriminating documents. And you had their last haul of cash. He wanted it all back, especially the money. He needed to disappear for a while after Anne's death.'

'He killed her, you know,' I said. 'He stabbed her with the shears. And my prints are on the shears.'

'We found your prints. But we knew you couldn't have done it. You were up a tree, weren't you? Unless you're an Olympic javelin thrower.'

'I'm hurt that you even considered it,' I said.

'Prints are prints,' he said solidly.

'But it wasn't just the shears, was it?'

'No, Anne had been throttled with something called a Spanish windlass. But the killer was disturbed and though

211

Anne was unconscious, she might have recovered if George Hill had not come along with the shears.'

'But who did this Spanish windlass? What is it?'

'A Spanish windlass is a loop of material placed round the victim's neck, something like a scarf, and then tightened with a stick. It's very quick.'

'I think it was a scarf,' I said, feeling sick. 'But you didn't find it, did you?'

'No, we didn't find the scarf but we did find a stick and some fibres from the material were on Anne's neck and the stick.'

'I don't think I want to hear any more,' I said.

'Are you feeling car sick?'

'No, I'm feeling scarf sick.'

James didn't understand that but I'd tell him later. We were nearing the outskirts of Latching and I knew by his route that he was taking me to Latching hospital. Perhaps I would let A & E look at my wrist. It was raw and tender.

'So did George Hill kill Anne Steel?'

'We believe we can prove it. The cadaveric spasm is clutching some dark hair, quite long hair tightly gripped.'

'George Hill used to have a ponytail. He cut it off.'

James droved into the hospital entrance and parked near the A & E Department.

'What about the 1 a.m. drop tonight? The last card in the windmill.' I asked.

'All taken care of. The six small figures were a map reference. You probably didn't know that,' he added kindly.

A map reference. It had never occurred to me.

'You won't have to wait,' he went on, opening the door. 'I'll go in with you and explain that you are under police protection.'

'There's something else you ought to do before some stage-hand throws it in a locker,' I said.

'Explain.'

'George Hill wore a black sequinned jacket for his last stage show. I saw him wearing it.'

'And?'

'If you send the jacket to forensic, they'll be able to find evidence of the man George Hill fed with ecstasy. The person he hung on the hook behind the dressing room door.'

'And how do you know this?'

'I've seen the jacket and I spotted some minute evidence. There may also be skin, saliva. The snagged sequins might reveal more particles of skin. It's on a stand in his dressing room at the Regal Theatre. And there's a speck of white.'

'What did you see exactly?'

'It's a feather, a tiny white feather. It's the kind of thing that could easily be transferred in a struggle.'

'And do you know the identity of the man in the morgue? The man that George Hill identified as himself?'

I paused. It hurt to say it.

'Yes, I do. Only one person would have had a feather on him after the show and that's Max, Max the magician. There were several doves in his act. He only drank juice. George Hill could easily have slipped in some tablets while Max was checking his equipment on the stage. He was such a nice person. And, James . . .?'

'Yes?'

'Could your officer please check on the doves?'

They did a good job on my wrist. Neat dressing. Told me to rest it and go to my doctor's clinic to have it redressed. I nodded and agreed to do that. It's easier to agree.

James came back into the cubicle, switching off his mobile. 'They are sending officers to fetch the jacket,' he said. 'And everything else in the dressing room. Forensic will go through the lot. We can match DNA with the victim and Hill.'

'Good. Have I earned bonus points?'

'A few . . .' Sometimes he could be so mean.

'Tim Arnold? Is he recovering? Can I go and see him?'

'You do push your luck. He's recovering and yes, you can see him. But I'm coming with you.'

I really wanted to see Tim Arnold alone but I guess I had to be thankful that DI James was allowing me this much leeway.

There was a police officer outside the private room on the first floor.

'It's OK,' said DI James. 'I am escorting Miss Lacey. We are only staying a few minutes.'

Tim Arnold was attached to lots of drips and tubes but his colouring had returned to normal and he seemed to be breathing easily. He opened his eyes slowly and caught sight of me.

'Oh, it's you,' he sighed. 'I don't want to see you. Dammit it. You arrived too soon. Why couldn't you have been late?'

'It was fate,' I said, drawing up a chair with my good hand. 'You weren't meant to die yet.'

'Yes I am. I can't go on living. I can't live with what I've done.' He stared at some point on the ceiling as if willing God to take him now.

'Is it about spraying the garden with weedkiller at Denbury Court?' I asked gently. 'It wasn't very nice but it isn't something you have to kill yourself for.'

'No, it wasn't that . . . I didn't do that. It was something much, much worse.' He seemed to be making a great effort, taking several deep breaths. I took a quick look at James. He was standing by the door, listening. He shook his head.

'Don't say anything if you don't want to, Mr Arnold,' I said. 'Wait till you feel stronger.'

'No, I'm going to tell you now or I may never tell anyone. Because I shall do this again, you know. As soon as I get out. Drive off Beachy Head on a wet day. I won't survive that.'

'There's no need . . .' I began.

'Oh yes, there is. You see, I killed my daughter. My daughter, my Annie. I killed her. My little girl . . .'

'Your daughter, Annie? The little girl in the photographs. A lovely child. She was Anne Steel?'

He nodded and seemed relieved that he did not have to explain. 'You found the photographs? Such a pretty girl, so lively and full of mischief. Her mother and I separated when she was only little. All I got were photographs and occasionally I managed to snatch a glimpse of her. Visiting rights weren't normal in those days. I was cut right out of her life. My punishment for straying.'

'And you bought The Corner House, hoping to see her?'

He nodded. 'I thought we might meet socially. But it didn't work out that way when they took all the plants.'

'Tell me why you think you killed her.'

'Think? I know I did. I had my hands round her throat before I realized who it was. I thought it was the other one, the one who has been spraying the garden with weedkiller. That skinny stepdaughter of hers, Michelle.'

'Michelle?'

'Yes, Michelle, she's the one. She's always hated my Annie. It was a way of getting back at her, to spoil her garden, to cause problems between Annie and Sam. She'd do anything to come between them. What were a few flowers if she could ruin their marriage? I wanted to give her a fright. But I got the wrong one in the dark. I got my Annie . . .'

He was so distressed that I stopped him from talking any more with my hand on his arm.

'Now Mr Arnold, listen to me very carefully. Was it your hands you used or a piece of material or twine? Think before you answer me and tell me exactly how you did it.'

He lifted his hands, then let them drop back on to the bed. 'These damned hands, damn 'em.'

I looked across at James for permission. Can I tell him, I asked silently? He nodded.

'Mr Arnold, if you say that you put your hands round Annie's throat to give her a fright, thinking it was Michelle, then I'm telling you that you didn't kill Annie. You see, Annie died in a different way, something quite different, information that has not been released to the newspapers at all.'

'Is that true?' he asked hoarsely. 'Are you sure? You're not just making it up?'

'Quite true. I'm not making it up. You didn't kill your daughter.'

'Thank God . . . thank God . . .' He sank back on to his pillow, his eyes closed.

'But someone else did, Mr Arnold,' said James, coming forward and speaking for the first time. 'And a man is in custody. He is going to be charged.'

'So you got him . . .'

'You should rest now, Mr Arnold, and think about getting better. Perhaps the nurse will bring you a cup of tea.'

'I deserve something a bit stronger,' said Mr Arnold, some of his old humour returning. He turned to me and took my hand. Only he took the wrong one. I flinched. 'What have you done to your wrist, girl?'

'A slight altercation with a pair of handcuffs.'

'Who won?'

I looked at James. 'I did.'

'So it was Michelle,' I said as we walked down the hospital corridor. 'Ruining her father's garden. I'd seen the red flash on her trainers but couldn't understand why she had to break into her own home.'

'She was after the floppy disk,' said James. 'At that point she didn't know that Anne was dead in the garden and she was trying to get the disk and make it look like a burglary.'

'And you know what's on the disk?' I asked, following him down the stairs.

'Yes, I do. Something Michelle wanted to destroy. It would have ruined her acting career if it was made public.'

'And you're not going to tell me . . .'

'That's right, I'm not. You're far too nosy for your own good. It should have been destroyed long ago but Anne kept it so that she would have some hold over Michelle.'

'So George Hill did kill Anne Steel and I had the scarf all the time,' I said, more to myself.

'The scarf? You've got the scarf?' James could barely contain his impatience.

'Not exactly, James. Actually you've got the scarf. I left it in your bathroom. Remember when I slept in your bath?'

*   *   *

216

I had not seen or heard of my trumpeter for months. It was like an empty ache in my veins. His music always soared in my head, making my spine tingly. But there had been no time for any jazz. My wrist was healing. My cracked rib had healed. Michelle apologized for booting me in the stomach. Mr Arnold came out of hospital and had gone on a late holiday to Italy. Samuel Steel was having his garden steam-cleaned to rid it of the poison. If that didn't work then he was going to have the entire top 12 inches of soil removed and replaced. It seemed a bit drastic.

He had forgiven Michelle for the destruction of the garden and was not pressing charges. 'I've lost my wife. I can't lose my daughter as well. She's promised to help me plant a new garden.'

He told me to keep the retainer. He said I had earned it. I was not sure about earning it. I did not want to fall out of any more trees. But I remembered the moonlight streaming across the sea like silver and the stars twinkling in a cloud of silent stardust.

'Stardust' is one of my favourite tunes. Hoagy Carmichael knew what he was doing when he plucked that one out of the sky. But I could hear strains of the melody right now, out in the street, in the late summer evening. Surely not? It sounded so close. I could not be imagining it.

My feet hurried towards the Bear and Bait. I knew those notes and could hardly believe what I was hearing. My trumpeter had returned from his travels and he was here, even now, playing to his devoted fans. I could not move fast enough. I flew along the pavement. My hair came out of its plait and fell around my shoulders.

As I hurried into the Bear and Bait, he blew the last few bars and triumphant notes on his gleaming trumpet, lingering beads of sound clung to the air. Amid the applause, he strolled over towards me, his arms open wide.

'Hello, sweetheart,' he said with such affection in his eyes that my bones melted. 'Where have you been?'

'Locked in a windmill. Chained on a ferry.'

'I wouldn't think of looking for you in a windmill,' he said, shaking his head.

'No one did,' I said. 'Till it caught fire.'

'Sweetheart,' he said. 'Doesn't anyone look after you?'

'I have to look after myself.'

I turned, radiant for once, and froze. DI James was watching me from the doorway but it was too late. I saw the expression on his face and my heart fell apart. He came over.

'The doves are all right,' he said. 'A stage hand took them home.'

'I'm glad.'

'I'm glad you're glad,' he said, glancing at my trumpeter. He nodded and walked out. My joy drained away with him.

Life was not fair. Not in Latching.